The ELECTRICAL VENUS

Julie Mayhew

HOT
KEY
BOOKS

First published in Great Britain in 2018 by
HOT KEY BOOKS
80–81 Wimpole St, London W1G 9RE
www.hotkeybooks.com

A CIP catalogue record for this book is available from the British Library.

ISBN: 9781471407048
also available as an ebook

1

This book is typeset using Atomik ePublisher
Printed and bound by Clays Ltd, St Ives Plc

Hot Key Books is an imprint of Bonnier Zaffre Ltd,
a Bonnier Publishing company
www.bonnierpublishing.com

ALSO BY JULIE MAYHEW

Red Ink
The Big Lie
Mother Tongue

For Thom

'In order to stay balanced, substances with a surplus of opposite charges will attract one another. The attraction may even be strong enough to make them stick together.'

— *Usborne Understanding Science: Electricity and Magnetism,*
Adamczyk & Law

'Behold this angel floating towards our earth!' announces the girl.

But the angel only wails.

'The pole!' This is what he cries. 'The pole, it will not hold!'

The disobliging parrot begins to chant – 'He is a kind of beautiful! He is a kind of beautiful!' – sensing danger, needing to voice it, but lacking the words.

The girl, her focus only on her own demise, her show so carefully crafted descending into chaos, does not see the situation – does not hear it, feel it, know it – for what it truly is.

'Crank the machine more!' she instructs, believing she is able, with the power of language, to make everything come to good.

But the fayre hawker's wife ignores the command. She stands frozen, eyes skyward, swallowing air at the impending horror.

'Lizzy!' the girl snaps. 'Lizzy! Are you listening?!'

She is not.

The next sound they all hear.

CRACK!

The pole gives way. Then comes the terrible scream of an angel descending as he was told to, but too fast, too fast.

1

'He is a kind of beautiful! He is a kind of beautiful!' gabbles the parrot as the angel tumbles through the air in the seemingly stretched-out motion of a dream.

The girl turns, likewise trancelike, to see that the bird's words are correct. There is a beauty – a certain majesty – to the revolutions the angel makes as he slips through the air, a delicacy to the dance of the silken threads as they tangle his wings, preventing him from making any effort to break his fall.

The green parrot takes flight, to coach his fellow, perhaps, on the magic of flying.

The audience's faces are upturned, a sea of expectant Os.

Then there is another deafening –

CRACK!

– as a body hits the floor.

Time returns to its usual pace with a wild howl of despair.

The dream ends.

An angel lies broken, bleeding, upon the ground.

ACT I

This is to give Notice to Gentlemen, Ladies and Others

that in this very Place before Sunset there shall be the Opportunity to see the most
EXTRA-ORDINARY *and* TALENTED *collection of wild Animals,* a

MENAGERIE as follows

Geese, that on hearing a Melody desire to dance the Hornpipe: A Learned Pig, capable of
impressive mathematic Feats: A Parrot from the South Americas that will recite the Poets
and the Saints with excellent Elocution: A Hare of Giant's proportions that itself is a Sight
to astound but will also beat upon a Drum at your very Command.

SECOND, you shall see

THE MOST STARTLING SPECTACLES OF

HUMAN BIRTH

A live DWAFF, which is a grown Man with the very dimensions of a Child, who can juggle
with Fire: the ONE-ARM'D BOY who does exist most jolly though missing one of his Limbs
and can do Feats of Tumbling to astonish and arouse; the NO-LEGG'D BRUTE who will
behave as if he is Hercules for your attending Pleasure by the lifting of several full
Barrels above his Head.

Many musical Interludes will follow.

~~THIRD, much anticipated and MUCH CELEBRATED, a true Lady, genteel in all~~
~~Aspects of Voice, Dress and Nobility save for her having the Head of a Swine.~~
~~It is a Spectacle never to be surpass'd.~~

~~HILDY~~

All followed by bare-Knuckle Fighting
for your Entertainment and serious Play!!!

The Proprietor – the most distinguish'd MR F P GRAINGER – wishes it be known
that he is willing to dispose of any of these Remarkable Beasts, including those of the
human Disposition, if any Lady or Gentlemen is so desirous of purchasing them.

LONG LIVE THE KING!

To begin with, there is the smell.

Of chicken shit and pig.

Of that particular perfume that simmers when the lowest ranks do hoard together.

In this gathering crowd you will catch a sniff of the brewer's armpit, the gelder's feet, the stench of the tallow-chandler's apron. They all mix strong with the fresh sweet scent of spring grass underfoot, and the vapours from the public dunghill that drift like intermittent farts across the whole proceedings.

The butcher, in all his meatiness, has arrived to swell the throng. The tanner, the wabster, the smiddy come too to this field on the outskirts of town, just where the road runs to proper dirt. They do their darndest to wash away the day's work done with the drinking of strong liquor and with the gobbling up of pure entertainment.

The band of performing rogues and vagabonds before them have paid their bribes to the observing parish wardens and so they may begin the evening's jamboree without any officious interruption.

So next comes noise – an earful of pipe-playing. A woman

of certain years and ample chest is behind the tune. She was introduced to us by the fayre hawker without the baggage of a name – she is simply his wife. Working her fingers inexpertly up and down the instrument, cheeks pink at the puffing, she barrels her hips along with a rhythm only she understands. It is a befuddling racket, but a sound not nearly so awful as –

SMACK!

– the impact of knuckles meeting jaw. It's a good sock – a marvellous strike! – and it acts like a conductor to this drunken orchestra of butchers and brewers, their wives and their cubs. (Just as it was supposed to.)

They rouse in unison, men and women, their mugs aloft and they cheer the punch –

ERRAYY!

– before settling into gleeful commiserations for the one who felt the pain.

That 'one' was the eldest of the two boxers – a bear of a man with a thick, bacony jaw. Red spills from the split skin of his chin.

The colour on his opponent's face? None. Only the scarlet bloom of youth and vigour. The boy, the one who dealt the blow, dances from foot to foot in the soil, all bare-chest and breeches, whooping at the sky. He is admirably lean with the beginnings of being tall, but what snags the attentions of this baying crowd is that he is boxing with only the one arm.

The other limb is gone, lost. Ask him for the tale of it, out of earshot of his master, and he will tell you of when he was a tiny infant and a cart could not stop, trapping him against a post. That accident, the subsequent amputation, is the reason he is here on this March evening, pugilising in a field. His mother gave him up, thinking he would never grow enough for hard work and earn his keep. She sold him to this fayre hawker who knew very well how to make a lad like him put coinage in the pot.

Now he is exhibited (inaccurately) as a 'spectacle of human birth', taught to juggle and tumble at an early age, teaching himself later the skills required to fight. The boy has been nothing but a financial success and, on this eve, one arm or no, he appears every part the winner. For unlike his opponent, the boy has legs. A phrase you are to take literally not metaphorically.

'You, sir!' cries the fayre hawker, our ringleader, an ageing man, an opportunistic sort in a greasy, second-hand periwig.

The crowd turns, seeking the 'sir' amongst them who has been singled out. And there he is — a fat sort by the farmer's gate, emptying his beery guts into the hedge.

'You sir,' the fayre hawker calls to the puker, 'you may be legless only part of the time, but this brute here is legless the whole damn day long!'

The crowd is one again, bellowing with laughter. The fayre hawker adjusts his ill-fitting curls, a little pleased with himself for tickling the audience. The 'No-legg'd Brute', our bear of a boxer, strikes forward in the mud in his wheeled trolley and snarls.

'Legless since he shot free of the womb!' the fayre hawker goes on. 'And though that makes him a lucky fellow in my eyes, never having to bother with the expense of shoes . . .' More laughter. '. . . it means he is no match for the nimble-footed. Or indeed the any-footed!' The cackling continues, enraging

8

the subject of this comedy routine. He growls at his audience, showing them his broken teeth, demonstrating how ready he is to eat them all up.

But the collected of the town only coo, pretending scared.

'So, 'tis time,' says the fayre hawker. 'Place your bets! Who will win? The one-arm'd boy or the no-legg'd brute.'

Into this scene comes a man no higher than an ell, a 'dwaff' as the handbill will have you know him, the fayre hawker spelling as he speaks – that is to say, incorrectly. This fellow of limited height entertained earlier with fire tricks and magic, and now he moves about the crowd at his master's command, taking cash and handing out the slips. But this mob ain't biting as eagerly as they should.

'Come on!' prods the fayre hawker. 'Don't be sorry you didn't stick yours in . . . As the abbess said to the fellow in the gospel shop!'

But the mob is muttering amongst itself, no longer in the market for wit. They smell a rat. Doubling your money is never this simple, as they know from bad experience.

The fayre hawker's wife stops her playing abruptly and puts down her pipe. She may not be one for tempo and pitch, but reading the thoughts of an audience is something she has a skill for.

'The brute is strong,' she calls out, throaty and convinced. 'He may have got hit, but I warn you, don't doubt him. I have seen him bend iron with his bare hands. I have seen him bite through china. One wrong step and that kid is the morrow's breakfast!'

The 'no-legg'd brute' revives at hearing his powers being

9

celebrated. He flexes his biceps, each as big as a loaf of bread. The audience is audibly impressed. The 'one-arm'd boy' momentarily retreats.

'Oh, shut it, woman!' snaps the fayre hawker, watching his carefully managed promotion of the boy slip like sand through the fingers. 'Don't listen to her!'

But 'tis too late; the crowd has turned for the wife. They jabber their agreement, as if they have too, with their own eyes, witnessed the feats of strength recounted in support of the man in the trolley chair. The fayre hawker's wife stands tall, proud of this knockout blow of sorts, revelling in the delivery of her husband's comeuppance.

The fayre hawker explodes with fury. 'You shrew!' he bellows. 'You snake! You grizly old hag!' But his wife only laughs, her new clan laughing with her. 'What?' blusters the fayre hawker, switching his attention to the crowd, spinning in the mud to address them all. 'What! You're going to take the word of a woman when it comes to sport? You're going to hark at this old Jade, this fussock, this mopsey. This truggish old crone with a bee up her chapel!'

The wife snorts, blowing at her husband with her tongue. The man's wig is slipping something awful now and is about to fall south. Because, yes – yes, they will take the word of this woman. The crowd is dead-set on backing the 'brute'.

That is until the boxing boy stops his jigging for the smallest of moments and bends close to the scavenger man on the front row. Like all those around him, he is craning for the attention of the small man with the ledger, itching to make his wager.

'You know 'tis all a show,' the boy says softly, snatching the scavenger's attention.

10

'Eh?' he replies from a smeary mouth of blisters. 'Eh? Wozzat you say?'

The boy takes a swift glance at his master, makes sure he is still engrossed in the argument with his wife and has not caught sight of this forbidden conversation.

'They make like this every time,' he goes on. ''Tis blaggery. They do it so's that you don't settle on me. So's that you don't get a farthing and neither do I.'

Realisation spreads gradual across the scavenger's dirty mush.

'I'm talking as one honest fellow to the next,' the boy concludes. 'Don't you be falling for any of this disgrace.' And back he goes to his boxer's bounce while the tip-off spreads through the throng as fast as a dose of the pox.

All money is put on the boy.

The round is called. The fayre hawker, with the ledger returned to him, stares down at the figures and wears the stoop of a beaten man. The crowd clocks it and they clap each other upon the back for a ruse well swerved. The 'one-arm'd boy' hops and the 'no-legg'd brute' does roar. They huff and they puff, putting on the most satisfying show, peppered with punches that are 'almosts' and 'oh-not-quites'.

And as they bob and jab towards their foregone conclusion, there is much that this mob, engrossed in the spectacle, will fail to see. Much that they will fail to feel.

For starters: the disappointment leaching from the richer folk who have come to this field too, willing to smut their hems and superior shoes. They hide at the back, keeping their distance from the contagious poor, fanning bad smells from the vicinity

11

of their noses, holding to their fair chests fading hopes of seeing the celebrated 'hog-faced lady', whose fame will grow even larger in their drawing rooms now that she has made no appearance. Their disappointment will grow stronger still when they arrive home to find their purses gone, lifted by the 'dwaff', who is as adept at picking pockets as he is at tossing flames.

The gathered will not notice the anxious sadness rising from the young girl of this travelling group, introduced with the fayre hawker's slippery tongue as his 'girl-exotic'. There she is, in an unbecoming dress, too nice for her standing and too big for her frame. She was the one who led out the geese and the pig and the hare for their performances, and then presented some skits of her own involving a brightly coloured and disobliging parrot. She has since fallen from everyone's memory though. She may be brown-of-skin in a way quite fascinating in a country outpost such as this, but all assembled were in agreement – her recital with the parrot was simply the largest pile of horseshit.

More impressive is her story of how she came to be here. Ask her, out of earshot of her master, and she would tell you how she is the daughter of a duchess. Though not the daughter of a duke. Her father was the lady's black slave brought back from a faraway island by the duke himself – a gift to his wife to decorate her parlour, to hold her train and to offer amusement while he was away on his recurrent voyages. Amusement, yes, but not like that. They fell in love, the gossips say. What is entirely certain is that the baby had to go, and once again our mercenary fayre hawker was in the right place at the right time. He swooped before the parish could intervene and, always with an eye for a bargain, insisted the chattering parrot came with the girl as part of the deal.

What else will they miss, this giddy throng?

The curiosity of the serious young gentleman in the good-enough frock coat, certainly, for he is trying hard to be invisible. He stands a short distance from the other spectators turning about plans in his head, reinventing them, reorganising them. If anyone was shrewd enough to give him even a casual glance, they would notice the unique way in which he observes this show – as if it were a book to be studied or a lecture most grave, rather than something jolly to pass the time.

And it is undeniable that all here present are too-far inebriated to notice the nod the 'one-arm'd boy' gives the 'no-legg'd brute', signalling that he may strike him now – use the new sleight they have been practising without end.

The young girl will wail, just as she has been told to, when the boy is seemingly knocked out – though no amateurish dramatics are required, for she feels the blow as if it had been real, as if she had taken the contact herself.

The crowd will then vomit their objections. All will be chaos.

'Oh, that was unexpected!' is the fayre hawker's next line as the boy lolls, apparently dead.

The seasoned old ringleader in the cut-price wig will then toss a wink to his comely wife to congratulate her for a part well played, before readying himself to brush aside the protests of the hoodwinked spectators.

Just as he does every other night of the week. And sometimes twice on the weekend.

MIM

George, you sod! You blighter! You useless pile of green! Zooks, I am so furious I could pluck you feather by feather! You might be named for the King but that ain't gonna stop me.

No! No shuffling away now. No giving me the sad-eye. You know our act inside out and upside in. Why decide on a whim that you don't? To make me look stupid?

You blasted parrot.

You let me down. There shan't be any seeds for you until you get that into your little blue head.

Oh, I am ashamed, in truth, sullied by the feeling of it. My master introduced me strangely and all was disaster from there.

His 'girl-exotic' he calls me now, my signal to get up and perform. That's a new one. A strange one. It's an improvement on 'oi', I suppose, or 'you' or 'shit for brains'. But still – what to make of it? I can only guess from the sauce dripping from his voice, and the *coo-ees* of the crowd, that he was saying it as a means to sell me high.

But then you, you idiot, you messed it all up.

Oh, those blank and silent faces! I reckon I shall never rid myself of the memory. Laughter is what the love of an audience sounds like, bird, either that or great rounds of cheering. But silence! You are to talk, George. That is your thing. You are to look all unusual and multicoloured, then talk.

My thing? Well, I am still getting a handle upon it. Perhaps 'girl-exotic' is to be my thing, since Grainger has made it my title. Though what that involves as an act, I can't say for sure. The 'One-Arm'd Boy' is a much clearer prospect, though Alex would have it different. He says those words alone don't mean much. 'Tis merely a description, says he, and one of the narrowest kind.

But he can take it with him. That's the measure, ain't it? I'm the goose-wrangler, the hare-botherer, the girl who leads out the pig. I'd be a whole big nothing without them animals. And here I am again, making the same bleeding mistake by relying entirely on you.

But please, help me, George. I cannot stomach any longer the way Alex looks upon me when the audience takes up their sniggering – sniggering done at the terribleness of our act, not the humour of it. His strangled expression now strays beyond the stage, and I will not stand for pity. His eyes go to me and he transforms somehow. Lightness goes, he sinks, and the apple of his throat does a great journey up, then down. When he talks to me, his words crack and stagger, like they did when he said goodbye to his childish voice. He is as embarrassed as I at my hopelessness. Me, with my full arrangement of arms, legs and height, yet no ability to lift, juggle or tumble.

Alex never fails to make the crowd gasp, kicking up each new ball until he has six in the air. He spins upon a toe beneath them, catching them in his mouth, his armpit, the crook of his

15

foot. That's what you get for a lifetime of training, for wasn't Grainger chucking stuff in his general direction from when we were just little chits, insisting he do not drop it, pick it up, get better. What did I get? Trained to fetch and carry for a selfish woman with a face shaped exactly like a pig. A girl ain't never gonna get a round of applause for that.

So, we must practise, George. We must get this routine exact. I'll start . . .

Grainger gives us our introductions – 'the girl-exotic and her most obliging parrot!' – and I step forward with a flourish – like so – bidding you to come fly upon my shoulder. As I walk about the performance space, I happen to say to one of the crowd, but for all to hear, 'What a fine introduction from such a man of clear distinction. Dost thou know whence my master fetched that excellent wig?'

And that's where you butt in and say . . .

'Skin of a dog. Skin of a dog.'

That's it, George! Yes! Keep this up, my yellow-billed friend and the cup of seeds is yours once more!

Onto my wrist now, let's have this looking proper.

So, I turn to you, giving it some bluster and I say, 'Shut your trap! Hold thy tongue, you feathered fop . . .' etcetera etcetera, until all the laugher has run its course. Then I go, 'Let us speak of the boy juggler instead, the one with the singular arm which we all did just see. He was most impressive, methinks? To what may he owe his wonderful talent?' And you say . . .

'To the gin. To the gin.'

'To the gin, why, you little tell-tale! I am sure he is too young to be quaffing. Well, perhaps just a finger for the purposes of medicine . . .'

'By the pint. By the pint.'

Yes, George! Yes! You clever bird! Why it was so bleeding hard to do this when folks were listening, I'll never know. Don't you dare go silent on me again. Give us a verse of the poem by the Earl and I might just consider the matter done and you forgiven.

'Her father gave her . . .'

You marvellous chuck! What did he give her?

'. . . dildoes six . . .'

Yes, he did!
Whatever they are.
Now, rub your cheek onto mine, dear George, and know that I could never live without ya. If I was made to go, if Grainger sent me packing, I would take you with me. Though he may not be as willing to part with you as surely as he's willing to part with me.

Did you see my serving of slop this evening? The geese got better helpings, the pig too, even though, yet again, it did all its mathematical feats entirely wrong. What does it matter, is what my master and his wife say, when the people watching can't do the sums themselves. But the fact remains, my worth to them is lower than a sow, less than half a dish of dinner.

'It's cos you're doing half the work you were before,' says my master's wife, 'now that Hildy's upped and gone.' Lizzy is accurate, of course. No more fetching and carrying, no answering Hildy's every whim, no cleaning her shifts and stockings or beating the bugs from her fine frocks.

She left me this dress, whaddya think? A little on the loose side, but I reckon it suits me well.

No more trimming her nails, combing and piling up her endless hair, placing the black spots on her great big cheeks and powdering that massive swine-faced nose.

Where do you reckon she is now, Georgie-boy? The gold streets of London? Got herself a dressing room at Sadler's Wells, I bet. She'll have a painter in there, putting her likeness onto pieces of ivory so they might be sold for three guineas after the show. Or maybe she's on her way to Venice, as that was always her biggest desire. Oh, Venice, George, can you even imagine! Venice – where they'd treat her like the celebrated person she is! Give her a life full of luxuries. There'd be no more rickety cart journeys, no more living cheek by jowl with birds and beasts, or suffering the bellyache of bad tavern food. Riches beyond your young imagination, is how she described it.

'But who'll look after ya, when you go?' I'd say, never thinking she'd actually do it, or at least believing she'd take me with her.

'My dresser,' she told me, 'my coachman, my butler, my cook.'

'Well, that's me now, ain't it!' I said. 'I'm all four of them people rolled up into one!'

That set her to laughing – *honk, honk honk.*

Was that the key to her success, d'ya think, George? Her being able to laugh as porkily as she presented?

'*I* look after *you*,' she corrected. 'I have been the mother you never had.'

I took that to mean she would never leave me behind, that she would always share the spoils. I thought it meant love. Stupid me.

'*Stupid you. Stupid you.*'

How easy it is to be wise, George, when all is said and done. Two mothers I've had now and I don't think I'll be looking for a third, thank you very much. My heart ain't broken, but I'm starting to think it has a bruise or two.

Now, if I was truly Hildy's daughter, all would be different. I'd have been born with a hog-face just like hers and Grainger would have had no choice but to prize me too.

'You were supposed to grow up all big and black and frizzy,' he is fond of saying, when the takings are low, 'a mysterious and terrifying beauty, but look at you! You're not one thing nor the other!'

I hate that man for the things that fall from his mouth. Hate him, yet depend upon him entirely. Don't think that the contradiction doesn't rub and cause a sore.

''Tis all fantasy though. My ideas have as many holes as my

stockings. Being Hildy's real daughter would not have saved me. She only looked the way she did because her mother witnessed a terrible coach crash while Hildy was in her belly. The shock turned the baby, that's why she came out the way she did. Looking pig-like ain't a skill you inherit.

'Perhaps it was the same crash what took Alex's arm,' I said when Hildy first told me. I was only little then, of course, all gathered up by the horror of it.

'Oh my dear,' she replied, 'if you'd received an education of the standard my father gave to me, you would find your arithmetic is somewhat deficient.'

It was one of those phrases of Hildy's, one of many, that I needed to take away with me and think about for a moment, untangle all the words to work out what she meant.

'Deficient' means 'lacking', George, in case you were too small-brained to know it.

And, as it was, I could do the sums just fine. I only spoke fast because my mind was whirring. Those sums I learnt from Hildy herself, what with her having so much unused education to spare. Her father, she told me, said she'd never find a husband, having been born grotesque, so she'd better get herself some brains instead. Very proud she was of her intelligence, though I don't see how it helped her any. All that teaching, and she ended up in the exact same place as me. You need the right face to become a lady proper. Hildy taught me an accumulation calculation for that one. Brains times face equals success. But if you multiply anything by nothing you come away empty-handed.

Oh, I miss her, George, and I hope the very best for her.

But also I wish her good riddance. She was a difficult bloody madam and I was tired of her horrible ways.

The skills I picked up looking after her shall not go to waste. I will bestow them upon others who'll appreciate them more. My needlework, made excellent from repairing her frocks, I am gifting now to Old Joe, sewing up his face each night from that awful first punch, the one what swings the crowd. I cannot say I approve in any way. I do not like our gentle Joe having to suffer such violence. I do not like the gulling of poor folk who come only to be cheered-up after a hard day's work. And I certainly cannot bear Alex taking that final blow. It sends a shiver through me, even though I know it's not thrown half as hard as it appears and does not do its promised damage. But I also understand that times are tough now Hildy has done her flit. Money is money, and money is food, however it's gathered.

This evening the sleight was off. Alex got hit harder than he should. His lip split wide, something dreadful.

''Tis but a flea bite,' he reckoned, the corner of his mouth bulging like a plum.

'Sit down!' I said, sticking the three-legged stool by the fire. 'I'll fetch the gin.'

And there it was again, that gaze of his upon me, something soft like sorrow, a gulp in his throat. I looked away, head bowed, and readied my needle. He sat, as if the blood had gone from his legs and he had no choice.

I leant down then and took his cheek in my hand, and – zooks! – did he flinch! Even before I'd touched the wound. When I dabbed the gin-soaked rag to him, he leapt so high I thought he might land on top of the fire.

21

'Holy mother, Mim!' he hissed. 'I thought you meant the gin to drink!'

'Yeah, like we need us another brandy face round here,' I said, and we shared a look that spoke a whole gospel on the antics of our master.

'You know the swelling will still be there at the next place,' I told him as I worked – little Xs of thread in a line travelling upwards from the top of his lip. Alex bit down, gripped the stool, sweated away the pain. 'Won't it blow the whole trick,' I asked him, 'if the next lot see your mush already good and thumped?'

'Nah,' says he. 'Shows 'em I'm happy for it.'

'And, are ya?' I wanted to know. 'Happy for it?'

'Course I am! You've seen the portions I've been getting since Hildy's gone, since me and Joe came up with this whole con.'

'Your brains'll leak out one of these nights,' I muttered. 'Now keep still. Can't finish this, can I, if you keep on blabbering.'

I took my time, was more delicate with my fancywork than I am with Joe. I didn't want there to be any scar. Old Joe's face is so battered by life it carries every mark it gets, most hidden in the beginnings of his beard. Alex, though, still holds onto his boyish skin. A cut upon his face seems twice as dire.

He watched me out the side of his eye as I stitched, checking, I suppose, that I could be trusted with the needle more than I can with a crowd to entertain.

'I'll share with you, Mim,' he said, once I'd cast off and stood back to admire my handiwork. 'My servings,' he went on, 'I won't let you go short.'

I nodded, ashamed all over again, that he had noticed the lack of food in my dish telling of what I'm worth – that his pity was coming out like this, in a way not easy to ignore.

But we did not dwell. He was all brightness quick enough.

'Whaddya reckon?' he says. 'Am I still handsome, even though me lip's the same size as a turbot?'

'Not sure how you could be,' I replied, calm as you like, 'when you were such an ugly bugger to begin with!'

Oh, go on, give us one of your laughs, George. Do Lizzy's great cackle for me. I was being funny. Alex thought me so too.

I don't find him ugly at all, you see, that's the joke. I have long thought him handsome. Don't look at me like that! It's nothing I keep secret. If anyone asked me for an opinion upon him I would say it. That freckled skin, the blue of his eyes – he is a kind of beautiful.

Yes, that's it exactly – he is a kind of beautiful.

For lately I do find myself staring at him. Not in the same way he looks at me. Different, I believe. I look at his left arm. Or should I rightly say, the lack of it. The deficiency, if you are wanting a dressy word for something quite everyday. And really it is the opposite, if you think on it. Because Alex is so much more without that arm. Distinctive.

Is it cruel of me to say so? Am I seeing the world as Grainger does?

How can I be? For Alex has been there all my life – all of it that I can remember. Yet it's only now he strikes my interest. Perhaps it's because I have the time, without Hildy to care for, to sit idle every so often and look about me.

If I see Alex at work, my gaze goes to his shoulder where

it curves down and the bone starts but doesn't carry on. It's as though he has tried to grow a new arm but nature has disappointed him, got distracted by something more fascinating, never finished the job. Someone as neat as me with the stitches must have been there when Alex had the accident, because the scar is quite smooth. Not that I would ever dare touch it, but this is how it looks to the eye. I find it sort of lovely. I know people pay to see him do difficult tasks with one hand – juggle those wooden balls and box Old Joe as if he had an arm tied behind his back – but in truth he hardly ever struggles. I watch him haul the ropes, roll the tarpaulin, that small piece of bone moving in the shoulder, trying to do what a whole arm should do, and I can only see him as capable. More capable than me.

Then I think myself bad for staring, just like the crowds in the fields do. Do they come and watch, I wonder, so they might feel better about their own unlucky lot in life? Am I the same? Only staring to pour damp on a raging sadness? It does not feel that way.

He caught me looking this evening, my gaze travelling down from his lip, all tidied up, to his left shoulder.

'What are you staring at, slave girl?!' he snapped.

And I went hot at the idea that he had seen the journey of my eyes, so I countered quickly. I stuck my bottom lip out at him, as if giving his question my serious thought, then with a voice all proper, as I do when performing, I told him, 'I can't say for certain for there is no sign hung upon this particular freak.'

His reply: 'As if you could read it if there were!' He is always doubting my claims that Hildy taught me my letters as well as my numbers. 'I should smack your brown bum!' he went on. 'I should give you a good hiding!'

Oh, don't look so shocked, George. The whole thing was done with the biggest of smiles. He chased me then, round the fire, though it soon wasn't clear who was doing the running-away.

'Which hand will you be smacking me with?' I teased, 'if you're gonna use the good one for doing the catching?'

And that was when I went over the stool and landed in the muck – serve me right!

'Mercy!' I wailed as he stood over me.

'Mercy! Mercy!'

Yes, George!

'Mercy!'

I was an actress in the middle of my death scene.

'Mercy upon me!'

Though I knew I was never in any real danger. We've played this game since we were children. There was a time when he'd have jumped on top of me, pinning my arms down with his knees, threatening to spit, until I flipped him over and did the same. On and on we'd go, tumbling through the grass, laughing like jackdaws.

I think I saw the idea of it cross his mind tonight, to carry on like we used to do, but he soon swept it away. Bit too grown up we are now to be playing like kiddies.

Mercy was granted, of course. He offered me his hand, his good one, excellent enough as it is. And once I was up and dusted down, he scurried away, reminding me of the mice that I disturb in the food store, the ones I catch in the act of nibbling at the bread.

ALEX

I've only gone and done it, pig. And I must speak to you of it, or else I'll hoot at the moon and wake the lot of 'em.

My master has ordered me to talk to you, after all – to smarten you up. They're losing hope that you'll ever get your sums right, let alone be able to play quadrille, or read a lady's mind, or whatever it is you learned pigs are supposed to do. You might wanna take my lead, mate, and get working on your show skills, if you don't fancy a spike up your backside and an apple in your gob. Don't think they won't do it, my master and his wife. They'll put you over the fire and eat you for breakfast, as fast as look at ya, if you ain't putting money in the tin. That's how this life works. And if you can't quite believe it, let this convince ya.

Tonight as Lizzy stirred the pot I overheard her ask my master: 'Oh, what're we to be doing with her now?'

I pricked up my ears at that, leant closer to the tarp so I could hear them on the other side. There is only one 'her' they could be gabbing about, only one 'her' of the human kind in our lot besides Lizzy since Hildy fled. Only one 'her' who ain't bringing in the pennies. She dies a little death in front of the crowd every evening because of that stubborn bloody parrot.

My master, already several gins down the alley, replied to his wife like so: 'Why, we'll sell her on. Put an advert in the paper.'

That alone should have set me to action.

'Sell her to who!' scoffed my mistress. 'It's black boys that are the fashion now. Mop squeezers like her, well, they come for free these days.'

So after a pause, my master offers: 'We'll marry her then.'

'Marry!' squawks Lizzy.

'To be rid of the expense of her, I mean.'

'Marry!' she squawks again. 'You blockhead! You're off the hooks! Men might wanna stare at her a while, all coffee-coloured and interesting, but who's gonna wanna marry a bastard girl like that? We've got no dowry to be offering. She's a debt, not a prize.'

All went quiet, except for the squelch of the slop and the crackle of the fire. I supposed that my master was doing some cooking himself, inside in his own head, thinking up a marvellous plan to save our Mim. Because surely he is fond of her, I thought. How could he not be, having raised her from a baby?

But no.

'She is pretty.' That is what my master murmured in the low-low voice of a devil.

'Pretty?' says Lizzy. 'What's that got to do with the price of . . .' Her voice trailed away.

'And there is another rewarding business, isn't there, dear, to be done with a young girl with a face like that and a cunny not yet been–'

'All right, Frank! All right! I get the picture!'

Lizzy sighed. There was more stirring of the pot, more squelching.

'You've had me do some terrible deeds over the years,' said she, 'but really, have I got the stomach to be that kind of go-between?'

I backed away from my hiding place.

It was as clear as daylight, though the night was black enough to stop me seeing my own hand in front of me face. I was the only one with a marvellous plan for saving Mim, and I would need to get a hurry-on, because it sounded like Lizzy's morals were loose-fitting and soon to be in the market for haggling.

Once my master and his wife were snoring, I fetched our longest rope and I went in search of two trees. You see, I have been sitting on this grand idea for an age, my mudlark friend, ever since we crossed paths with those amazing Turks in the West Country. But that's all I have done – sat on it, like a daft chicken warming eggs that have had no help from the cock.

You see, this is the thing about me, pig – I am a boy what waits. I wait until there is absolutely no other bloody choice but to do the thing I rightly must. And tonight was that time.

I had to, so I went and I did.

As soon as I'd got the job done with the rope and the trees, I went and fetched Mim from the animal trailer. She beds down in the straw with the hare and the geese now. No more kipping on tavern room floors since Hildy's cleared off.

'It's late,' she argued, groggy and soaked in sleep. 'What the bleeding hell do you want?'

There was the print of stalks on her face and her hair was

wild from the brushing out she does at night, cursing as she goes, but still I could see it – exactly what my master was getting at. She is pretty, pig – very – and it is as though she has all of a sudden become that way. Or I have been blind to it until now. The bones of her cheeks have risen up, her eyes deepened in colour. She stands out so tall, so different, against all those other lasses we see from field to field – them white ewes with their shelves of milky breasts. My mistress compares Mim's skin to coffee, but having never drunk the stuff, I cannot say. Lately I find myself staring at her, when she isn't watching, at her smooth brown skin, trying to work out a way to describe it, like a poet might, though I ain't no sort with words. Is she the colour that leaves turn come September? Like the shine on the soil of a riverbank, or the tawny stuff inside of willow bark? No. Nothing like them. And I feel ridiculous for suggesting it. Should we want any proof that Joe's punches have turned my brain to mush, there it is – me pretending I could ever be some kind of versifier.

'Whaddya want?' Mim crowed, up on her elbows in her straw bed. 'Get that candle away! Or this whole wagon'll go up!'

'I know it's late,' I said, 'but come 'n' look at the moon. The clouds have shifted from earlier and it's glowing huge.'

Light like that don't come often, pig. I was taking it as a sign that my timing was just right. And it convinced her too, for up she got, following me out, wearing just her white shift. The moon made a full shadow of her body through the linen – the whole scene! The lot! – but I didn't make mention of it because I reckoned she would be red-faced to know it.

Mim weren't immediately pleased on sight of the rope,

30

even though I wasted plenty of breath wowing her with my story of it – how I'd sneaked out unseen, how much trouble I'd gone to to get the thing hanging at just the right slackness.

She nodded with half-heart, asked: 'So what are you going to do with it?' She gave the rope a gentle push, watched it swing all sad in the silver light. And this was when I wished I had a stash of words in my gob like Mim does. Always ready with a fancy word or six, is she. I wanted to describe to her those Turks in their silky trousers and what they did, make her see it as clearly as I had. I wished for the tongue of a hawker like my master, who can sell anything to the first man who comes walking. I wished to be that poet, that versifier, that I so clearly ain't, a man who can describe a girl's particular beauty so it feels as though she is right there with you, close enough to touch, if you dared, if she wanted you to.

But I have always been better with the doing than the saying. So I took a running jump at that rope, hit it at its lowest curve, landed my belly upon it, feet lifted. Using my hand to steady myself, I flew. Just a little.

'We swing on it,' I said, smiling, doing my hardest to put a smile on her face too. 'At first, that is. Like this. And then after that . . .'

Well, I had to step down for the next part. I had to rely on my words, because I don't yet have the bodily knowhow to show her, and I didn't want to shame myself. Falling and cracking my only wrist is my greatest fear. I see the way Mim looks at my shoulder sometimes, at what's missing below. I imagine her pitying thoughts. A split lip will heal but that arm ain't never gonna grow back, so I do everything I can to distract her from it. I stand at the right angle, act like no task is ever any bother. My master whipped me as a young 'un until I could juggle and tumble for that very reason – to turn all eyes away from what I'm lacking. It's a clever con, just like the boxing trick, just like convincing the crowd that Abel is small and harmless, then having him rob 'em of their money with a hand, furtive-like, into their pocket, or by getting him to challenge 'em to a game of cup and balls that they never can win.

'So yeah, we swing first,' I told her, 'and then when the audience thinks, *oh, is that all they're gonna do, what a bleeding disappointment!* we hop up and lie on the rope, act like it's the easiest thing in the whole world, like we're as comfy as a captain snoozing in his hammock. Then before the crowd has time to put another doubt in their heads we're up on our feet on it.'

'Our feet!' she cried and I made her shush. I didn't want anyone waking. Didn't want the game to be given away. 'But it moves about!' was her protest, quieter now. 'It's nothing like balancing on a log across a stream.'

'I know,' I tells her. 'I know!' She's smart is Mim; she understood the difficulty. 'And ain't that what makes it so impressive! But I've seen it done. Seen it with me own eyes!' And that was when I got so gathered up in my excitement that I grabbed hold of her hand. She looked down at the joining up of our fingers with the strangest of faces, making me snatch mine back, as quick as lightning.

'I'm sorry,' I said.

'Oh,' she said. 'Are you? What of?'

'Nothing!'

I pulled myself up tall.

What followed was the most awful of silences. I don't go in for them much, big batches of quiet. I might not be good with words, but if there aren't any passing back and forth it can make me right itchy.

'So then what?' she asked, breaking the moment, looking at me straight with those dark brown eyes.

'Then we walk on the rope,' I said. 'And then we dance, and then we do our somersaults which we know are easy upon the ground but we find a way to do 'em up there on the rope . . .'

She made to tell me that she cannot do those things even upon the ground, but I stopped her – shush! Sniv it! – told her she was spoiling the picture I was trying to draw.

'Then we balance all sorts of things on our noses and chins,' I went on, 'without them things or us falling down. And then we juggle and then we sing, and then we might even shift the rope higher if it makes the audience gasp and then . . .'

'And then?' Her eyes were all a-fire; I could see it.

I'd got her!

And then we do a flit, just like Hildy, I could have said. 'One-arm'd boy' or 'girl-exotic', that would be just extra fruit upon the tree if we pulled this off. It's an act that goes with you, I could have said, just like you wanted. We'll head to that Bartholomew Fayre we've heard talk of, cross the seas even, to Paris, Venice, make our own fortune without any master taking the lion's share, us always being the goats and the sheep. But I didn't say that, because it seemed too much to drop into the lap of a girl in the moonlight. I only shrugged.

She nodded a while, grew quiet, wasn't agreeing as such, only considering. Finally she said: 'We?'

One word. Hanging in the sharp air.

It made me scared. Maybe she wanted to do it, but not with me. Maybe she would like my master's idea of marrying out, someone with the full arrangement of arms. Perhaps I should have told her what else they had planned, only to nudge her to my side, but I couldn't. I knew it would make her cry, something she'd done plenty of since Hildy had gone, though she tried her best to hide her tears. She wouldn't understand anyway. For all her fancy words and abilities with the sums, Mim is an innocent. Hildy only taught her ladies' ways. There'd have been no talk of men and their nature. I have bunked with the likes of Abel and Joe all my life, been given a whole different education – Abel always joking about the one part of his body that is most certainly full-size and what he likes to do with it given half the chance. Joe I've caught plenty of times letting a girl have a taste of that bear growl at close quarters, his visitor bouncing on top of him as joyful as the hare at mealtimes. Me and Mim might have been brought up in the same family, if that's anywhere close to the right word for it, but it's not been the same family at all.

After the longest bit of thinking Mim said, 'He'll kill you one day not meaning to.'

'What, Grainger?' I asked.

'No,' she said, 'Old Joe.'

So we were back to my brain spilling. And then I clocked it – she thought I was saving myself with these rope tricks, that I was the one desperate for a new act, not her. I did not set her straight, let her have her pride. All I wanted was her 'yes'.

'And they won't be letting me back on the cart when the slop runs short,' said she.

A tear made its way down her face and I wanted very badly to wipe it away, but of course, I didn't dare.

'Don't cry, Mim,' I said, 'I don't think I can stand it if you . . .'

And that was when Abel's snoring started up, scaring small creatures back into the scrub. I'm telling you, pig, that fellow might be half your size but his snorting is twice the racket.

Perhaps I would have said something kind to Mim if we'd not been interrupted, something nice. I ain't sure what exactly, I just felt it rising up, like a bubble of air ready to burst on the surface of a stream. But we fell to laughing instead. Shaking with it, since we couldn't make any real noise.

'We need to get practising, slave-girl,' I said once the joke had worked its way out of us, 'if we want our names to be writ biggest on our masters' next handbill!'

'Too right, stumpy!' she said, and I should, by rights, have given her a fierce pinch for saying that, and I would have done, if she hadn't taken a run at the lowest curve of the rope, given her whole body to it, lifted her feet in the moonlight, and flown.

The new moon appears again, bold and fresh, after an almost-month spent folding itself away then unpacking its circular self once more. In those in-between times, when the moon was not generous, candles were lit – many of them. At night, the rope became an altar, each flame an earnest prayer. The consequences of such decadent tallow-burning they left for the morning.

The fayre hawker's wife wakes and sniffs the air, suspicious. She pulls the tarp close to her nose, the undergarments too, strung wet in lines above their camp. She knows it is there, the echo-scent of fat only recently lit, and she knows who to go to with the blame.

'Oi,' she will yell. 'You! Girl-bleeding-exotic! Get your arse here!'

And the girl, in her too-big dress, will report to her mistress, all virtue, shaking her head at the accusations, claiming she witnessed her master going a-bed in his cups, without bothering to extinguish the lights. But still, she receives an extra beating, in addition to her customary one. The fayre hawker's wife chants to the rhythm of her strikes.

'Well. You. Ought. To. Av. Blown. Em. Out. Then!'

These particular punishments the girl finds she can endure, for pain that has purpose is enviably more bearable than the random sort. She is past believing, as she was told as a youngster, that a thrashing from your mistress is a sign of good care but still, she is able to see these sufferings as part of a process. She screws her eyes tight to the sting and thinks of the night-time secret she shares with the boy and how, in keeping it safe, she is bringing herself closer to a thing more longer-lasting.

But what that thing is, precisely, is difficult to articulate.

Closer to better portions of food, is how she levels it to herself and to the boy. Closer to escape, is how she sees it within the quiet confines of her own mind. Closer to London, Paris, Venice, perhaps. But there is more . . .

When she is out there, sharing the night with the small insects and the newly fascinating boy, she has grown aware of a feeling. She is moving – nay, hurtling – towards something, fast. She cannot pin this feeling down, cannot sound it out with a neatly elaborate phrase, or one singularly impressive word. She can only confirm there is indeed a sensation and that it is thrilling. She receives it as it comes, discovers it part by part.

Oftentimes the boy will stand between his furious mistress and the cowering girl during an attack and make his speech. 'Oh, do me instead, Lizzy,' he'll say. 'We're both as innocent as each other so what's the bleeding difference!' And the irascible woman, not particular who receives her anger, will oblige the boy with a wooden spoon, sharply about his head.

He takes the dose, not covering his crown with his one good hand. Nursing a sore head, they can continue their night-time practices. But with broken fingers, the challenge would become insurmountable.

And already it is proving to be a task that desires to defeat them.

If you had been with the owl in the tree or the hedgehog in the brush observing their very first rehearsals, you would have thought you were witnessing the birth of a new comedy routine – one that does not require the witticisms of a parrot.

The girl attempts to lie upon the rope; the rope flips her to the floor.

The boy and girl run for the rope to execute alternating swings; the rope flies back and thumps them across the face.

They both try over and over to stand upon the rope; and over and over the rope insists they fall.

One tumble sees the girl land badly upon her ankle, making it swell so wildly she suspects a break.

'Oh, it is no good now!' wails she, as loudly as secrecy will allow. 'And *never* will it be any good!'

But the boy-what-waited has become the boy-what-does, and he will not stand for this talk. They shall not knuckle under. He gives the girl his good shoulder, despite her protestations – a flinching that he misinterprets as revulsion – and with her limping close to him, the warmth of her on his hip, the boy takes her the few lurching steps to the site of the fire and the stool. Water is heated on the embers, a cloth soaked.

'Take your stockings off,' says he, affecting a physician's voice.

'I cannot do that!' exclaims the girl. 'In front of you!'

The boy buries his one useful hand in the opposite shirted armpit, dips chin to chest.

''Tis dark,' he argues. 'I'd hardly see. And you're hurt, in't ya?'

But the girl's chin sits high in contradiction, she is not to be moved.

'Come on, Mim,' he reasons. 'Let me fix you up, like you did for my lip. I mean, what's a foot to a lip. It's all part of the whole, innit?'

'But a lady never shows a gentlemen her–' begins the girl, parroting back the manners she has learnt from her hog-faced mistress.

'Well,' cuts in the boy, taking the briefest pause, thinking how to place this. (She is a girl, he wants to say, not a lady, but he has little desire to lengthen their arguing, so he takes a different tack.) 'Well, a lady don't go throwing herself off a rope all hours of the night either, does she?!'

This is always the best defence, to scold her in this playful way – and it saves him now. She pushes away a smile.

'I'm a good boy, Mim,' he goes on, 'and you bleeding well know it.'

She does. The girl does know. So, while he sets his gaze off course, she unfastens the garter rag at her thigh, and in the quiet of the night, rolls back the wool. The boy turns back and the sight of her bare ankle sets a ripple through the muscles of his throat, a reflex he wishes he had some power to master. He removes his hand from the opposite armpit, warmed from its time there, and places it against the smooth brown skin of her foot. Neither of them dares to breathe as he kneels before her – making a new altar of her, perhaps – and lifts the leg so it rests upon his lap. Then with gentle palpations he discovers the extent of the swelling, working from toe to shin until the girl gasps a small strangled, 'Don't!'

He stops, asks gently: 'Am I hurting you?'

She shakes her head, her breath coming in a tremble. And then in a move that is curious to both of them, she leans forward, takes hold of his hand and shifts it upwards, onto her knee, then to the beginnings of her thigh and then . . .

The boy assumes she must be taking him away from the site of the pain, for what else could she be . . .

There is a stirring within his breeches and, in one swift and terrified movement, he places her foot onto the ground and leaps to standing, busying himself, his back to her, with the practical nonsense of preparing a hot compress. Poise restored, he goes and hands it over.

'Place this where the pain is worst,' says he.

As little children they tumbled and brawled together, thinking nothing of it. (Both revolve this memory in their minds as the girl presses the warm bundle of cloth against her ankle.) Yet here they are now, lost for their wits after the touch of a thigh. What on this green earth has changed between them?

Once the tended-to ankle is elevated upon a resting place, the boy ventures, 'You might wanna lose the stockings altogether.' He leaps back in, ready against her offence, 'I mean, you need to have a good grip on that rope. Them Turks what I saw had these thin socks made of leather or skin or somesuch.'

'I can sew us a pair of them,' says she, 'steal some corners off things here and there, piece them together, treat them with oil.'

'And what about your petticoats and stays?' he says, bracing himself again for objection.

But there is none. She smiles at him in the strangest fashion.

'What of them?' she asks.

'Well, stays won't let you move freely. And I don't wanna seem vulgar or nothing, but when we get to hanging upside down . . .'

The girl posts the fabric of her skirts between the flesh of her thighs. That word – vulgar – reminding her, all of a sudden, to be prim once more.

'You wanna get some breeches like mine,' says the boy. He stands so he can strut a cock-walk, lifting the tails of his untucked shirt, allowing her to see the garment in its entirety. 'I wear mine a bit looser below the knees than others so I can do me handstands and whatnot, but every pair's got space around these parts for running and jumping.' He gestures to the generosity of fabric about his crotch, safe as it is now to do so, and the girl permits her eyes to go there, as directed. But the lingering spirit of her hog-faced mistress is again in her ear, chiding her for such indecency. She shifts her eyes, only to land on the flat, tanned skin of the boy's bare belly where she should not be looking either.

'I find them most tolerable,' she says quickly, pushing her attention to her now less-swollen ankle.

'You could botch a pair from Hildy's leftovers,' suggests the boy and the girl nods slow. That she must dress as a man – as someone else – leaches even more of the joy from the night than her injured ankle.

'Oh, but it is taking us so long,' she sighs. 'Even longer now I must rest this foot.'

The boy does not miss a beat. 'All the best things do,' he returns. 'I reckon cheese left a little while to soften and ripen is much the better for it. I dunno. It must work with things aside from grub. Meaningful things, I'm saying.'

Their eyes meet at the understanding of this.

Now, if you had been there with the rodents in the rough and the moths about the flames observing the rehearsal when the pair at last mastered the knack of standing upon the rope, then you would have thought to be witnessing a lottery win amid the trees. They rose together, slowly, from a crouch to legs straightened, wobbling upon the line, dressed in breeches fashioned from leftover silk, and once they were up, they met the other's victorious gaze with the widest of smiles. Then they leapt, in harmony, to the ground, so they might celebrate by grasping the other's hand in a kind of flourish – for cheering was not allowed. Then they fell to embracing riotously, before springing apart, remembering themselves – still unsure how to behave since the boy's hand had felt the warmth of the girl's thigh that night.

They coughed away their embarrassment, kicked their strange oilskin booties in the dirt.

'Think what we can do now, Mim!' said the boy, fanning the flames of their enthusiasm.

'We could toss things to one another, catch glass marbles in jars.'

'Then spear fruit upon forks.'

'I'll fetch Hildy's fan.'

'And balance it upon your conk?'

'Or even upon my toe.'

'Then I will juggle with fire.'

'And I shall slide right down into a perfect front split.'

'You could stand upright on one foot in a front split, Mim, I'm sure of it.'

'While I recite a word-perfect poem by the Earl!'

'Then I will join you in a ditty.'

'Oh, save us! You sing like a cat!'

'Then I'll play upon Lizzy's pipe instead, while you dance along.'

'And then . . .'

'And then the crowd will cheer.'

'And we . . . ?'

'We . . .'

The boy was not lost for an answer but rather too full of them.

The girl needed no answer at all. There was that mysterious sensation again – that thrilling feeling of hurtling, too fast. And here was a way to better describe it: being out in the night air with the small insects and the newly fascinating boy felt exactly the same as when making up a story with someone else, trying to imagine what marvellous thing might come next. It is not the knowing of what follows, only the understanding that something will, and that you wish to stay to see what it is.

'And then we go to bed,' said the boy. 'To get some kip,' he quickly clarified. 'We'll need plenty of vim for our next practice.'

The girl nodded and bade him goodnight, retreating to the animal wagon where she swapped breeches for a shift. The boy loped back to the farty confines of the covered cart to claim a space aside his adopted brothers, who when awake and watched become the 'dwaff' and the 'no-legg'd brute'.

Then both girl and boy fell asleep apart to dream of a future together, one painted in much brighter colours. A dream that swung and sung and somersaulted and swelled.

Oh, what a shame that you did not witness that exhaultatious rehearsal, for truly it was a joyous one. And, of its kind, it was the very last.

MIM

Here's a lesson for you, George: we are to observe, collect and organise.

I have restored Hildy's standing mirror and set a candle before it for this very task. Perch atop my shoulder and let us begin. No dropping husks from your beak though, no fouling from the other end either. My dresser-of-sorts will be arranged with many a valuable whatnot once I've decided which objects to collect. Not valuable in the money-meaning; valuable in the learning sense. I am to continue my education even though Hildy's gone. Tonight brought a way for me to do that. To truly better myself.

But for now, you are it. You are the first curio in my collection.

George the Yellow-billed Amazon.

George the *Amazona collaria* of the Psittacidae family.

Aren't I clever for memorising something as tongue-mangling as that?

Say it with me, for it's your family name, not mine.

Psittacidae.

Si-tass-ee-die.

Si-tass-ee-die.

'Sit down! Sit down!'

No, George.

'Numbskull! Numbskull!'

George!

'What a nob! What a nob!'

Wherever did you pick that up? Quiet with you! Observe! Look into this mirror and tell what you see. Do you see an 'oi'? Do you see a 'girl-exotic'? Or am I now something else?

When Hildy was still here, I was a girl travelling fast in the direction of becoming a lady. We can agree on that much, can't we, George? Being a lady was all she ever stood for. How could I have been heading anyplace else?

'Don't you ever feel like hitching up your skirts and running about a bit,' I'd ask her, 'making a racket? Laughing like a cuckoo?'

'Of course,' she'd reply, 'but being a lady is always more important.'

I'd even asked her if she considered doing the other thing – you know, what we hear Abel and Joe getting up to with the lasses who loiter after the crowd's gone home. What we hear Grainger and Lizzy attempting on high days and holidays. I asked her if she'd ever thought of doing it for the money, if not for the fun – since fun wasn't something a lady should be in the market for.

I'd clocked those painted girls, you see, winding through our audience looking for a little bit of business of their own. Hildy

46

wouldn't have had to bother with the looking. Gentlemen (if that's the correct word for them) came hunting for her after almost every performance, wondering if possibly, maybe, if the price were right and the circumstances suitable, etcetera, etcetera . . .

Pigginess, it seems, is a thrill in more ways than one. The sums of money they suggested, it seemed quite brainless to refuse. But refuse them she did.

'A lady should be chaste.'

Ha, George! Yes! It's like she's still bleeding here!

But I pushed her. Wouldn't the money she earned go directly in her hand, not through Grainger, and wasn't the having of money the only way the likes of us would go up in the world? She laughed at that, loud and long, so I knew just how stupid she thought me.

'A lady should be chaste,' said she, thick with clarification, 'but that isn't all she can be.'

I couldn't get a handle on it. Those painted girls get called 'women of pleasure' and the last time I'd felt it, pleasure wasn't something to run away from. Yet I could see that those girls weren't the happiest hens in the nest.

'Chastity is your strongest asset,' said Hildy. 'Your only asset. Use it to marry the right gentleman, someone of standing. That way you'll achieve your true potential.'

But hadn't we gone round in one huge, unsatisfying circle. She weren't mentioning the most obvious thing – the thing staring back at us in this here mirror. Neither of us would ever qualify as a lady. Pig-faced or brown-faced, it didn't matter: we were rejects, poor. Men of standing did not look at us and

47

see us as the marrying kind.

Or so I thought.

Let us return to our observing.

If I had kept this glass in place, not packed it away in my sorrow with Hildy's other leftovers, I might have seen how my appearance has changed of late, how I have been travelling in the wrong direction, away from being a lady. I have become a girl who seems out of place in a frock, one who forgoes stays and petticoats for shirts and breeches. I bind my hair so tight to my head it might as well not be there and sometimes I've stuffed the whole lot of it inside a cap, before thrusting on my leather booties and heading out to work the rope. I confess, George, I've also, in the briefest of moments, let myself bend to the idea of certain pleasures, ones only men should want. Though I've not allowed myself to do the complete back-bend, if you get my meaning.

Had I lifted my nose from that dirty rope for just a second, I would have seen it – the error of my ways. But mercifully, it was pointed out to me this very evening. By a gentleman. He saw me for what I am beneath the grime – a lady, potentially, and one that might be described as a beauty.

'You're a beauty.'

All along you've been telling me, George, and now I see it may be true.

After our usual show tonight, after I had packed away the geese and the hare, and set the pig in her pen, I headed back to the fire, to our tarped-over quarters between the carts. There I met with Alex, to talk of the rope, hushed of course, until

Lizzy arrived back, catching us conferring, catching me with my hand upon the wooden spoon, stirring the slop which she had left to stick to the pot.

'Put that down!' she shrieked and I dropped that spoon as fast as a horseshoe fresh out the brazier. 'I got you pegged,' she hissed, rounding on me, 'I know what you're practising for.' Which of course I thought to mean the rope, that she had overheard and we were now discovered.

'It's only rope tricks,' I muttered, and this set my mistress to laughter.

'Oh, there's a coy term for it!' she cried. 'Rope tricks! Rope tricks! I know your tricks, missy. I see you. I know what you're aiming at now your position's in doubt.' She put her face close to mine. '"Pretty" he called you the other night, "pretty". Where the bleeding hell is he getting that from?'

I shook my head, knowing nothing of what she was saying.

'He ain't interested!' she spat. 'I do that. I do *all* of that. So you stay out of it.' She tapped the sloppery spoon against my head. 'Get this into your thick skull,' she jeered, telling me what I just told you, 'you are not the marrying kind!'

Then came another voice, 'My lady?'

It was our gentleman, suddenly upon us, with his lovely vowels and his excellent shoes.

'My lady,' he said again with a gentle bow, now Lizzy's attentions were all upon him.

And I ain't never seen a transformation as miraculous as the one that came over Lizzy then. Her spoon was lobbed, her skirts flicked, her furrowed face was all at once serene, as if someone had taken a flat-iron to it.

'Oh, sir,' she quivered, her voice high and dancing, 'you did quite take me by surprise. Have you come visiting *per*chance to *pur*chase something from our most wonderful menagerie?'

'I do beg your pardon,' said the gentleman with another bow, a knowing smile spreading wide across a face that was not too-old, not too-young. 'It was never my intention to startle you. I desire to speak to the proprietor. Mr F. P. Grainger, I believe?'

His way of speaking, George! I wish you had been there so you could mimic it for me now. No amount of practising will have me uttering my *aahhs* and *ooos* like that. It's something you are born to. Lizzy roundabout swooned at the sound of him.

'Bien-y sur,' she cooed, tripping over her own curtseys and her terrible French, scurrying backwards in the direction of her husband in the tavern. 'Uno memento, silver-plates!'

That left the three of us – me, Alex and the gentleman – staring at one another. The words were stolen from my mouth – Alex's too – by the shine on the man's buttons, the firmness of his unpowdered brow, the whole picture of him. He thrust his hands into the pockets of his spotless breeches and took on a bold stance with hips shoved forward. Then seemingly without thinking, Alex did exactly the same – plunged a paw into his dusty pockets and arched his back like so – as if he'd realised all of a sudden this was the right way to hold yourself.

When Grainger finally arrived, his wig all askew, he had plenty of words to make up for our lack of them. Spilling from his gob, they were, askance. The pong of the liquor was so strong upon him we could have lit him as the evening's illuminations.

'I hear you wish to purchase one of our fine beasts?' he

slurred, forgetting the courtesy of a greeting. Our guest laughed, polite-like, as if my master had issued a witty little epigram. Remnants of a tavern dinner sat at the corners of Grainger's mouth. There was a boozer's drip at the end of his nose, a still-wet piss stain at the front of his breeches.

'I could not help but observe,' said our guest, 'the way in which you collect your wagers for the fight of an evening.'

Well, this comment worked like an instant sobering tonic – a magic spell, if you will. My master's words became immediately violent and precise, as much as he could make 'em that way.

'Oh, I see . . .' he said, puffing out his chest, 'I see what you're after and it's a no. No, no, no. All bets are final, I make that clear. God can't abide a bad loser, sir. Thank you. Now, be on your way.'

Our gentleman stayed put. 'I did not gamble, sir.'

'Eh? Did you not?' Grainger swayed in his boots, confuddled. 'Well, then, you missed a bloody good chance to get rich, didn't ya.'

'No, it is I, Mr Grainger, who comes to you with the offer of riches.' That knowing smile went broad across his face again. 'A "bloody good chance" of riches as you so illustratively put it.'

'I'm not following . . .'

'Well, you seem to be a man, correct me if I am mistaken, who takes a great joy from the accumulation of money.'

'You what?' Grainger swung his head from Alex and me, to Lizzy, then back to the gentleman, desperate for a grasp on what was happening. 'Sorry, which horse are we saddling here?'

That was when the gentleman remembered good manners for us all and handed out beautifully printed calling cards – one to Grainger and one to me. To me, George, he chose me!

Mr Sebastian Theodore Fox

SCHOLAR, INVENTOR, NATURAL
PHILOSOPHER, ELECTRICIAN

❧

*Dedicated to the noble art of observing,
collecting and classifying the wonders of
science, nature and*

That was as far as I got before the card was snatched from my hands by Lizzy.

'I have visited a number of the great fayres, Mr Grainger,' the gentleman, our Mr Fox, went on, 'London, Paris, Venice ...'

'Venice!' squealed Lizzy, expressing much of what I was doing my darnedest to keep inside. I elbowed Alex in my excitement, knocking him from his pose of thrusted breeches. Hadn't I talked to you, George, of one day doing our rope tricks there? Or did that conversation only go on inside my head?

'Quiet, woman!' snapped Grainger.

'And I have also been following the travails of your fascinating cornucopia of acts through a number of our country towns,' continued Mr Fox. 'I have enjoyed your offerings most delightedly, yet I cannot help but notice that you are altogether lacking a headline performer.'

This was another phrase that cast a spell upon my master, a hex of vexation.

'Well, excuse me!' Grainger's already pink face went a dark shade of crimson. 'No headline performer!' he cried. 'No headline performer! You do not know what you're blabbering about, man!'

So Abel was fetched, Joe as well, to be paraded before our guest. Alex n'all. Even though Mr Fox had explained very clearly that he'd seen our show numerous times and knew it well. Joe's strength and number of absent legs was reported over and over, as if repetition might make it more astonishing, and throughout it all our gentleman remained ever gracious, ready with comments of 'most remarkable' and 'very unfortunate' in just the right places.

Abel's shortness was explained in much detail, as if to a fool, and this was when our Mr Fox ran short of civility.

'I have seen someone of similar stature before,' he said, 'but *they* had the most astounding skin. Piebald is how it is described, brown and white, as if they were wearing the patterns of a dog.'

'Ah, yes,' argued Grainger, thinking he had the winning ace, 'but could the spotted kid do magic?'

'He did not need to,' came the curt reply.

Silence.

'So tell me, Mr Grainger, of all these fine specimens, which one do you consider to be your headline performer?'

Grainger cast his disappointed eye over the lot of us, his jumble of children, fathoming which one he should prefer best. Or dislike least. Mr Fox, very clearly, was not interested in the answer; he had proved his point. So instead he asked: 'What does she do?' He was looking at me.

'What she's told,' snapped Lizzy.

That smile of Mr Fox's – which I saw now was a defence against the awful commonness of my master and mistress – lit up his face once again. 'I am referring to her role within your show, my lady.'

'Well, you've seen it,' Grainger chipped in. 'She does bugger all.'

'We took her in good faith,' went Lizzy, 'but we was diddled. She was supposed to grow bigger.'

'Blacker,' said Grainger.

'Be summat worth looking at.'

I shrank.

Grainger slung an arm across the shoulder of this elegant man and pulled him bodily into his confidences. Our guest right-out winced at the stench of his breath.

'We think we shall probably get the head of a cow, sir,' whispered my despicable master, loud enough for us all to hear, 'hollow the insides and stick it over this here existing head of hers. There is a market for that, I have found. Proper half-breeds.'

I swear one day I will find a way to let my master's insults wash over me without leaving any marks.

Mr Fox did not nod his approval. Instead his eyes stayed on me – taking some kind of inventory. Hair, eyes, neck, chest, legs.

'I find her most tolerable,' he decided.

'You what?' spluttered Lizzy. 'She's a tawny, you know.'

'A mulatta,' corrected my master.

'I see that,' said our gentleman. 'An exotic case.'

That word again. So maybe, George, it's true. That is what I am.

'Her parentage has gifted her the most arresting features, don't you think?'

Our Mr Fox addressed this comment to Grainger. He had escaped my master's friendly arm but was still keen on his attention, eager for his accord. It brought to mind a memory of Grainger bargaining over our most recent horse, the conversation in the stables. Would I next be asked to show them my teeth?

Lizzy threw a look of knives at her husband, ordering him to disagree with Mr Fox's decision upon me, and I started to get the gist of who had called me 'pretty' and why it upset her so.

'She is a beauty,' Mr Fox said, certain, raising that fine, dark brow of his, urging Grainger to fall in.

And I don't reckon I took in the meaning of it, right there and then – that word, George, 'beauty' –

'You're a beauty! You're a beauty!'

Yes, but I was too busy noticing the way our master's face was shifting – pennies dropping into the slots. I felt very scared. I may have wished to be free of Grainger and Lizzy too many times to mention, but it is all I know, and in that there is a strange sense of safety. As for my musings on those women of pleasure, I could see starkly, there and then, that my grasp of it all had been something short of shallow. It dawned on me what was happening and the suspense I couldn't bear. So I hurried it along.

'Do you wish to buy me, sir?' I asked our Mr Fox, meeting his smiling gaze with a confidence I didn't rightly own.

Grainger, his eyes a-shine, rubbed his hands together, ready for the bidding.

'Now there's a thought,' he said to the gentleman, slipping close, that arm going across his shoulder once more. 'What do you reckon she's worth?'

ALEX

Hear this, pig: no longer am I the 'one-arm'd boy'. No longer shall you know me as a 'spectacle of human birth'. Now I am a 'specimen'.

A 'specimen', I ask ya!

Even you, pig, at your very worst, get called a 'tasty dish'. But there shall be no such favourable terms for the likes of me.

A 'specimen'!

I may not know the accurate meaning of the word but certainly I know the feeling of it – especially when it comes from the gob of a fella who believes himself to be the cat's long-lost bleeding uncle.

'What a fascinating specimen,' said our gatecrasher when I was paraded for his approval, the man fingering the various parts of me like I was an apple to be checked for its badness. 'What happened to the bones they removed?' asked he, none of his questions being offered in my direction. All of 'em went to my master for the answering. Tongue-less he thought me, no doubt, as well as being short of a limb.

'I'd give a good price for them,' said the cat's uncle, believing this left arm of mine was somehow still about the place, locked in a trunk, perhaps, or hanging off a hook. 'I am most interested in the intricate workings of the hand,' said he, before listing off other bodily trinkets he was sure to be in the market for – bladder stones, twisted spines, skulls of particular shapes. 'They contribute to my learning,' said he, as if his type of graverobbing was superior to the usual kind.

I should have contributed to his bleeding learning all right, by smacking the intricate workings of my hand against the underside of his ridiculous chin!

And you wait to hear what he had to say about our Mim. Slavering all over her he was, as if she was one of your sort that had been salted plenty so was good for the crackling.

'Her arms are not as filled-out as they should be,' said the cat's uncle, no shame in the uttering, 'but her feet are well-turned.'

God bless Lizzy for answering as she did, if only to throw him off the scent.

'How on earth can you tell,' said she, 'when they are so covered in shit?'

Then God bless Lizzy once more for what came next. My master ordered her to fetch water so Mim's feet could be washed. Lizzy pulled a face, of course, made her protest. 'I think . . .' she began, but my master was fast back at her, his hand raised ready to strike because she had gone against him in front of a stranger.

'That's none of your business is it, woman!' he yelled, 'to be bothering yourself with any kind of thinking!'

So off went Mim and a hang-headed Lizzy, out of view, so Mim's boots and feet could be made clean without any men's eyes peering on. Of course, I could not help but think of how I had already seen her foot, held the smooth skin of it in my hand, felt the warmth of her leg too, her thigh. The memory of it has given me some comfort these last few weeks, I don't mind admitting. Comfort and, shall we say, personal relief, when all is quiet, in the black of the night. Not that that puts me down the same dark alley as that cat's uncle, that dandy prat. It ain't hurting her, is it, just to think of her sometimes? He, on the other hand, wants to steal our Mim with the fat of his wallet. He wants to buy her, pig. Buy Mim.

Oh, he didn't say as much. When my master asked him to start the bidding, he only laughed and changed the subject. He distracted with talk of machines, things he reckons my master should be putting in his show, things that might bring him riches. Full of the patter, he was – all his geese were swans! – but it was only for stalling. I'm the boy what waits, as you right well know, so I can smell shilly-shally a mile off.

My master though cannot hear the promise of a round sum and walk away. He egged on this dandy prat, begged him for a look at these contraptions he'd described – contraptions, I was starting to suspect, didn't even exist.

'I shall require a boy and a lady to demonstrate them,' said our numbskull and, as you'd expect, I was shoved forward. Our stranger objected. 'This is no boy!' said he. 'This is a grown man!' – the first bit of sense he'd uttered since trespassing on our camp. I looked to Mim, who had returned, her heavy boots still broken but clean now, to make certain she had heard this verdict upon me. She had and was looking my way, not entirely in agreement, not laughing though either.

'Use the pygmy then,' says my master – which got the nod – 'and as for the lady, well, there is only my beautiful wife.'

Lizzy fell into a flurry of curtseying, still charmed by our stranger even though she'd been disgraced in front of him. But numbskull had eyes only for Mim.

'She's a child!' went Lizzy, doing all she could to snatch back his attention.

'Hardly,' said he. 'This is a woman of marrying age.'

It was my turn then to do what Mim had done to me – to look her way, not entirely in agreement, not laughing either. Mim, a woman? It didn't seem possible. But then if I am a man, there it is, I suppose. These things happen when you turn away.

'What year were you born?' he asked her, making Mim shrug. Maybe the parrot knows the date of her arriving. I was too young to remember and my master is too heartless to care.

So it was decided: Abel and Mim would be used for the demonstration. Of what, we still don't know and I dread to think.

'Fetch your machines then, man,' my master urged, a horse eager for the offing. 'Go fetch them. Where are they?'

But we were told we must wait until tomorrow, that preparation was needed. The machines, it turns out, are not being kept at the tavern close to our camp. Oh no. That tavern ain't good enough for the cat's bleeding uncle. He's boarding much further away in town.

'I have there all my books,' he told us, 'and my cabinet of curiosities.' Whatever one of them is. 'I must choose places to stay where I can trust the proprietor when I am carrying with me such precious cargo.'

I glanced at Mim, who was drinking this all up, her eyes a-shine, not realising that she was about to become a piece of bleeding cargo herself if she weren't careful.

'A gentleman can be judged on the quality of his library,' goes old shiny-buttons. 'Ignorance of the world will lead to social demise.'

It was all I could do to not bring about his demise right there and then, by kicking him in the cods, flattening him in the mud. What a nob! What a complete bleeding nob!

'You must take the girl to see these arte-farts,' says my master with a giant wink, Abel sniggering at the fumbling of the word. 'Immediately! Take the girl with you to your lodgings a-while, see how tolerable she is there.'

'Oh, it's not necessary that I am accompanied. I shall return,' replied our Fox.

More of his stalling. But I was stalling no more.

'We should all go,' said I, stepping up, a hand thrust into my pocket, casual-like. 'If anyone is to go.'

The eyes of the lot of them fixed upon me.

'We should all see this stuff if it's supposed to be so educating.' I shaped my words in a way that might pluck this crow. 'We should all make sure it actually exists.'

Abel and Joe gave groans and weary looks, in no mood for sermons more from this visiting nob, eager as always to return to the grog. Lizzy had my corner of course, but it was Mim's face what hurt me so. She was furious that I had tried to prevent the disaster of her going, seeing it as no disaster at all. She hadn't the foggiest idea what would happen when she went back with that man to his far-off lodgings, when he had her locked up in his cabinet of whatevers. Or perhaps she did. Perhaps that's what she was after. Hildy no doubt taught her that a lady should be chaste, but wasn't it Mim who had moved my hand up her thigh that night . . . Maybe girls do what boys do in the dark when all is snug – give themselves a bit of pleasure when they're there all alone.

'I shall be the envoy,' is what Mim said, shutting me up, using on purpose a word that I would not know the meaning of. 'I will report back,' said she, 'I believe that I am the most capable.'

My heart was fit to burst at how proud she was of herself, at the efforts she was making to speak right for our slippery visitor.

And it won him over – I saw it happen. When she talked in that way of hers, his gaze was all transformed. He hadn't valued her right the first time. She was a thing for using not moments ago, but now . . . Now he would take her. Short of throwing myself to the ground and fixing a hand to her ankle, there would be no means for me to stop it either.

Talks were had to convince us not to move camp, to stay in town another night, so that our nob could return with his machines and give us a show either side of twilight when we would see the effects of it best. If he ever did return. Might he not just run off with Mim, pig, into the rest of the night? I trust you further than I do that fool and you've bitten my hand more than twice.

'The girl will be fine!' is what my master bluffed, patting me on the back, a friendly gesture he never would have bothered with if we weren't being watched and judged. And I was too busy correcting him, telling him that Mim is not a girl no more as we had just found out, that she is a grown woman, but it was all to nothing, and it was an argument that went against me anyway. She had gone. Off on the arm of a stranger.

MIM

So what was I worth, George? Enough to walk out on the arm of a gentleman.

I cannot tell you how wonderful it was – and how bleeding awful, all at the same time.

As we took to the cobbles, he steered me house-side so that I got no carriage-splatter, nor shocks from above. And half of me – perhaps the half that was born of the gentry – felt, at last, that I was in my rightful place. Hildy had taught me to be a lady, and here I was as a lady being treated.

'A lady should be chaste!'

Well, quite, George.

But the other half of me, which tends to be the whole bleeding story, was really very grateful for the dark. We slipped from the hopeless glow of one street candle to the next, with no danger of anyone seeing my unpowdered nose, my shabby bonnet, the dress what didn't fit. I'd thought this gown a right natty piece when I'd pulled it out of Hildy's leftovers, but walking next to our Mr Fox, him cutting such a flash, I could see it made me no lady whatsoever. I'd fooled myself. For we know what proper ladies look like, don't we, George? They loiter at the back of our shows, fanning bad smells from their lovely washed faces.

'Show us your ha'pennys!'

And Hildy was a lady too, of course, from the neck down.

I, meanwhile, am a half-measure.

There was a particular look the landlord gave our Mr Fox when we arrived at his fancy lodgings and headed for the stairs. I had talked my own self into this outing certainly, wooed by the cultured chatter of our visitor, but had I gone and talked myself into my own demise? Mr Fox went rightly cold at Grainger's offer to sell me, but a thought came creeping when I saw the curl of that landlord's lip – might Mr Fox take his pleasure anyway, without paying any charge at all?

But guess what his first question to me was once we were upstairs in his room? (The warmest, snuggest place, by the way, I think I have ever been.)

'Shall we take tea?' That's what he wanted to know.

'Take it where, sir?' I replied, too distracted by the situation, by the fine rug beneath my boots, the shapely desk, the shuttered windows, the flowers dried and the portraits hung. Mr Fox laughed at this joke (made quite by accident) before leading me to a seat at the round table set a short distance from the hearth. He took on a gallant pose aside the fire – a fire which must have been coaxed alive by someone who knew we were to return, for it roared at such a lovely height.

The last thing I wanted to do was sit. All about me was so much to see. I was necking for a glance at his books, at the things upon the desk and dresser, arranged so pretty, as if those surfaces were a theatre stage ready for an opening scene. I did try to behave disinterested, as Hildy had taught me, for too much eagerness in a lady is a vulgar thing. But you know me, George, patience and moderation ain't never been my strong skills. And, anyway, our Mr Fox did not seem the least part bothered by my craning. He urged me to get up, look, even touch, if I wished.

He had asked Grainger, you see, right after they had finished agreeing on whether I was a beauty –

'You're a beauty!'

– if I had been educated any.

'Of course, not,' crowed Lizzy, and though I am all too aware of how it upsets my mistress to be contradicted, whether polite company's present or not, I had to speak out.

'I am confident with my alphabet, sir,' I told him. 'I am able to read tolerably well and have been taught the basics of arithmetic.'

Lizzy's face darkened like the skies before a storm, while Mr Fox's gaze became the sunshine what follows.

'Marvellous,' said he.

Hildy had warned me to keep my teaching a secret from men of standing. They won't like it, she said. But here was Mr Fox proving her wrong.

'Entirely marvellous!'

Upon his desk in his room, I found shells of the most astonishing sizes and designs. I've only ever seen the flat, ridged shells of oysters, discarded in the alleys, their insides sucked clean, so I thought these to be pale, knobbly snails until Mr Fox set me right. They come from the sea, said he, and not the sea what laps upon our shores. Shells from the likes of your home, George, and beyond. There were eggshells too and mottled stones, the bones from some poor dead fellow's head. In jars floated strange small creatures in murky liquid. Regular rats or frogs they seemed at first, until you clocked they had the wrong arrangement of tails and heads. There were certificates and lists written in a hand so very different from Hildy's loops and swirls, and a small wooden chest of bottles filled with mosses and dusts that could cure you of almost anything. This one for the coughs, that one for the squirts, another for the falling downs.

'Bless you!'

And you, George.

He also had this large painted ball that spun around on its stand, and Mr Fox explained that it was the actual earth upon which we walked every single day. He put his finger on a spot and said – 'There we are!'

Well, it was my turn to laugh then. How boggling!

'Can we really be there?' I said, pointing to the ball then to the boards beneath our feet, 'when we are also stood right here!'

Again he gave a great guffaw, this time calling me, 'a wit, to boot'.

'Comedy requires a certain logic and quickness of thinking,' said he, 'and I perceive that you are in possession of such a brain – even though you are not in ownership of an obliging parrot to help you in its service!'

If you think I blushed at that, well, let me tell you, I turned full-beetroot at the next thing I spied among Mr Fox's collection of curiosities. Propped upon the dresser was a book laid open at a picture of a man and women entirely without their clothes. The man had his hands spread wide, everything on display – the whole scene, the lot! The woman had her apple dumplings showing, a hand of modesty placed across her very private parts. I gasped – as Hildy would have wanted me to, though perhaps not as swiftly as I should have – and I stepped back. I certainly, absolutely, did not lean in, much as I was tempted.

The curl of the landlord's lip returned to my thoughts on seeing those drawings. Would my pitcher get cracked this eve, whether I liked it or not? (Though liking it ain't something that I'm ever supposed to do.) And how I did I feel about that? Scared, of course, all a-tremble, but still able to apply some small measure of reason. Mr Fox is a highborn gentleman, learned and clean, and definitely handsome. If it had to be done, could it be done by anyone better?

'Adam and Eve,' said Mr Fox, explaining the drawings, not embarrassed in any way that I had seen them. He flicked through the pages to show the man and woman's inside parts too, their livers and giblets. ''Tis a book on anatomy and dissection by a learned man,' he explained, 'for the enlightenment of surgeons and natural philosophers.'

'Like you,' I added, remembering those titles written upon his calling card.

'Indeed!' said he, the smile going all the way to his lovely eyes. There was no more of that polite gringogging done for my master.

On the mantle was the next object for me to observe – a piece of glazed pottery shaped into the curves of a lady's body, completely lacking its head, and its limbs.

'The Venus,' said my Mr Fox, 'revered in Rome as the goddess of love, beauty, fruitfulness, desire and . . .'

He did not finish, leaving me to wonder what else a headless, armless, legless women might manage. For certain she could be no goddess of juggling.

I did not wish it, but my mind went to Alex on sight of the Venus. That boy (that *man*, as I must now say), he annoyed me greatly when he tried to prevent my trip to Mr Fox's lodgings, trying as he was to scupper my opportunity. After this evening, I now believe Alex is envious of my quick-thinking, my logic and my beauty, and being resentful is something I had never thought him capable of. If he loved me well, like a sister is what I'm saying, like family, he would have helped me in my prospects. Still, the Venus did make me wonder about the potter who had been inclined to make a figure like this one, a body missing all of its parts. If that potter believed an absent arm to be a thing quite beautiful then I cannot be alone in how I see Alex.

And I suppose Alex cannot truly be envious of my beauty if he has a beauty all of his own.

'Here,' said Mr Fox, returning to his painted ball, placing a finger on another spot. 'This is Rome, Italy.'

'You have been there, have you, Mr Fox?' My eyes must have had the most eager of glints. Never have I met anyone who has travelled to other countries, apart from you, George. Yet he did not seem as thrilled by the idea as I was. In fact, if I had to pick a mood, I'd say he looked a little sorry about it.

'Yes,' said he, spinning the ball then stopping it, spinning then stopping it. 'Yes, I have travelled to Rome.'

A knock upon the door came then – the tea arriving, smelling exactly like perfume. Albeit a perfume you might want to drink right down. We sat and supped and I did my very best not to make any kind of slurp.

'Pardon me!'

Exactly right.

And I also did my best to ask the sort of questions a lady with a certain logic and quickness of thinking should be asking – like, why the bleeding hell have you got all this stuff?

'Because we are to observe, collect and organise,' was his reply.

I assumed by 'we' he meant me too, so I put down my cup and started listening very hard, waiting for instructions.

'It is our duty to study the world around us,' he went on, 'all the phenomena we encounter. For naming what we see and seeking classification of it leads us towards greater knowledge.'

'But ain't that the job of God?' I asked. 'The deciding of what is what, and so on?'

He gave a snort and I felt I must expand: 'I ain't the most church-fearing type, Mr Fox, and nor are my master and his

70

wife, as you might have gathered, but they have always rightly taught me that when something don't make sense, or it can't be changed, or it ain't what I'd hoped for, then I have to accept that it's down to Him upstairs.'

'*Whatsoever Adam called every living creature, that was the name thereof.* Genesis 2:19,' he said with a dose of scorn, 'if you require some scripture as your reason.'

And the conversation was briskly changed.

Mr Fox questioned me quite thoroughly about our menagerie and all the other parts of the show that he had seen, if only to add to this God-given right for knowledge, I presumed. And as I spoke, he took notes in a lovely leather-bound book, making me all the more nervous about what I said.

He wondered aloud how the geese were trained to do their dance and, though I probably shouldn't have given away such secrets, I told him that we heated the bottom of the metal pen until they had no bleeding choice but to jig along to Lizzy's pipe.

'It makes them cross though. Turns them into nippy buggers,' I said, forgetting where I was, not minding my language.

'*Ah, fuck off!*'

Enough of that!

I did praise you to Mr Fox, you know, said many glowing things about you being born with the knack of the mimic, how feeding you wine had made that skill come along all the faster. In return, he told me some things he knew of you – for you are quite famous. You're in one of his books.

Amazona collaria of the 'Psittacidae' family.

71

Let's try it again, shall we?
Si-tass-ee-die.

'Sit down! Sit down!'

Hmm, well . . . He wishes to see these amazing mimicking skills of yours at much closer quarters when he returns to our camp with his machines. He used to keep a bird himself you see. A robin it was.

'Ah, fuck off!'

Well, I do admit to spluttering some tea myself at that. A robin is not a bird for keeping, is it? And that much I told him.
'My father was of the same opinion,' he said with the saddest of nods, 'and so he chose to let the cat upon it.'

'Mercy!'

Sorry, George, 'tis what he said, and if it's any consolation he appeared to be in deep mourning still for the poor blighter. I told him of the pig, to cheer him, explained the way she'd been taught maths with a rope about her neck, with little tugs and rewards. Though I did also confess her training had not been entirely successful, that our particular mudlark weren't the cleverest of its breed.
'Alex,' I explained, 'the young gentleman you met, the one with the blue eyes and the freckles upon his face.'
'The one with the singular arm?'

'Yes, him, well, he has been talking to the pig in the evenings so as to smarten her up.'

Mr Fox snorted laughter at that and I joined in, for it was quite contagious. I added that Alex weren't the cleverest of his breed either. Not to be bad-mouthing him, George, that weren't my intention. But Mr Fox wanted knowledge, after all, and that was the truth. 'Tis a thing Alex would rightly admit about himself.

'Numbskull! Numbskull!'

He is not, George! You've gone too far!

'Alex's mother was not a highborn lady like mine.' I dropped that in, subtle-like, so Mr Fox knew I could be handled with a little extra respect.

From there we talked of Hildy, to which he asked: 'Was she truly a bear shaved?'

'A what?!' I spluttered, more tea spilling onto the saucer.

'Was Hildy in truth a bear that you had shaved,' he said, 'then nudged beneath the table to growl at your command?'

'No, sir!' I was quite upset by the accusation. 'Hildy was a lady of her own mind, a lady who I daresay is responsible for much of the sharpness of this brain of mine right here. A lady who upped and left of her very own accord, no prodding needed, no trick at all!'

At that he hooted so joyously he even slapped his thigh.

'We had a sheep with two heads once,' I went on, keen to shift him from the subject of Hildy, for though it made him merry, talking of her did still make me sad.

'A beast with two heads?' he said, that smile spilling upwards again. 'Are you sure it did not have two backs?'

'Two backs?' I asked, setting down my cup. 'How on earth would that be possible?'

Then off he went again, cock-a-hoop, calling me a wit once more for a joke I had no clue I'd made.

Then came silence, and though it made me uncomfortable to have a gentleman, a serious one, not at all at the mercy of the beer, to be so uncontrolled in his laughter, I liked it least when the room went still. In those gaps, I felt as if I were standing in a ring of people, their blank faces upon me, and that I must entertain, keep the show a-moving.

'Where's your bed?' I found myself blurting into the quiet.

Oh tragedy, George! What had I said? I'd as good as offered my maidenhead on a silver dish! If I could have shoved those words straight back down my gullet, I would have.

'Her father gave her dildoes six!'

Shush, George. You see, I was curious – about the bed, I mean. The likes of me, who is used to sleeping in an animal wagon, would have had no misgivings about kipping on a rug in front of that fire, done it plenty of times in Hildy's lodgings, but I couldn't see our Mr Fox carrying out such a thing in all his fine rags.

'In the next room,' he said. Subject done. There was no, *Would you like to see it?*, no, *Follow me, little girl*. And I think it was then, George, that I truly believed I was in the presence of a gentleman, one who had not lured me to his lodgings for his own devilish pleasures. But more than that . . .

You see, I am so very used to considering myself beneath all those around me, for my master and his wife work hard for me to see it that way. They are below most others we meet, which makes them mightily bitter, so we must provide them comfort – me and Alex and Abel and Joe – by being lower still. Yet this highborn fellow did not treat me as something unpleasant at all. Perhaps it is his study of the anatomy that has made his opinions differ. For something I have learnt just this evening from Mr Fox's books and diagrams is that we are all the same on the inside, if not on the outer, if not in our situations. We all have a heart for beating, I mean, and lungs for breathing. Perhaps this is why he did not behave like the goldfinch to my lowly sparrow. And perhaps because of this I found the bravery to ask him something further, the curl of the landlord's lip not entirely banished from my thoughts. 'Is it not improper for you, sir, to be entertaining a lady in your room?'

He shook his head. 'You are a student.'

A student.

'You're a beauty!'

Yes. But can I be both? Is one a little more than the other? I can't say I've quite worked it out yet, George. I reckon I'm a caterpillar in a cocoon right now, not knowing exactly what kind of butterfly I'll be hatching into.

'I am entertaining a student in my room,' he said, 'and entertain you I shall.'

He brought out a bright yellow stone flecked with black,

which he polished hard with a silk kerchief before placing it close to my face. And do you know what happened, George? You never will believe. The stray hairs outside my bonnet lifted up all by themselves and went towards it.

'Are you a magic man, Mr Fox?' I asked. 'Is this what you will be demonstrating for us all tomorrow night?'

He thought about this a moment, the idea dancing across his face – a face that was, for someone a few years ahead of me, in most excellent nick. No boils to be found, no pox had left its scars.

'I suppose that I am,' he said. 'A magic man. A conjuror! Yes, I like that! So tell me, my lady Mimosa . . .'

'Mimosa?' I squealed, cutting him short.

'Mimosa! Mimosa!'

Oh, that's right, George! Do you like it too?

'I apologise!' said my Mr Fox, 'I assumed that Mim was a shortening of the flower's name.'

'I dunno!' I answered back. 'The name came with me, my master says. Though I've always thought he must've heard it wrong, that probably I've been a "Mary" all along and never known it.'

Mr Fox shook his head, as if I was too good for a name as simple as that. 'You are named for the *Mimosa pudica* perhaps, the touch-me-not of the South Americas. An exotic flower.' And on he went to describe a very special plant that moves all by itself if anything should go near, closing its leaves as wondrously as my hair moved towards that precious stone.

'It is so sensitive,' said he, 'even the gentlest caress will make its fronds close as if in prayer.'

'Goodness,' I replied. So I tried it out for myself, my new full name. An exotic one, I suppose, if I have got the grasp of that word at last. A special one. Something I have never been. *Whatsoever Adam called every living creature, that was the name thereof.*

'Mimosa. Mimosa.'

'Mimosa! Mimosa!'

I think I like it.

Then back we went to the question I had so clumsily interrupted.

'Do you desire,' said he, 'to do something great with your life, something greater than providing animal shows within a field?'

Such a thing to ask! I, at once, felt guilty. Had he spied upon us, Alex and me, doing our rope tricks at midnight, in the same way he had observed our daylight shows? Or was the heaviness I felt due to the great weight Mr Fox had given to his question, and to my reply? I returned to the safe teachings of Hildy.

'Ambitions, sir?' I asked. 'Should a lady be having them?'

'Ambitions of power, perhaps not, but of betterment, improvement – these pursuits are most agreeable in a woman, I believe.'

'Then, yes,' I replied, though still cautious. I did not approve of him doing you down like that, George – you and the pig and the geese and the hare. 'But ain't it also a great thing,' I told him, 'to make people feel happy after a long day of toil.'

By rights, he could have been cross. Had I challenged my master or mistress's line of thinking in that way, I'd have been given a sharp smack across the cheek. But he only nodded, as if chewing on my words, working out exactly how they tasted. Then, making very sure he had my gaze, he said, 'Is it not a great thing.'

'Yeah, it is,' I said, 'I just said it was.'

'No,' – he spoke more gently now – 'you said "ain't it a great thing", but the phrase you require is, "Is it not a great thing".'

'Oh, yes,' I replied. 'Thank you.'

And I meant it, George. Without Hildy around to pick me up on my ugly speaking, it seems I have slipped right back to it.

'Well,' said he, leaving behind the delivery of the conversation and returning to the matter of it, 'if you had toiled all day and had money to spend, my Lady Mimosa, tell me what you would pay to see?'

The answer that came first, landed hard, like a stone going plop in a pond: my mother. I would pay very good money, George, to see her, to know her how she was, and to find her proud of me for trying to be a lady, despite all, one who can read and write a little, one who walked on the arm of a gentleman this very evening. But to confess this to my Mr Fox seemed too much. He wanted an answer more sober. So I said something to please him – student to teacher – yet something I did still believe.

'Magic,' I said. 'I would pay to see real magic.'

The fayre hawker and his wife are evicted from camp.

'The no-legg'd brute and the one-arm'd boy must be gone too!' says the visiting philosopher and out they go, the boy huffing and stomping, making sure his sulk is visible for all to see. Why should he be sent away from his own home (of sorts)? And at the order of this sneaksby, this gil, this numbskull, this nob!

''Tis essential,' insists their visitor, 'for preparation is all.'

The fayre hawker's 'girl-exotic' – the philosopher's new 'girl-student' – remains to assist this temporary master. Her first task: to slaughter one of the geese with a twist of its neck. The girl's reluctance is met with a reminder that the birds are, by her own admission, 'nippy buggers', and that the defeat of one might reinstate her authority over those that remain. Eager to demonstrate the ambition she has recently been permitted to feel, she obliges, and returns pink-handed to carry out the next of the philosopher's tasks: 'Bind the limbs of the dwarf.'

Long, silken threads are used to do the job, wound around the small man's wrists, waist and ankles.

'I am trusting you, Mim,' he says, as he watches her loop

the fine strands, leaving long lengths attached to each part of his body. 'Don't let me regret it.'

'You won't,' says she, a converted disciple. 'Forget your fire tricks and your cup and balls, Abel. We're about to witness real magic.'

The philosopher sets out his paraphernalia, transforming the covered area between the carts into a laboratory (of sorts). Tubes of glass, a block of resin and a strange machine with a handle to be cranked are all put in their place. A shiny disc is suspended from on high, and at the sides, on the ground by the tarp drapes, just in case, sit lead-lined jars.

All her silk-binding done, the girl leans in as the philosopher makes his final rearrangements, and he leaps upon this opportunity to provide her with a lecture. The dials upon the jars, he explains, allow him to adjust the strength of the instrument. At the first notch, the substance within will dissolve wire. At the second notch, it might murder a small beast.

The remark sends the disobliging parrot up into the air, fanning green, settling for the safety of a much higher perch.

'I wish you'd showed me this before,' says the girl to her new teacher. 'You'd have saved me much wrestling with the goose.'

And there the lesson must end, for beyond the tarp the audience grows restless.

'You're a St Paul's workman!' calls the boy. 'You're taking a bleeding age!'

'We'll be at the tavern!' yells the fayre hawker in accord, tempted by the stale scent of beer that drifts upon the breeze. 'Come find us when you're ready!'

'No!' cries the philosopher. 'I need you sober. This is a sight best seen on the level!'

So presently the tarp is pulled aside, and in the four loiterers troop and roll, not used to being the ones what watch. Before them swings the fayre hawker's 'dwaff', who the philosopher will soon have them know by a different name, suspended from silken threads tied to a hastily erected bracket. The girl-student, meanwhile, has been instructed to take on her girl-exotic persona once more. Not knowing what that requires, she sits upon her stool, a metal crown decorating the free-falling waves of her hair, and attempts a demeanour suggesting royalty.

'Stop yer hanging about, Abel!' bellows the bear-like boxer from his trolley, his cackle diffusing the air of gravitas that the philosopher has worked so hard to affect.

So he begins with no more delay.

'Gentleman and ladies!' cries their visitor, cutting through the collected guffaws.

'And others!' adds the parrot, god-like, familiar with this part of the script.

'We gather you here tonight under the folds of this unremarkable tent to show you something we know to be, on the contrary, most remarkable!'

'Gedonwir'it!' heckles the fayre hawker, not as unfuddled by booze as the philosopher had hoped.

'Sir, prepare to have your eyes confounded by the most extraordinary electrickery of Dr Sebastian Theodore Fox!'

'A doctor he is now,' grumbles the boy, but no one pays him any mind for the philosopher-now-doctor is brandishing a long and impressive glass tube.

'Behold this angel that comes floating towards our earth!'

The girl leaps from her stool to loosen the pulley of threads, as she has been directed, allowing the 'dwaff'-now-'angel' to lie, belly down, but an ell from the grass below.

'Angel?!' The bear boxer starts cackling once more. 'Angel?!' The boy cannot help but grin.

'We shall fashion him a costume,' explains the doctor quietly, in the direction of the fayre hawker – for he is the only person present, in truth, that needs to be convinced.

Then he proceeds: 'And if I do charge up my large and magic wand . . .' a phrase that sets the fayre hawker's wife to tittering, escalating to a cry of, 'Oh, eh!' when the doctor takes a leather cloth and begins to stroke the shaft of the glass tube most rhythmically.

All threatens to descend into filth and fun, until the doctor intones, 'Spread your wings, dear seraph!' and places the glass wand against the taut silken threads of the suspended angel, and . . .

There is a collective gasp.

'The feathers!' squeals the fayre hawker's wife.

'Good lord!' says her husband, fit to swoon. 'I've drunk so much I've bunged my eyes!'

'No,' says the boy, in spite of himself, ''Tis true! 'Tis happening!'

Feathers, that had once belonged to a dancing goose, placed in pots beneath the suspended angel, are, of their own volition, beginning to fly – snowflakes returning themselves to the sky. They cling in small drifts to the angel's hands.

'How are you doing it?' demands the bear boxer.

'I ain't doing nothing!' the angel insists.

'It's witchcraft!' hollers the fayre hawker's wife, angry and afeared. ''Tis the devil! He's brought old Harry upon us!'

'No, madam! No! Please do not worry yourself!' The doctor grins, not really concerned by this excess of emotion, only pleased for it. This is something he can shape to his will. ''Tis but an æther,' he explains. 'Small particles pressing upon gross bodies.'

His audience is not enlightened, their faces remain in the dark.

'The feathers are forced,' he tells them, 'by an unexpected, natural flow.'

'But there is no wind, no draught,' says the wife, licking a finger and testing the air.

The doctor grins once more, amused at their misunderstanding. He rounds upon his quarry by another route.

'Tell me, madam, do your stockings ever crackle when you remove them in the evening?'

'How dare you!' she cries, terror lost to indignation. Her husband's face sets furious on her behalf and this the doctor takes as his cue to move on and show them magic more.

The angel is set back upon the earth, and the girl returns to her stool. The audience is asked to help with the extinguishing of all but one guiding candle, at which they grouse, convinced that they will not be able to see. The doctor smug in his knowledge rejects their protests and begins to crank the handle upon an impressive machine of wood and brimstone, as if winding a music box or milling the grist.

'Gedonwir'it,' calls the parrot in the fayre hawker's voice, and the doctor, beginning to understand how an entertainer must behave, fills the empty stage with enough tongue for two sets of teeth.

'Here sits the beautiful Miss Mimosa Pudica,' he croons. The girl draws herself up taller on her stool at the hearing of his monologue. The serrated crown upon her head inches closer to the disc suspended above her, a disc that by a wire is connected to the machine, which now whispers in readiment. 'She is an angel of a different kind,' the doctor informs his audience. 'She is a princess! A deity!'

'What a beauty!' adds the parrot, before putting in: 'Numbskull! What a nob!'

The boy, who had gone grey at the doctor's patter, at the way the girl had sighed a little at the wording, gives the parrot a smile, a colluding eye.

'And this is how we know for sure that she is of celestial lineage,' the doctor continues, still winding the crank. 'Because of her . . .'

And the place is all cries.

A startling blue light fires through the air, fizzing, spattering, jumping from the hanging disc to the crown upon the girl's head. It illuminates her fully, drowns her in a blissful glow.

'Lord, save us!' howls the fayre hawker's wife, throwing her hands together at her breast in prayer.

'She is on fire!' caws her husband, his gob falling cave-like.

'Mim! Mim!' yells the boy, leaping forward in rescue, 'Are you hurt?'

'Stand back!' orders the doctor, a hand meeting firm the stage-invader's chest.

'Stand back! Stand back!' echoes the bird above, carried away with the moment.

'What's happening to me?' asks the girl, no trace of pain in her voice.

'You're glowing,' says the boy. 'Like a firecracker!'

'You got a crown of lightning, girl!' says the bear boxer.

'You're the true angel, dear,' adds the small man. 'It certainly ain't me.'

The girl's face glows now with a new light, one from within. 'Oh,' says she, 'how I wish I could see!'

But 'tis too late to fetch a mirror. The cranking of the machine is stopped. The light sputters and dies. They live once again by the sorry illumination of a single candle.

'Well,' says the fayre hawker's wife, truly winded, 'what are we to make of all that?'

'Oh, the performance is not complete, my lady,' replies the doctor. He has discarded all pretensions that this is a learned demonstration, a lesson in nature – it is a routine now, 'tis a show. The doctor is the one who has gained the greatest education from the eve so far. Now he knows what it feels like to hold an audience in his hand, to guide their sensations. The control of nature is one grand thing; the control of the human heart is quite another. This, he decides in that moment, is a line of experiment that he must pursue with all seriousness. And with that he looks to the girl.

'I will now ask our beautiful Lady Mimosa to stand upon this dais,' he commands, keeping his eyes upon her. Not understanding his words, the girl follows the doctor's gestures to know that she must step up onto the large resin block.

'We shall decorate it,' he whispers to her, taking her hand to steady her as she climbs. 'We shall fashion you better. A fine dress, stockings, a nosegay. Dress you with majesty.'

'Are you for real, sir?' she replies, quite breathless, but she gets no reply. He has placed her hand upon a spike of the machine, bidding it with small pressure to stay right there, while he cranks the handle at the required tempo, makes the brimstone spin.

'Now,' says our doctor, 'who would pay a farthing to kiss this most illuminating lady, this girl-ethereal who can pluck gold from the very air?'

At the word of something that might grease his palm the fayre hawker gets vocal, realising the trick without further explanation. 'Oh, I should imagine they'd pay a baubee, maybe even a win.'

'Quite right!' says the doctor, gathering the gist of the man's words if not the particulars. 'Who would not wish to know the sensation of kissing a monarch, an angel, a sorceress of the sun? Tonight the experience shall come for free. So who will step forward?'

The fayre hawker lurches towards the makeshift stage but the fingers of his wife are fast, snatching at the scruff of his jacket. 'Don't you dare!'

'Go on, Alex!' urges his boxing pal, pushing the boy forward.

'Well,' says the boy, fumbling with both speech and feet, in awe of this girl who is now so obviously a woman, and one who is capable of resisting fire. 'If there ain't anyone else to . . . I mean, if I'm the only . . .'

He has her eye and he is frightened, terrified that he too, by the power of his own emotions, will explode in a shower of sparks, burn the whole tent to ash. Likewise petrified, the girl can only imagine what will happen should their two mouths meet. The touch of his hand upon her thigh was mighty enough, a force so strong it sent them flying apart.

The air grows dangerously charged. The look they share threatens to be more fascinating than anything the doctor can present. So he cuts right through it.

'Oh, listen!' he goads, remembering how the fayre hawker had taunted his crowd, winning over the many by insulting the few. 'Listen how he talks of this as a task that must be endured!'

The spell is broken. The pair snap from their trance.

'I weren't!' objects the boy. 'I didn't!'

But, 'tis too late. The girl has turned for the doctor's learned take on proceedings.

The boy does not wish to kiss her. How did she not see? How had she fooled herself to the contrary? She knows she is not special, no girl-exotic really, no matter how many times they say it, no matter how hard she tries, so why would she think herself desired? Shame rises within her. At the boy, she scowls, no glow of lightning now. She is reduced to the solidity of clouds.

'Kissing a deity should not be considered a chore!' the doctor continues, winding up his machine.

'Mim! I didn't!' begs the boy, appealing to the girl direct. 'I was only–'

'Shut up!' she snaps – a small jagged voice. His words feel like pity, a prize of consolation. 'This is my act,' she tells him, 'and you are interrupting.'

The doctor lets the machine handle fall. There is quiet. He has done enough.

All eyes are on the girl.

So when the voice comes, so clearly hers in sound, everyone sees that her lips have not moved.

'He is a kind of beautiful,' says her voice.

Is this the trick, they think, some kind of ventriloquism?

'He is a kind of beautiful.'

No. It is the parrot mimicking the girl. The bird bobs a little dance and repeats it once more: 'He is a kind of beautiful.'

The girl's gills, already reddened from the earlier misunderstanding, deepen at the indiscretion. She meets the gaze of the boy and takes a breath to explain, then stops, realising silence is her better ally. She owes him nothing.

The boy looks from the girl to the showman and back again. He has heard his own words for the doctor – Numbskull! Nob! – issue from the parrot's beak, and these new words, he believes erroneously, are the girl's appraisal of their interloper. She has fallen, he decides, she has been beguiled by this trickster with his fine breeches and his endless spouting. The boy retreats, beaten, back into the shadows.

'So *I* will step up,' exclaims the doctor. '*I* have no fear.'

With the girl raised upon the block, their lips will meet easily, squarely. Seeing what is to come, she shivers. Never has the girl known a man this way, not even in tender privacy, and now she must do it for an audience. The doctor – this gentleman, this teacher, this master of electrickery – he places his face close and she feels the warmth of his breath as he chants his next piece of prose seemingly all for her.

'I will place my lips against the softness of yours, Miss Mimosa Pudica, my angel, the touch-me-not of the South Americas, and it will feel . . .'

He kisses her. There is an audible –

88

SNAP!

– and a great flash of light as their mouths meet in the grey-brown dusk. The girl has never felt anything akin to it before in the entirety of her life. She is stunned yet manages to speak, to finish his sentence, the sensation of the spark still echoing on her flesh.

'It feels, sir,' she says, 'as you promised. Like magic.'

ACT II

This is to give Notice to Gentlemen, Ladies and Others
that in this very Place at Sunset the Proprietor Mr FP Grainger
is honoured to present

MAGICKAL ELECTRICKERY

with the distinguished

DR SEBASTIAN THEODORE FOX

him being a Natural Philosopher, Inventor and Electrician of great report who can command the very Forces of Nature and Lightning for the Purposes of amazing and enlightening his Audience. First, you shall see as follows:

A PHYSICKAL ANGEL

who shall descend from the Heavens at the Doctor's request to mesmerise lifeless Objects to fly about the very Air. Second, you will see:

THE ELECTRICAL VENUS

Miss Mimosa Pudica is a Lady of CELESTIAL ROYALTY, who has travelled from the Islands of the Caribbean to astound thine Eyes. She can pull Stars from the Sky to light her golden Crown and on the payment of ONE PENNY will allow Gentlemen to kiss her upon the Lips so that they may understand the shock of true Love.

All followed by bare-Knuckle Fighting for your Entertainment and serious Play and the sale of REMARKABLE ANIMALS for collecting or slaughter, including a learned Pig, dancing Geese, a musickal Hare and a green Parrot that does speak most well.

LONG LIVE THE KING!

MIM

Honey is too sticky, George, 'tis beeswax we need.

I have tried all of the powders, the pastes, the mosses and the dusts. That stuff within Mr Fox's lovely wooden chest does more harm than good. Mix 'em together and you bring yet more harm upon yourself, of the foul stinking variety! The concoctions are so noxious I daren't put them anywhere near my mouth. For if I did I would surely drop down dead.

'Stand back! Stand back!'

Either that or fall asleep for a thousand years, stuck that way until some prince comes and wakes me up. I feel rather like one of them fairies from the folk tales right now – albeit one with agreeable intentions. The way I pestle things to dust, combine them with this and that, then boil them up as potions to apply, once cooled, with all my good hopes. 'Tis the work of a sprite. 'Tis not magic though. Mr Fox says we are only to use that word for the purposes of the performance. In the cold light of day, it is forbidden.

'Everything can be explained,' says he, 'with a degree of

investigation and a certain amount of perseverance.'

This cure for cracked lips, I have decided, shall be no exception. If I am to kiss so many men an evening, my poor chops will not stand for it.

'Skin of a dog! Skin of a dog!'

Ain't that the truth! So let us investigate and persevere – like stubborn bleeding mules.

Right now, I believe the cure lies within a substance that I might lay my hands upon without the handing over of coins (Mr Fox's coins, that is). I don't need bottles of whatnot from across the seas. Crushed berries might soothe, perhaps, if heated and mashed, or combined with the fat discarded from the liver of a cow. That sap that oozes from tree trunks has got me wondering n'all. Yet beeswax still is the stuff mentioned most as a balm in Mr Fox's books – the ones I have stumbled through thus far.

Hildy only had two well-fingered books, as you know, stories of virtuous girls and dastardly libertines that you liked to chew the edges of when no one was looking. Both times I got to the spicy bit only to find you'd swallowed the most important part of the plot.

'Pardon me!'

You are forgiven. For I have Mr Fox's books to savour now, and all his back issues of *The Spectator* and *Tatler* – though they may as well be written in French. I have to go most slow with my finger trailing upon the page even to get the gist. I have read reams and reams but am still to find a line telling me how the bleeding hell you get this lorded beeswax out of a honeycomb.

I reckon the fancy sorts what write those books have a slavey to do the piddling tasks, much like Mr Fox has me bothering rat catchers for any mice caught alive, so I might keep them boxed above the fireplace. He likes to stick the poor blighters inside the chamber of his new air pump and give them a taste of rarefied air. That stuff does the strangest things to sound and fire, and to mice it makes them lurch and droop until they faint.

I am not Mr Fox's servant though, even if I am to be found running his errands. He has not bought me into his service. No money has changed hands.

'You are a student of the arts,' that's how he describes it. Or other times: 'An apprentice to the arts'. And some things, if you hear them said enough times, start to feel true.

In actuality, being a student or an apprentice reduces down, as any murky liquid will above a flame. Dirty water becomes sludge. Student becomes servant. But my prospects look exceedingly good. All I need, says he, is a show of willing, a fondness for hard work and a certain spirit, then I am guaranteed a position in life better than any I could ever have imagined before.

'All leading thinkers are supported by wives who are in possession of their own adequate minds,' Mr Fox told me, the night of his first demonstration. 'I have thus far worked alone but as my endeavours gain momentum I am in urgent need of an assistant.'

So, that's me, innit?

'Stupid you! Stupid you!'

Hardly, or else why would he have chosen me?

So immediately, I suggested an experiment, one of my own, to display this willing he seeks and to demonstrate my adequate mind. I requested that I have a commonplace book, like his. No need for the leather binding – something simple would do, as long as there are clear pages for me to record my findings. At first he weren't certain.

'I cannot see how the curing of roughened lips will send ripples among the great and the good,' said he.

My first instinct was to ask how the torturing of endless mice was doing any rippling better, but I swallowed my impudence and told him instead: 'Well, the great and the good can't have felt the burn of the sun then, can they? Nor the chafing of the wind. Not like the rest of us.'

This had him cocking his head on one side – a clear marker, I have learnt, that he is in the market for persuasion. And while I waited for him to sway, I added, genuinely curious: 'Is that why we do it then, all this experimenting? Much like the show – to seek out the applause of others?'

'Of course not!' he said, as sharp as a smack – though whose proverbial backside was getting the beating wasn't clear. 'We do it for the advancement of civilisation!'

And the commonplace book was mine.

There is a method quite simple, I believe, to the wringing of beeswax out of a comb. I'm sure you would only need to be told once. Lizzy would have a grasp, no doubt, but Lizzy won't talk to me no more, not even to trade in insults.

'You're his business, now,' that's what she says, if ever I do approach. 'I wouldn't wanna stand accused of tainting royalty,' she sneers. Then off she'll wheeze, that rump of hers swinging.

I suppose I should be grateful she don't come within spoon-swiping distance, yet there's a certain something in the way she sets out her position. It makes me ill at ease. You'd think she'd be all loud and pleased about palming me off, but the look she saves for when I'm in her vicinity is wary now, like how you draw close to a strange dog while working out if it's gonna lick your hand or bite your nose.

'Stand back! Stand Back!'

I think she is sulking, George, about my master's swift decision to change the handbill and make me the biggest act.

'A pale slave as the main attraction!' she crowed. 'Who'd pay to see that?!'

But what else could my master have done after witnessing Mr Fox's fabulous demonstration, then hearing him lay out his quite reasonable terms for the sharing of profits? The same terms stated that I was to fall under his supervision for the ongoing benefit of the act, that I am to stay in rooms, as he does, when we travel.

'Oh, is that what this is about!' said my mistress, a-nodding and a-winking. But Mr Fox didn't let her pick apart his dignity.

'A small room of her own, madam,' he corrected. 'Our profits with this new show, I assure you, will extend to that. She will join me only in daylight so I might improve her understanding of the arts.'

'The arts! Oh, is that what you blunty sort call it!'

When Lizzy grabs hold of a thing she simply don't let go.

'The study of electricity and the related sciences,' Mr Fox expounded. 'This knowledge she will need if she is to ably assist me upon the stage.'

Lizzy snorted, still disbelieving, though I reckon her look was a yellow one too. All the things I would get to learn that she never would.

'I also want to keep her feet and hands from the sun and the dirt,' Mr Fox continued, 'so they might stay . . .'

'White?' Lizzy finished with a smirk.

'Oh, it don't wash off, sir,' I chipped in. 'Not all of it, anyways. And I don't believe it's the sun what caused it in the first place, if it's the science of stuff we're to be concerned with.'

'If you had let me finish,' Mr Fox said, one of his own clean white fingers raised in my face, 'I was to say desirable, attractive.'

And how could I object further when he described me like that?

My master shoved in, always needing to meddle, proposing that I bleach my hands because he had heard word of fine women doing it. But Mr Fox was aghast at the suggestion, reminding Grainger that I am an 'exotic case' (which now I am to understand has a good deal to do with the brownness of my skin) and that is something which makes folk much keener to part with their money.

'*Show us your ha'pennies!*'

And parting with their money they are.

Lizzy might be as fond of coin-getting as my grabbing master – who insisted the price for a kiss should be set at a penny and not a farthing less – but she is all the more fond of being right. She wished for our trial shows to fail, I know it. But even without the decent costumes we're busily acquiring now, and despite your rude interruptions, George,

'Gedonwir'it!'

the tin overflowed in ways we ain't never seen before, not even when Hildy was still with us.

'I believe we have created a future sensation,' said my Mr Fox in a tone of giddiness more fitting my master. He was even convinced those first few nights to take ale at the bar to celebrate.

So Lizzy is stung and, I warrant you, she's scheming my downfall – which is exactly why I insisted you stay with me when I moved into lodgings. If anyone is to come asking about the note at the bottom of the bill saying that you are for sale, I can tell them some useful lies.

'Oh, take him for free!' I said to last night's showy madam, who came fluttering her beautiful fan depicting a brutal battle. 'I cannot bear the biting of that bastard bird a moment longer!'

I pushed the slip from my shoulder so she might see some old scars left from Lizzy's beatings and think them done by you.

'I swear that evil bird'll peck out one of me peepers before the summer's done!' I cried.

'Mercy! Mercy!'

No, no mercy at all, not when it's you, George, who's at stake.

I saw how ashen that lady went beneath her powder and her lead. And though I find it hard to pick up speed in these new lacy bootees of mine with their stubby heels, that woman proved it's a skill that can be acquired – with time, perhaps, or the right impetus.

The handbill does not please me in any way, and not only for the casting aside of you.

I understand the liberties taken with my skills and my origins – it helps sell the act – but I cannot say that I'm happy with my name. The Electrical Venus.

My master was after calling us: *The gimcrack on fire and the man what done it*, while my mistress offered: *The heretical witch and the devil what created her*, so I suppose I should be grateful for the mercy of Mr Fox's suggestion.

'Mercy! Mercy!'

Yet I can't help thinking of that porcelain woman without her limbs over there on the mantle, the one you like to perch on top of every now and again, making it look as though she has a great green something growing out of her neck instead of a head and a brain.

The goddess of love, beauty, fruitfulness and desire, she is, and a something else that Mr Fox didn't like to mention. But she is nothing but a pair of apple dumplings, a belly and some very private parts – so it don't take much investigation nor perseverance to deduce what that something else is, does it?

'A lady should be chaste!'

I know, but don't everything lately seem to come right down to it?

I have tried asking my Mr Fox to explain – as a teacher would to his student.

'Men pay money to kiss me because they want to know what true love is like,' I said.

'Of a sense,' was his reply.

'And the men what do it, do they fall?'

'Fall?' he asked.

'Yes.'

He laughed. 'Some of them do stumble and go weak at the sensation, indeed!'

This was not what I had meant and he knew it. I would not laugh too and make everything well for him.

'What about you?'

'Me?'

'When you did kiss me for the very first time, it felt . . .' I was reaching for words I did not have, George, so Mr Fox filled the space.

'It was electricity, passing between two bodies.'

That was the correct description, of course, philosophically speaking, but as an answer to give you a better grasp on life, well, it weren't worth a farthing, let alone a penny.

'Yes,' I said, 'electricity, and it was a sensation most wonderful! I ain't never felt a thing like it, not before nor since, not with a one of them others what pays for a go.'

He did not reply immediately, only observed, his brow pulled tight in thought. He does this a great amount, even when he is not deliberately writing notes about me in his commonplace book, asking me to describe my upbringing, sketching the parts of my face, testing the swiftness of my actions to things, as if a woman is a species as worthy of study as a parrot. If I was a plant, he would pick me and press me. If I was a coloured stone he might describe me as fascinating.

When he did speak, he did so stutteringly, and only to correct me. '"I have never felt anything of its like," is the phrase you require, not "I ain't never –"'

'Yeah, yeah,' I said, no desire for a lesson in talking proper. I was urgent for an answer. 'But what we felt, passing between us two, was that, is that . . . Is that what love feels like?'

I expected him to dash for a book to explain the phenomenon. I was certain he wished to do that, for he was twitchy in his chair, his collar growing damp, but I don't rightly think he has a book on this particular subject.

'Of a sense,' was his reply – those words again, urging the moment to die, to fizzle to nothing. But I can be as eager to hang onto a thing as Lizzy. She has taught me perseverance well.

'Do you understand me, Mr Fox? What I am saying? That when you kissed me, I felt . . .'

'What?' he croaked. And I could see he had become quite breathy, his chest rising in shifts, even though I was the one who was speaking so pleadingly.

I thought for a moment that he might lurch forward from his seat and kiss me again or perhaps drop to the floor, as faint as a mouse. He did neither. With an unexpected jerk, he stood and strode away across the room, angry all of a sudden.

'What is your question exactly?' he snapped from all the way over there, as if his time was expensive and I was running up a debt I'd never be good for.

Oh, I could not say any more, George.

'Stupid you! Stupid you!'

Quite. But I did not rightly know what I was asking.

Or perhaps I was too afraid of the answer.

Let us cross honey from my list.

I wish you could pick up a quill, George, and do writing as well as talking. It's a right inconvenience having to down tools and wipe my hands each time I must put a new discovery in my book. This experiment requires a speedy solution. For here I am fashioned so beautifully, thanks to the fat of Mr Fox's wallet, thanks to his share of the profits, but this soreness of my lips is threatening to spoil the picture.

'You're a beauty! You're a beauty!'

Thank you, George. Though, in truth, I am still not sure of it. The face I see in the glass is the one I have always known, albeit now with powder and rouge. And since when does the everyday and the ordinary catch anyone's eye? For that is all I am to myself.

To Alex, I believe I have become quite ugly.

'Look at you,' he remarked yesterday when I passed him on the camp as he did his warming-up ready for his tumbling. Knee-tucks, stretches, jumping in a star-shape, one ray missing. He had spoken with scorn yet still I was grateful. Like Lizzy, he rarely wishes to talk any more and I have missed the easiness of our conversations. 'Is this what our coppers get spent on, now?' he said between leaps, nodding at my new fine frock, my bright white stockings, the laciness of my boots.

'Look at you,' I said teasingly in return, hoping we might go back to our old ways of mocking one another. He'd call me a slave, then I'd say something rude about his arm and off we'd tumble into the grass.

He carried on with his stretching.

'The extra coppers mean you've . . .' I started, then I stumbled on my words. Alex took my pause as a signal that he should pause too, and he came towards me, shirt off, sweating in the sun, a swagger to his walk that felt something close to a threat.

So often I have watched how he angles himself away from me, making sure his right side, his 'good side', is the one forced forward, but not this time. He stood square, as if I was supposed to see everything, pulling back his shoulder blades, rolling them, oiling them flexible.

I wished to say to him that the extra coppers in the tin must mean that servings had improved, for he was bigger. Not fat, not bacon-fed, far from it, but . . .

'You have definition,' I said, which felt like saying too much and not enough all at the same time.

He nodded at that, a sort-of agreement, but silent he stayed, looking at me so directly he sent me to blabbering.

'Last night I learnt how to start a fire,' I said. 'With the electric, I mean, not the usual way.'

'Oh, yeah?' said he – a flicker of light.

I was so eager to share it with him, with someone, aside from you, George. Keeping all this new knowledge to myself can feel selfish at times, painful even.

'Mr Fox soaked one of his handkerchiefs in gin –' I went on, gabbling, nervous '– then I took the charge as I do, but from one of them storage jars with the dials, which are far more powerful, can I just say, than the usual machine –' The light in his face was fading, so I speeded up my words, if only to get it all out before he could peel away. 'And instead of giving my usual kiss, I touched the handkerchief with my fingertip and –' I pressed my finger against the sunny skin of Alex's forearm to demonstrate, the arm he had casually hooked across the flatness of his stomach. But at my touch he whipped it away, put it behind his back, chafed it against the skin there as if trying to rub the presence of me gone.

'Then, whoosh,' said I, my voice quite flat, 'up went the handkerchief in flames.'

He nodded, not moved at all.

'I could do it for you now,' I said, a little desperate. 'Grainger or Lizzy will have some . . .'

He was shaking his head, his gaze on his bare feet.

'That's what you get up to these days, is it?' said he, 'when the moon is out?'

'I am a student of the arts,' I replied.

He shook his head once more, unimpressed despite everything.

'Mr Fox believes we shall become a complete sensation,' I went on. It was very important to me, right there and then, to make him pleased, to insist upon it. I would have grabbed his hand so I could press the idea on him physically, if he had not hidden that hand away. 'We shall all be quite famous and living much the better because of the doctor,' I said.

'That so?' he replied.

I could not say 'yes' for definite, of course. I still cannot. This is just an experiment, after all. Each turn we take in our lives requires an investigation, a perseverance, a testing of the outcome. Yet I did promise him, for if you say a thing enough times I believe you can make it so.

'Yes, we will,' I said. 'Quite the better.'

'Better.' He tossed the word about, considered it. 'Better.' As if it were a new ball to juggle, a thing he must get a feel for, assess the weight of, before he might work it into his act.

He let it drop.

'We'll see,' he said as he wandered away, returning to his stretches. 'Let us wait and see.'

A GENTLEMAN'S VIEW

MONDAY, September 6. 17——

Being a person who does, on occasion, find himself *a la deusea ville* among the fields and the ditches, I rarely return to the hurry of the town with much to report. Time spent amongst milkmaids and country Harrys does not lead one towards great enlightenment; or furnish one with stories suitable to entertain the coffee house rabble.

But serendipitous occurrences did direct me Thursday last to the rookeries beneath the fine bell tower of Evesham where the passing out of handbills was taking place. This task of distribution was all happening under the leadership of a young fellow who had, at some distant time, been reliev'd of one of his arms, and another poor unfortunate invalid who, having neither of his legs, moved about the uneven streets by means of a raised trolley.

I confess to being charm'd by the one-arm'd boy who much compensated for his shortfall of hands with an over-flowing of patter, superior to the inarticulate bellowing typical to our London street hawkers. His pleasant demeanour was also aided by a handsome visage and of him being of admirable, good height, allowing you to momentarily overlook the deformity of his body.

I was also not a little curious about the acts of 'Magickal Electrickery' promis'd upon the paper thrust into my hands. All was to be presented by a Dr Sebastian Theodore Fox of these isles, who the bill said was 'a Natural Philosopher, Inventor and Electrician of great report who can command the very forces of Nature and Lightning for the purposes of amazing and enlightening his audience'. His name was not familiar to my tongue or ears and I understood very well that his claims were of a bold and inflated nature, yet some sense instructed me to stay on within the town's environs to witness this advertis'd Magick.

And I was not alone in my decision. Word of the Doctor and his electrickery had spread to homesteads far and wide in anticipation of their arrival. What occur'd was a very near storming of the hall when it became apparent not all who had gather'd would be allowed to enter. I was only able to secure my place in the raised seating for the better classes by greasing the singular palm of my one-arm'd acquaintance from earlier in the day, who then attempted to calm the impatience of the assembling throng with acrobatics and juggling.

Now, I need not go on here of the advances being made in this field so-named 'Electrics', a subject my colleagues have cover'd with much explanation and examination of consequence on these very pages previously.

That the concepts of Newton, Boyle, Hawksbee and Gray move on apace will not have escap'd any of us who have experienc'd an after dinner show involving the miraculous relighting of candles or ladies being made to quiver at the showering of sparks.

That our eminent Mr Fox desires to bring this complex knowledge to the fayre-going folk of the lower orders is what perhaps intrig'd me most about his reported display. I was adamant to discover if this was a demonstration of great ingenuity or, indeed, stupidity.

Certainly when our leading man took to the stage at seven of the clock precisely, his talk of 'effluvia' and 'gross particles' did nothing to enthral the collected masses, even though he was of well fashion'd appearance, five foot eleven in height and most expressive with his limbs. The crowd did talk most rowdily throughout his oratory, stopping only to laugh at the interruptions of a green parrot, train'd, I am sure, to demonstrate such impudence for our amusement.

This boisterous audience did calm, however, at the arrival of an 'angel'. This was but a dwarf draped in linens, wearing a most impressive pair of wings, fashion'd it seemed on sight from the feathers of innumerable geese. Yet his appearance was most suggestive of the heavenly sphere that I found my belief could be very easily suspended. (As was the poor small man! From the very rafters!)

As the first conduit of the Doctor's act, the hanging 'angel' did indeed, as promis'd, cause 'lifeless Objects to fly about the very Air'. In this case flakes of seeming gold.

But it was the act's finale that did engage the seedy masses most. The Electrical Venus was a negro but of paler skin and lacking the round'd bodily parts expect'd of a girl exhibit'd as an exotic subject. Her beauty was, I must note, exceptional, allowing us to be carri'd along by the Doctor's narration that she was of celestial royalty and therefore able to teach us of the exact nature of true love – a suggestion that caus'd much hilárity amongst the men of the audience, the implication being that her particular strain of love was not of the godly kind.

After the girl was dress'd in the most astonishing crown of sparks by our showman Fox, the collect'd men were invited to pay a penny to kiss this girl-exotic. For the purposes of investigation I, of course, volunteer'd to step up and found myself decorating the one-arm'd boy's palm once again for the honour. It was a decision I was to regret on closer inspection of the girl's mouth that appear'd most red and sore from continuous contact with the mouths of the lower classes. Yet too embarrass'd to turn away, I oblig'd with my caress, but to one of the girl's powder'd cheeks.

In return, I received my own short, sharp taste of 'electric' which I can confirm is painful and shocking. Those married to a scold may say this is indeed the sensation of true love! This remarkable and at turns lurid act is to be seen in the capital very soon, I am assur'd, and I would urge all gentlemen (and ladies of a robust disposition) to experience the garishness of it with their own eyes.

As for the claims made by Dr Sebastian Theodore Fox during the performance that he is a fellow of the Royal Society who has studied at the shoulder of many of our eminent surgeons and naturalists, I have found no evidence on my return to support this.

Investigation of renown'd families with the surname Fox reveal no son of his twenty-something years with philosophical leanings – or at the very least no family willing to claim him as their own.

A KISS ELECTRIC: Or a Cautionary BALLAD to all fair
gentlemen and ladies on the ILLUMINATING THRILL OF THE VENUS

I

Good people listen closely on a warning
I embark,

Of a fellow named Fox who they call the
bright spark,

He will tempt you with enlightenment by
heaven's cherub and queen,

But once you have look'd it cannot
be unseen,

More to the worry is the penny you give him,

For the delights you do purchase you may
never forgive him.

> You lose more than a coin for a
> kiss that's electrick,

> Love will please you no more if
> 'tis tame and domestic.

II

The Lady Mimosa Pudica is of an
isle Caribbean,

Don't be fool'd by her smile she is the eve's
tragedian,

Her savage beauty we do not oft see the like,

Be thankful, good people, for to your hearts
she will strike,

> Or to the heart of your beloved –
> ladies beware!

When the firey light falls from the
sky to her hair.

> You lose more than a coin, &c.

III

'The force comes from nature' is how the
doctor describes it,

But refuse every dose until a Physician
prescribes it,

When your lips are placed on those of the
emblazon'd lady negress,

Nothing will prepare thee for the shock
of this exuberance,

The mouth doth sing with dizzying effects,

And with all kisses thereafter, these thrills
you will expect.

> You lose more than a coin, &c.

IV

Now hear of a fellow who dared embrace
with the Venus,

Then travell'd home to his wife to tell of it in
all truthliness,

'Your honesty is worth more,' said she, 'than
a kiss given lightly,

> 'Come close, my dear, let us caress as
> we do nightly.'

But the man found wifely love was
no longer exciting,

Believing now that a kiss must be thunder
and lightning.

> You lose more than a coin, &c.

Jamieson, Printer, Nottingham

ALEX

Perhaps it's cos I'm no longer black and blue. My lip ain't split and my conk ain't busted.

There's little light left at the end of the show for boxing these days. Either that or the hall don't allow it. Oh, yes, pig, you heard me right. We get invited inside now. Cadgers like us! That's why you're sometimes stuck, alone, outside in your pen of an eve, not called on to mess up your sums. You can't be trusted not to shite upon the floorboards.

Maybe it's cos I'm hoiking that machine about, that resin block what weighs several stone. It's me who makes the bulky poles stand up tall when we do the show outside. I climb 'em, the tarp in my teeth. It's my job n'all to hoist Abel high – and though he may look nothing, I'm telling ya, pig, he's as heavy as a fattened calf. All this I do, and my usual tumbling and juggling to warm the crowd. All this and my midnight rope-walking. It has given me muscle. It has given me . . . What did Mim call it that last time she could spare a precious moment to speak, a crumb to toss to this sparrow? Ah, that's it – 'Definition'. That's what I got, pig. I am definite. 'Tis how I feel, as well as how I look.

That's why the ladybirds do come and stand too near, twittering their fans at me, fingering their buttery curls, because they can sense this 'definite' rising off my skin like steam. It makes me vivid. They offer themselves up, no persuading needed. It's me who gets pushed backwards into the animal trailer for a flourish in the straw. I am a man now, I suppose, and all because I have become shaped like one – wider across the chest, narrower at the middle, the strength in one arm to make those with two look pitiful. I have become shaped in the mind too. Hard.

The girl what just left, her hair all tumbled, her skin like milk that will soon turn sour, she reckoned she loved me. But I do not love her. She is one of many, all much of a muchness. They can call me handsome, call me mighty, a darling and a duke, while we do it bread and butter fashion, but their words don't sway me. If any of them make mention of my arm, even to coo about it, I bid them a swift 'fuck off'. There's a queue of lasses waiting where the last one came from.

It all means nothing. After years of wondering what it would be like, feel like, to be that way with a girl, it's a surprise to find, despite the joy of the moment, that it don't mean a thing, not when the morning comes. Not with them waxen girls, so bloodless that they come leaching mine.

All it goes to show is that they don't want the doctor. That's why they gather in the first bid, pig, I know that. Word of our electrickery has spread like a bad cough, and every little town tweet thinks she must come along and bag herself a learned husband – the distinguished Dr Sebastian Theodore Fox! What rot! As soon as they get close, gaping as they do in the front

113

row, they realise they're close enough. He jaws 'em half to death with his 'floovias' and his 'gross particulars', then all their attentions go to me. I am the one with physical skills, the one not locked away in his head. That quack is as wooden as the frame of his machine.

So I crack their pitchers, but only the nice ones. I've heard too much from Abel and Joe about how you'll end up pissing needles if you ain't careful who you lay with.

And why shouldn't I, pig? Why shouldn't I dance with those girls and have me some fun? Why should I stay lonely? Mim said we would all come to good off the back of the doctor, so this is me taking my slice. And I am due the largest. All that tough graft, what with us moving every single day cos we're so in demand. Abel is no help with the lifting; Joe is no good with the climbing. Lizzy has some heft in her, but the master's always too diddled, or too busy recovering from the diddling, to do anything but shout the orders.

As for Lady Mimosa herself, our celestial royalty, well, she's too busy resting her fine-stockinged feet in her tavern castle. It happens that kissing all those strangers is exhausting. Funny, cos I find locking mouths with a different bit of bloss every night to be something right uplifting. She tells me that her days are filled with study – another sparrow-scrap of information she cared to toss in my direction – but I reckon it's only study of that doctor's two-faced mug. And other parts of his body what I don't wanna be thinking about.

She does not love him.

She lies with him, I don't doubt it, despite all his protesting to the contrary, despite what Hildy would have taught her about guarding her goods. He has used his zapping power to make her faint. Lizzy had it straight – he's an infidel and he's lured Mim with magic.

Or else she lies with him for the gain, for the money, for the title. If coming to good is all she cares about, then there's the quickest route. It's a route no more royal than the one taken by them painted girls what work our crowds and sell themselves for less than a shilling.

But still – she does not love him. Even if they marry I will not believe it's so. Women only get wed to be kept and men do it because the fools think it cheaper than employing a servant.

Ah, fuck it, pig! What would I know about love anyway? Not a one of us cast-asides in Grainger's lot has felt it for what it really is. If I expect to ever get a taste of it I must be weak-brained as well as lank-sleeved.

Good riddance to her! For what is she to me? What was she ever?

We all of us travel up and down the oily pole of this wretched bleeding family. We rise, then slide, knocked down by another climbing behind us. Then we ready ourselves to shin skywards again once we've got our breath together. I'm gathering mine now. When I was taking those punches and it filled the tin, my slop servings were double hers, I know it. I might never have been prized enough for a tavern roof, but that was only a matter of me not being a woman, so not fussy about those things. Hildy was highborn, both mother and father, she had to have herself a mattress. Now that Mim is labelled a queen, I suppose she can't be seen bunking up with the hare.

What I don't like is how quickly she's believing all this

queen gab. Only yesterday, it feels, she would laugh when I called her slave-girl. Now it's all:

'My mother was a lady, dontcha know.'

'I'm top billing and shall soon need my own servants.'

'Let me educate you, oh stupid one, on the decadence of setting fire to gin, for I am The Electrical Venus!'

What a name. My master was after titling her something more humble. My mistress, well, she was after leaving her behind in the mud. Me, I was after robbing the nob of his machine and doing it all by ourselves and never handing him the cut. But, no. Our Mr Fox gives us a sheen we could only ever dream of alone. Doors open when he knocks upon them, no bucket is emptied upon his head. All our Lammas days have come at once, my master says. The pocketbook grows fat and the new order of things is this: Grainger, Fox and Mim ride up front in the covered cart, Lizzy and Abel go behind in the next, Joe and me are in with the animals. That says everything you need to know.

I don't understand what people find so fascinating about this electrickery anyway. I've had my fill of it. The feathers fly up. The crown goes blue. Beyond that, it's just a jostling of men, the ones who can afford to waste a penny on it. They push and shove for their turn on her lips, leaping off the ground and howling like dogs stung by wasps when the stuff shoots through them. A 'vertue' that's what Dr Numbskull calls it. A vertue, eh? If that's the case, then these days, with all my lasses, I'm the most virtuous of them all. Even Mim can't better me on that.

Truth is, pig, I can hardly bear to watch. Can't bear to see her proud face painted white and spotted, believing she is a lady when she is only a harlot by another name. She even wears a wig, covering the long black wildness of her own hair, more beautiful beneath . . .

Ah, enough, pig! This talk is making me watery-headed.

You'll be gone soon. You're up for selling. They don't care no more if you can count or spell or pick a club from a heart. All bets are on Mim and the doctor. I'm with them – on their opinion of you, at least. What have you ever offered me? An ear is all. Your advice, let me tell ya, is something fucking terrible.

I sometimes wonder if this kind of chatter is what others might do with their fathers. Is that what I need? Someone to tell me to pull myself together, to choose mind over matter and be a man?

So, I'm off to walk the rope. I can stand upon it well, put one foot in front of the other, for I have worked out how to cheat the balance. With the bend of my knees, I can make the rope swing, harder and harder, until I'm a ship in a swell, except I absolutely refuse to let it knock me over.

On the rope I am upstanding. On the rope, at least, I am king.

MIM

Talk to me, George. Please. It gives me the wobbles when you go like this.

Are you sick?

You lose your fluff when that's the case, go greasy and start pulling at yourself. But right now you're looking dandier than ever.

This is nothing but a sulk.

Do you wish to take your chances in the animal trailer with the others, cross your feathered fingers some customer don't take a shine to you? The audience is getting richer, in case you haven't noticed. One of them might want to stuff and mount you so you might never misbehave again. Or do as we have done – put you in a cage. 'Tis how all other parrots do exist; I am assured of it by Sebastian.

This is what I call him now. I am allowed to because I have proved myself, as you should try to. I assure you, bird, your liberties would be much improved.

I am celebrated in the pages of Sebastian's favourite periodicals, take several bows at the end of our shows before the applauding will quell and I have barely said 'I ain't never' once in his earshot this last week. He has leafed through my commonplace book and seen my adequate mind at work, seen how I have raised myself to his level. To the same standing, at least, as a prospective wife of a learned man. That I am to call him 'Sebastian' was the obvious next step.

It occurred only the other evening, as we were leaning into the light of the tallow, trying to revive an air-pumped mouse by using one of the electrical jars. The moon was helping us none as we bound the creature's tiny limbs, just like we do the wrists of Abel before a show. As we worked, peering closer and closer, our heads did touch. Our eyes met. We stayed like that for what seemed the longest moment, our skin pressed together, neither of us daring to move, as if frozen by the error. Then my Mr Fox, my Sebastian, inclined his head so that his cheek might slide against the skin of my forehead, enjoy the sensation maybe. So that I might feel his hot breath across my face and then . . . He got up. To search aimlessly in the dark for more silken twine. His voice came tentative from the gloom.

'You should call me Sebastian. I do not think it inappropriate, do you?'

'Not in any way,' I replied. 'And I reckon,' said I, 'that you should call me Mim in return.'

What do you make of that, George? Come on, give me your take. A witty comment. I'd stand for something rude. Nothing?

Sebastian says all other parrots live behind wire for a good part of the day and are let out only occasionally for the spreading of wings. You have a bell and a fine perch; much expense has been gone to. Your sulk is without substance. By rights, Sebastian could be wringing your neck.

No giving me the sad-eye. No waddling off and away. You have brought this upon yourself. You interrupt his show – the learned men who write our notices have remarked upon it. You did bite a hole in Sebastian's best jacket. And then the book . . . Well, that was the final straw.

My Sebastian is a collector in a long line of very distinguished collectors what have gone before. John this and James that – I forget their other names – and a Mary Somerset, Duchess of Beaufort, meaning it's not beyond my grasp either.

That book you spoiled was of Sebastian's own making, George, plants picked and pressed upon his travels all over, drawings done so very carefully of creatures and leaves. For you to just fly above and drop one of your wet and messy turds upon the open page . . . Oh George! He works so hard to keep the weevils from eating them books, then 'tis ruined in one quick squit.

So the cage it is.

'Tis such a shame, especially as he did like you very much to begin with – as something to study, that is, as something to look up. He once talked very gaily of you, about how your girl version has the same coloured feathers, two peas in a pod, and how in the wild I would find you in a small flock on an island, travelling long distances to find your food. There is no time for mimicking there. You do not copy other birds and animals, only us people when we take you as companions. Isn't that something curious to ponder? Then when it's time to have baby parrots, you go to the forest to live with your very special one.

'That's why me and George get along so marvellously,' I told Sebastian.

'George and I,' he corrected.

'George and I. Because our lives are so alike. I know how it is to travel in a flock and to wish for a special one to marry.'

I watched my Sebastian very carefully when I said that, and received a certain smile.

'George and me,' I said, 'George and I – we are the same creature in different forms.'

I thought our talk might continue then with the subject of marriage and all its possibilities. I felt the shadow of Hildy watching over me somehow, even though she ain't dead, slowly nodding her piggy head to say well done for how I'd steered him to my favour.

But no. We talked more about parrots.

Up he leapt in a frenzy of books, as he does so often with little provocation. Much of my chatter – even the chatter meant idly, just to pass the time – sends him fluttering through the pages, questing for some titbit of evidence he believes I should know.

Sebastian says, it does not work that way. You and me, George, cannot be the same creature, because you are from a different family – the Psittacidae family, as he has explained before. He set in front of me a chart in one of those great books of his, and on this chart – this ladder, if you like – it showed how all the living things in the world are separated out. We are of the same kingdom, George, the animal kingdom, and we do also share the next rung of the ladder, for we both have a backbone. But that is where it ends. That is where we must divide. You are of a different class – *aves*, which is a fancy word for birds. I, meanwhile, am *mammals*.

It is like the ranks, I suppose. You are either highborn or you're poor. I should like to sketch a ladder chart of my own within my commonplace book. Sebastian would be right there at the top, and me, well . . . I say I have climbed high enough to look him in the eye, but still, I do not feel that Sebastian and me are of the same kind.

My hypothesis is this: all of us in Grainger's brood need a separate ladder of our own, upon which we rise and fall only in relation to each other. We have more money than we did, yes, but still we stay on the cliff-edge of poor, still the scullery maids and the horse boys would think themselves above us. Are we not still vagrants, wandering abroad, gaming in the streets, peddling our subtle crafts? One wrong step and we face hard labour or a stint in the clink. Because it's not just the having of money, is it, George? – Hildy was correct – but the how you got it in the first place and what you choose to do with it. And if all that's the case, how many broadside ballads must be written in my honour, how fancy must my shoes get, before I am truly able to climb?

Come on, George. Give me your sway on this, some pithy comment.

Well hear this, then: you are going down the rungs, no matter how well you fly. Continue on this path of wilful destruction and I will fail in my attempt to turn Sebastian's affections back your way. I have stroked your cheek so dearly and talked of your great intelligence.

'A dog might fetch or sit or come when you tell him,' I have said, 'but that dog will never repeat the order for you, like my George.'

You have heard him scoff. 'Mimicry is not intelligence! If that is so, then we should congratulate the mirror for giving us back our own reflection.'

I am not of the same mind. You have been able to learn the language I speak while I have not learnt the meaning of a single one of the wordless squawks that issue from your yellow beak. And if mimicry ain't intelligence, then Sebastian can stake no claims to cleverness either, for all his experiments are copied from the pages of books and gentlemen's periodicals.

'I wonder,' I said to my Sebastian, defiant, 'if George believes that *you* are intelligent!'

Oh, he liked that. He laughed at that. He even scribbled it in his book, which we must take as a positive move. Things do not exist for Sebastian until he has studied them in great depth and written of them upon the page – a yellow stone or an air pump, a mouse or a shell. A woman. Love.

His study of me continued the other evening by making me take the charge from the jar, my feet upon the ground. He increased the setting of the dial and noted my reactions – the loudness of my cries, that is, the ripeness of my tongue. He wished to set the dial to its highest settings but I begged him 'no'. The sensation became quite impossible to bear, the sting upon my hand nothing compared to the terrible anticipation of the pain to come when I touched the bottle next.

'I think we can accurately record that as my limits,' I said, in gasps, though I did regret not pushing myself to endure it a little longer. I later caught sight of a phrase in one of the letters he writes to his learned friends. *A wife should have a certain strength of will. I require a woman who is delicate & diffident but ultimately robust.*

Had I done enough to show him that this was me?

If only Sebastian were more trusting of his instincts, more willing to believe what is right there in front of him, without a footnote, or a scholarly paper to support his choice.

'Be instinctual!' I wish to cry in his very face. For this is how I have decided to be. I have decided to trust what I felt the night of the demonstration, when Sebastian kissed me upon the lips. It was love. Yes, love. Nothing in Sebastian's books can confirm or deny it so I must rely only on the feeling. A shot of lightning goes through me every time I look at him, this highborn gentlemen talking to me in that way of his. I glow at the thought of becoming a lady. When have I ever felt anything else to compare?

You have rubbed your head against my face and I have thought, oh, this is it, this is love, for it makes me warm. But then Lizzy has thrashed me hard and told me that's how true care is shown. My mother did not love me or she would not have sold me, and for all I know my father never saw me once. My master has room in his heart only for the chinking of coins, while Hildy talked of being my dear guardian, then off she went. As for Alex, he has just bitter words and the shaking of his head for me now. The feeling of that, let me tell you, George, is worse than the pain of the most powerful charge. And it's not supposed to hurt, is it, love? It is not supposed to be confusing.

Oh, please, talk to me!

I have done my best by you, tried to fasten you and Sebastian as friends. I have urged him to *parlez* a bit of foreign with you, knowing how much you miss your Frenchified chatter with Hildy, as Sebastian must miss the using of his fluencies too, in French, Italian, German, Latin and all the rest he boasts of. But he will not have it.

I believe he is too shy to speak that way in front of me, not wanting to seem a show-off. Being a braggart, I'm sure, would not appear in a list of appropriate behaviours for prospective husbands, if such a corresponding list for gentlemen does exist.

On stage, of course, he has no problems playing the showman. But isn't that how it goes? Abel and Joe have entirely different ways of being when not performing. Joe is a snarling bear for the punters, but gentle and funny for us. Abel is cheeky, a prankster, but brash and short-fused when the clapping is done. I am a queen and then when the wig and crown come off . . .

Wait. 'Tis a bad example. Because here I lie in an actual bed with an actual roof above my head. Last month, in Banbury, I had an actual bath in an actual tub in front of the fire instead of jumping in the nearest stream or doing a daily brushing off of the bugs. I am eating so well I will have to adjust the waists on my gowns to enable proper breathing. And doesn't Mr Fox, in every lodgings, give coins to the woman of the house so she will be my Abigail and lace me up. He has even talked of employing a girl to travel with us always and behave as I did for Hildy, managing my wardrobe and toilet. There will be more dresses n'all, for we must keep the act looking fresh. Soon we will have run out of people who haven't seen our electrickery, Sebastian says, and then we will be in need of more original ideas. We head slowly London-bound and once we've done it there, well 'tis done.

'Exotic girls such as you,' says Sebastian, 'are a novelty in rural environs, but it will not be so in our capital city.'

We will have to move on, he says – and not in the packing up of the horses sense. A new show is what we'll be after. That's why he always has his nose in a book or is skipping away in the bigger towns for some kind of lecture. I have asked to go too, so I might assist him in improving the act, but he refuses.

'There is no point,' he says as he puts on his jacket. 'It will be presented in terms too complex. I will only have to explain it to you, as I do anyway, in layman's terms on my return.'

He is right. I understand a book better when he reads it aloud to me first, so I get to hear it in full flow, not the stuttering progress within my own head. Yesterday he read from the latest book in his collection, the one I have here in my hands. I'm giving it a gradual go myself, so don't cock your head if I begin to stumble. In it, a learned reverend writes about an island called Nevis.

'. . . *the vast Atlantic ocean (which looks of the finest Azure blue colour occasioned by great depth and exceeding transparence of water) might abound at bottom with large growing trees . . .*'

'That is a description of your home,' Sebastian said when done narrating. Into my hand, he dropped some small speckled shells, each with a grille of teeth along the middle. 'These,' he said, 'do come from its shores.'

'But I ain't from Nevis,' I told him.

'You are *not* from Nevis,' he replied – a correction of my speaking not a note of agreement –'but 'tis the same region as Jamaica.'

'I ain't from there neither,' I went on, 'I was born in Birmingham as far as I know it. You're confusing me with the parrot.'

I cannot get a fix on it, George. He wishes for me to be just like him, speak proper, become cultured, watch my manners. In all senses, I must mimic him like a parrot. But whenever possible, he mentions our points of difference with triumph. Perhaps he does this so I understand that I am special and unusual, for haven't I searched for the longest time for my own unique quality, something to mark me out in Grainger's lot and stop me being kicked off the cart? If that is so, then why does it feel the opposite? Why does it feel, when Sebastian tells me of who I am, like I am being boxed-in, caged-up?

I offered to sing *Rule Britannia* when we last discussed ways to make the performance go better. My voice is tolerable enough. I thought it would lift the crown-sparking part of our demonstrations, but he brushed the suggestion aside. He said that that part of the show, and all its other parts too, were far more singular because I kept quiet.

'It's distracting,' said Sebastian, 'when a woman opens her mouth.'

This book, George, should mean more to you than it does to me. This is your home, not mine. Do you remember seas that are a colour called 'azure' with trees growing out of them?

My youngest memories are of brown roads that kick up too much dust in the summer and are too sticky come wintertime. I have endless recollections of hot gloopy food eaten around a fire with the moths, nights slept on the boards by Hildy's bed, play-fighting with Alex in the grass . . .

If someone were to read me words about that, by a learned reverend or not, and I happened to live very far away from it, I suppose I would have a sort of sadness. Is that how it is for you, George? You cannot go back. Your wings will take you on long journeys for food but not that far.

I wonder sometimes if I have not travelled too far since meeting Sebastian, gone away from where I once was. Not that I should ever wish to go back.

I am The Electrical Venus. Celebrated, applauded.

Yet I'm not sure if I ain't more lonely than ever.

I have Sebastian, of course, and you; it's not company I'm lacking. It's just that I used to stare through the windows of fine carriages passing by, whenever we were in the bigger towns, and think that those people sitting upon their nice cushions did see the world in an entirely other way. That they felt things different to the likes of me. That no cares ever came near them.

It is true that the view is not the same from this slightly higher perch, but . . . You can't change your insides, can you, is what I'm saying. Your anatomy, if you like. The way you always thought, the way you have been loved, or not; mind and heart, they stay the same.

I think I shall take my blanket and sleep upon the floor tonight. Don't think me odd and don't you dare tell my Mr Fox. I shall open up your cage door too so we both are more comfortable.

There is just one more thing I must share with you before I close my eyes, something you must not tell – and with you so mute, I suppose I shall not have to worry.

It used to be that in the early morning when I was half

awake, half asleep, my mind would go to Alex, our feet up on that rope, or his hand upon my leg that time. This would make a wonderful sensation flush through my body, make me press myself down into the hay, against my hand, so that the sensation would spread. Perhaps it was a wrong thing to do, wicked. It's not ladylike of course, to have that amount of pleasure. But still, I was not so awake I could reason on it. Lately, though, George, my sleeping mind does go to Sebastian, the fine frame of his face and the line of his lips, the shape of his hands and the cut of his breeches. The moment when he first kissed me – the memory of it does not fade. Oh, the power it still has to make my whole body sing. I press and press and press upon myself until I could cry out with the swell of it.

Do not judge me, George! I cannot control it! I do not ask for these feelings to come. But what I'm saying is, this feeling, is it love too?

Sleep on it, George.

Tell me what you think in the morning.

In the market place at Buckingham there is a scene.

When the cry goes out from the fayre hawker – 'A penny, sirs! Just one penny to kiss our Lady Mimosa and experience the sparkling electricity of true love!' – a skirmish ensues.

One that quickly becomes a battle royal.

'You've had yer taste,' spits a fellow in the crowd – this is how it starts. He delivers a dig to the shoulder of another who he believes to have pushed in front.

'Out of it, she's mine now!' comes the reply, hands reaching forward for a grubby fumble at the ankles of The Electrical Venus. He yelps with stung fingers when he feels her charge, but 'tis no dissuasion.

'Don't think so,' says a further voice, piling in, barging the quarrelling pair from the front of the stage, shoving the ankle-fumbler to the floor. He is eager, this new one, not for the kissing but for the knocking down of some skittles. 'Outta my bleeding way or I'll snabble ya!' he crows.

And that is all it takes. The market place boils quickly into a sea of fists and boots. The ladies do shriek and swoon, the men do roar. The crowd pulls weapons from the building work that goes on about them – sticks for swaddling, bricks to be launched.

The Venus does not move from her resin block. She is stoic perhaps, or the reverse – stunned into this rigid state. Even when a heavy rock whistles past her ear and relieves her of her towering wig, she does not shift. The doctor is so aghast at this change in the tide that he cowers behind the shelter of his machine.

'Enough of this!' he calls from his hiding place. 'I will not have this sort of behaviour!'

The boy in the wings, meanwhile, pulls up his one useful sleeve with his teeth – he understands how it will go. This sotted lot have had a taste of the riot and nothing will make them stop. They'll drub, lump and quilt one another until the parish officers arrive to drag the ringleaders to a lock-up. So he goes in swinging, his goal clear – to rescue the girl. And though his intentions are good, his outcomes are not so. A fellow he clouts falls backwards, onto the stage, and the resin block is shunted. The girl's legs go with it, flying from beneath her –

CRACK!

The back of her wigless head connects with the wooden edge of the doctor's machine. Her eyes do roll and in a dance of eyelashes, her consciousness flutters away. In dives the boy, up onto the stage, fast, scooping up his prize, whisking her from the melee. There is no time for decorum; the Venus, his girl, is slung abreast the ledge of his shoulder, petticoats displayed. The boy's one arm holds safe the back of her legs.

'Wait!' cries the doctor, scurrying from his trench, ducking

131

the missiles and following the boy at a trot. 'Put her down at once!'

'Why?' asks the boy, not slowing his jog through the candle-lamped streets. 'You volunteering to heft her home, are ya?'

'Certainly not!'

'Di'nt reckon so!'

'We should wait for a physician, I am saying!' The doctor is panting now, not used to any kind of chase. 'Or at the very least, transport her to her room via carriage.'

'We'll wait until holy bleeding Sunday for a medicine man to show,' shouts the boy. 'And I ain't suffering no basting from that lot while I sort out the horse. Go on with ya! Rescue your machine, before the rabble in there make firewood of it.'

The doctor skids to a halt in the gravel: the thought of his instrument turned to cinders is the stopping stuff. The boy runs on, alone with the girl, towards the south of the town, beyond the river, to where the doctor and his muse have taken their lodgings. The learned man, meanwhile, runs in the direction opposite, to save what can be saved.

At the Mitre, the girl is placed before the fire in the small lounge and given liquor strong enough to kill the devil. Alone with her rescuer, she begins to revive.

'Sebastian has a cure upstairs, I'm sure,' she says. 'In those books of his, there is a cure for almost everything.'

The boy notices how the doctor no longer goes by 'Mr Fox' on the girl's tongue and this confirms so much of what he had feared. He takes a dram himself from the pot left by the bar girl at the landlord's insistence.

'Yeah, well, he ain't here,' says the boy, wanting that point logged. *Worried more for his machine than his lady*, he might have added but the girl is smart, she'll grasp the inference. So instead he says, 'Warm in here.' Though the comment comes out harsh, bitter-sounding for what he does not have.

'Oh, the weather ain't that bad,' says the girl, keen to level it. 'You lay it thick.'

'It turns at night,' he mutters, though he wants to be kind, 'in case you've gone and forgotten.'

They stare into the fire that licks the stone, sputtering and popping behind the grate.

'More slop for you now we're making a mint,' the girl offers, 'now that I'm off camp, doing my eating in the tavern.'

'Don't be so sure.' The boy shakes his head. 'A one-armed juggler ain't so exciting in the presence of angels. I'm treated no better. I'll be the next one off the cart, you'll see. Better hope a workhouse somewhere will bend the rules and take me.'

They look at one another now across that dim room, absorbing who they have become, familiar yet so transformed, their roles, perhaps, exchanged.

'Your place, meanwhile, is safe,' he says, a voice of sorrow.

'Well, ain't that for the good?' says she. 'For me, I mean.'

A shrug from the boy, his honesty spilling free. 'I dunno.'

'I was but a caterpillar, Alex, and now I'm a–'

'You ain't no butterfly, Mim.'

'Excuse me!'

'He won't let you be one, will he? Don't you see it? He wants that role all for his preening self. You've turned proper slave now, if you ask me. You're nothing but his trinket.'

The girl's face falls furious. She rises suddenly in protest, only to wobble with her dizziness.

'Where you going, kid?'

'Up-stairs,' she says, both syllables a knife.

'I'll take you, Mim.' The boy rises too.

'No.'

'You need someone to look at that head before you go asleep.'

''Tis but a flea bite,' she tells him darkly, the boy's long-ago words being used back at him. She makes to leave.

'Well, then I'll help you on the stairs.' He reaches for the soft, dark, reflective skin of her arm, that skin for which he has found no comparison despite – as some might call it – a most thorough search. But the girl snatches the limb away.

'Ah, come on, Mim!'

'No!' This is final. There is bite to what she says. 'A lady does not allow someone such as you to accompany her to her room. It is hardly appropriate.'

'Hardly appropriate?' he repeats, watching the way she looks at him, upwards and then, more importantly, down. He can see the shift, her vowels pinched tight, now that she's gone back to the pretensions of being a doctor's muse. The accident did not knock into her the sense that he had wished for. 'Hardly appropriate!?' he says, his anger growing. 'So says the girl who kisses an 'undred men a night for pennies!'

'*They* kiss *me*,' she says, her eyes but slits.

'That makes some kind of difference, does it?'

'It is a distinction!'

'Oh, a "distinction"! There's a fine word for it! I know another word, Mim, that's much more bleeding accurate.'

'Oh, yes! Well, there's a word for the likes of you too. All those poor girls you take advantage of!'

'Go on, then!' he goads. 'You tell me. You tell me what am I, eh? Cough it up! What exactly do you make of me, Lady Mimosa? Am I just some lank sleeve to you, some sad dog, some specimen for the jar? No one could ever rightly want to lie with me, eh? Better I just take myself to the slaughter yard, is that what ya reckon?'

Their eyes lock. The air fizzes hot and dangerous. Kiss or kick. Embrace or die. A mutinous tear spills down the girl's cheek and one falls down the boy's in return, though he is fast to wipe it away.

'I am to bed,' she says, quiet, picking up her skirts so she does not brush him as she passes, as if she is carrying a residue charge from the stage and sparks might fly.

'The rope is still there,' he says to her back, desperate, making her halt. She does not turn, but waits for more, motionless at the base of the stairs. 'I can walk on it now, Mim, jump, spin, rock it beneath me . . . You should see.' Still, she does not move. 'I can imagine it, our act. You climb first, walk the rope, speak to the crowd in that way of yours. Then up I climb to join you and . . .' He sees her ribs spread wide within her loosened stays – the taking in of a breath – then, tiredly, those ribs collapse. 'We don't take it to Grainger, Mim, this is what I'm thinking. Once we're perfect, it's a ticket to London.'

'We're already heading to London,' murmurs the girl. 'Hadn't you noticed?'

'To Paris! Venice even!'

'I'm the Electrical Venus now.'

135

'But you're not, are you. That's what I'm saying. That's not you! That's done to you. You're but the sideshow of a bleeding sideshow. You're worth more than that, Mim. Why give half to the doctor and then let our master drink the rest? It ain't fair. I mean, what do you get out of all this, aside from a round of applause at the end of the day?'

'Love.'

'Huh?' The boy chokes as if the word had come from his own throat, got caught on the way up. 'Love?'

'Sebastian loves me.' Still she does not turn.

'But . . . I . . . I mean . . . How do you know? Has he said as much?'

'I feel it. I felt it right from that very first night.'

'But that's just electrickery, Mim, he said it himself. Look . . .' He dares a laugh of sorts. 'He ain't gonna marry ya now, is he?'

And this is when she turns, rounds upon him as if she might drive her nails into the flesh of his neck, though she stops herself from violence at the last moment.

'Must we all be so miserable!' she screams. 'Must we all be so sorry for ourselves for ever more! Must none of us ever come to good!' Her face is dark and wet, her body shakes.

The boy is open-mouthed, destroyed by his own clumsy words. Sobs tremble within his chest, wishing to burst free, so he clamps tight his lips, holds a fist white by his side.

'I am to bed,' she whispers – an end to it – and she is away again.

But he must say something. He will not part with her in bad air, let her sleep upon this quarrel. What can he say, though, that will mean anything, that will make her change her mind?

So he decides to speak idly, playfully, if only to hear her reply that way in return.

'Will ya give my goodnights to George?' he manages, his voice a quaver, his skin glistening with the tears he cannot keep back.

'I can't,' says she. The soles of her brand new boots, bought that day in this cobbler's town, not yet worn into the shape of left and right, sound upon the wood.

'Why?' asks he.

'Because –' and these are her last words, ones she delivers with a terrible gasp before she disappears from view – 'the bird has flown away.'

ALEX

So, pig, this is goodbye.

You're to stay in this half-built town, and we're to go. I did my best to sell you as a mudlark with skills, but I can't make no promises. The future ain't commanded by the likes of me. The man what bought you said he was to keep you, but his belly might win him over. Either way, 'tis all a new beginning. And if you do end up as bacon, I reckon I still shall envy ya.

My future's black, pig, black as pitch. The boy what waits, well, he waited far too long. The rope weren't the answer. I thought it the most frightening thing I could do – go behind my master's back, plot with Mim, take her there at midnight and chance a nasty tumble. I thought, if I was to go down while balancing way up high and break my fall with my good hand, snapping my wrist as I did, then Mim would see me at my very worst – no hands at all. That, I'd convinced myself, was the risk I was taking, the illest consequence. Of course, it weren't. I did those rope tricks with Mim only to avoid doing the truly terrifying thing. I travelled around the alleys and back again, when I should've taken one straight route. I should have just said it. I should have just told her.

My lesson's been learnt the hardest way. Now I will know to grab a thing if I want it. Not in the actual sense, but in the honest one.

Ah, hark at me, pig, speaking in riddles.

So this is how it went, this was how the final nail was driven in. After she went up them stairs at the Mitre to bed, I didn't leave. The boy what waits decided to do just that. I stayed by the fire and drank, and not for the numbing of the booze, not even for the warmth. I waited so that she wasn't alone. Someone needed to be there. If the doctor didn't return soonish, I would be the one to go silent-like upstairs once she were a-kip and make sure she was still well, still breathing.

The landlord had been in, you see, no doubt because he'd heard Mim's voice raised, mine too, and sensed there was trouble brewing. He wanted to know where she had gone. The 'woozy girl', he called her. And when I said a-bed, he was surprised.

'What? Without her husband?'

Now, I could have set him level there, said no vows had passed between them, but I supposed he might be a starched sort (in his mind if not in his dressing, for his shirt tails weren't long enough to broach that gut and meet his breeches). He was likely the kind of fella who thought that people should be in the married way before sharing any rooms.

'Well, she shu'nt be going a-bed after a blow to the head,' said the man. He was wiping down tables which were clean enough already, his excuse to come in and see that all was well. 'I heard of a poor fella who slipped the wind in his sleep – gone! And all cos of a crack in the face in a fight before bed.' He shook his head at his sorry story, cheeks wobbling. 'I would be staying awake if it were me,' he went on, 'to make sure I didn't die.'

I must have gone pale at that for he followed pretty swift-like with: 'Not that that's gonna happen to your . . .' He stopped, not knowing how to finish the thought.

'Sister,' I put in, being canny. He wouldn't be letting me up them stairs later if he was a straight-lace and I was a nobody to her. Mim was right I suppose, it's hardly appropriate for a lady to be accompanied to her room by someone such as me.

He stared, narrow-eyed, his brain in a knot.

'Funny colour skin she's got compared to you,' he said.

I nodded, told him he was most observant, flattered him some, but gave him no details more.

'And you,' he goes, 'you've only got the one arm.'

Oh, there spoke a genius! And it ain't the first time, pig, that someone has felt the unquashable urge to point out the bleeding obvious. Right tempted I am each time it happens to look down at my empty sleeve, give a scream of shock and start scrabbling upon the floor in deathly search. It would have cheered me no end to have done it then, but as I said, I wanted up those stairs. I needed the fella on my side.

'Yeah, I lost it,' I told him with a cool shrug. 'In a knife fight with a hackum. My attacker, well . . .' I whistled my sorrow '. . . he weren't so lucky.'

He let me be after that. Better than having the clod on my side was to have him a little bit afeared.

Once the fire had fallen to a height that told me time had passed, and there was yet no sign of the doctor, I took a candle and made for upstairs. At the top I found two doors, went for the one not closed. On the table was a spread of books and on the dresser lay all the things Mim had spoken poems about – shells and stones and jars full of all-sorts. I'd feigned a kind of boredom when she'd boasted about them. It weren't that I had no interest, just that I cared little for their owner. So I took my opportunity then for a quick nose about, had a flick through the books, making neither head nor tail of any of it, what with me never being taught to read. I went towards the notebooks instead. These were full of writing still, handwriting, but also pictures, sketchings, dried-out plants all stuck upon the pages. Mim had taken a liking to doing this kind of thing lately – picking flowers in spare moments and working out ways to squash 'em. Now I understood what she was aiming at – copying the doctor. I'd seen her pick up eggshells too, try and get Joe to join her in a conversation about the colour they were, because blue couldn't be just bleeding blue any more, not since that nob arrived. It's 'periwinkle' or 'turquoise' or something called 'azure'. Joe would be too soft with her, humour her.

'Oh, ain't that right!' he'd go. 'It does have something of the grey skies about it.'

I caught her almost dancing a jig one day to find a robin dead on the ground with hardly a mark upon it. In her pocket it went, and never mind the maggots.

'We must observe, collect and organise,' is what she kept saying, as if it were a tune that had got stuck in her head.

I could only think that we were doing it already, and had been for the longest time. Observing, collecting and organising is my master's game. That's his bread and lard. For hadn't he always got his peepers peeled back for a weird-seeming animal or a strange sort of person – an Abel, a Joe, a me, or a Mim. Someone he can hand over notes for, add to his collection, organise into a show that's entertaining. Mr Fox is doing nothing new, nothing special, though he likes to think he is.

In this big notebook of his, was a drawing of George done from the side, then another from the front. There was a close sketch of the bird's eye and another of a wing outstretched, with plenty of scribblings I had no hope of understanding.

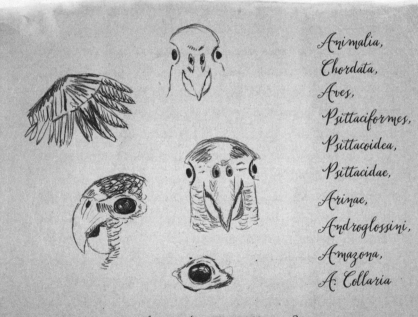

Animalia,
Chordata,
Aves,
Psittaciformes,
Psittacoidea,
Psittacidae,
Arinae,
Androglossini,
Amazona,
A. Collaria

Do parrots believe that WE are intelligent?

Poor George.

He loved Mim so hard, was always with her. I can't fathom a situation that would make him fly away. I reckon the doctor was behind it because he didn't like the heckling. That bird is at a tanner's now for its embalming, you mark me, having his insides swapped for horsehair so he might never squawk again.

On the notebook pages after George, there were drawings of a deer with two heads and one body, like what we have seen before with sheep and cows at fayres along the way. Then on the next page was Mim. He'd drawn pictures of Mim – exactly like he'd done with the parrot. Mim, all dressed up, full length, taken from every slant. The close things he'd decided upon were the shape of her lips, then the place at her collar where the skin dips and the bones show. The paper was uneven on these parts, shrivelled, as if something filthy had been dropped upon it then wiped away. The drawings weren't worth saving though, if you asked me. They gave no sense of her. I only knew for certain it was Mim because the frock was a familiar one. In the margins there was more scribbling that I wished I could get the gist of. What did he have to say about her? What words was he using for the describing? Had he summoned up the perfect way to get across the colour of her skin? I doubted it. He was writing about her as if she were nothing more than a parrot, a poor deer born joined to its brother. If the man had been there in that moment, I would have held his arm painful behind his back and made him read it all aloud.

Then, if that weren't enough, if I'd not been made sufficiently fierce by what I'd seen on paper, my eyes went to a piece of shiny white pottery above the fireplace. Standing in among those jars of lizards and the insides of frogs was a statue of a woman, all naked – the whole scene, the lot – but she had no legs or arms or head. On her base she wore a label.

Now, I may be no reader but that word I knew, because it is writ big across our every handbill

~ VENUS ~

This thing, this saucy bit of clay, was supposed to be Mim. I gripped it ready for the throwing. I was gonna knock down the doctor's jars as if they were pins. I wanted water and frog guts to spill across the floor. I know I may have taken a bit of joy in the naked shape of Mim myself, watched her move through her nightdress when the moon is right, but to set the idea in pot, remove all the parts of her except the ones you want to peep at then stand it upon your mantelpiece . . . Well, it weren't right! I raised it up, ready for the lobbing and that was when the nob returned, cradling his machine in exactly the way I had cradled his not-so-really wife.

'It has but a scratch,' he said, his words of hello, as he slid the machine all gentle-like onto the cabinet by the door. He made no comment on my arm raised, which only maddened me more. I wanted him startled that I was there, furious about it, ready to fight. If he had proposed a duel and he had the weapons there for the doing of it, I would have agreed without a blink.

'We lost one glass tube,' he went on, so calm that I considered saving the specimen jars and lobbing the Venus straight in his self-satisfied mug. 'I have given my full report to the authorities. 'Tis a miracle not more was lost.'

144

I let my hand, and the Venus, fall by my side. The only duelling this fella would agree to was the sort that was done with words.

'Mim has more than a scratch,' I said, a comment I fashioned more pointed than a very sharp stick, 'in case you were getting fretful.'

He took my meaning. ''Twas but a knock,' he said.

'Yet it was you who was calling for the services of a "physician".'

Still he would not rise.

'In a fracas such as that,' said he, 'tempered speech does not flow freely.'

I mean, honestly, pig. Who talks like that and thinks it normal!

I stood the Venus on the page with the drawings of Mim, deliberate-like, so he knew exactly what I'd seen and how I felt about it.

'It's not good for her to be asleep,' I told him, taking charge. 'Where's your bed? She needs checking on.'

'*My* bed,' he said with great weight on that first word, 'is this.'

He pointed to a cot in the corner. Not quite a bed but twice as decent as anything I have ever slept on.

'Mimosa has her own bed,' he added, 'in the privacy of her own room.'

That shoved me off centre. 'But I thought . . .'

'I'm sure you did!' he went.

So I struck back. 'What – don't you like the girls, mister? Bit of a Molly, are ya? Should I be careful for myself?'

'I have admiration for the female form,' said he, acting the judge, making me the defendant, the drunkard in the dock. I was so eager to punch the nob but also certain I mustn't do it. It would only prove him right. 'You know of my appreciation,' he went on. He nodded to the Venus. 'You can see it very well with your own eyes. You have had a feel of it with your own grubby fingers.'

Both of us looked at the statue and I felt a shame crawl over me, for picking the thing up, even though it was him what owned it. I was cornered, and I thought of cutting my losses, leaving there and then with my tail between my legs, but sometimes I find my mettle.

'She reckons you're going to marry her.'

I said it. I said it.

And it was worth it, in that moment, to see the gulp ride his throat, the white sweep across his cheeks. He looked behind him at the door, as if she might be standing there to witness this, instead of a-kip in that room across the hall.

'Does she now?' was all the answer he had.

'And it ain't fair,' I said, 'to lead her by the nose.'

'Is it not?' said he, pulling himself together, as much as he could. 'Thank you for your learned opinion on this matter.'

'She thinks you love her.'

If this was to be our duel, I would stand my ground, I would fight.

'Love her?' It was news to him, I could tell. News he'd been doing his best not to listen to.

'And do you?' I jabbed. 'Do you love her? Are you going to marry her?' I was after his refusal. I was sure it was there, that I could drag it up, protesting, to the surface. And after I'd got it, I would burst into Mim's room, tell her how it was, and carry her away from this nonsense, just as I'd carried her free of that riot.

But the doctor was blushing. Blushing, pig! He stammered

and placed a hand against his heart. 'I . . . She is . . . I mean, she is charming, certainly. More charming than I could ever have anticipated, but . . .'

I realised then how I must have appeared that night of the demonstration when I did not dare step up for a kiss. The doctor wanted her, but could not say it. I had thought that she was nothing to him, a creature to tame to his will, a means to something else.

He cleared his throat. 'But I don't see what business that is of yours.'

Then came a change. The doctor lifted his gaze to meet mine, a nasty little smile spreading across his face. 'Unless, of course, you have some kind of vested interest of your own.'

'What are you saying?'

He looked me up, then down, and I saw what he saw – a vagrant, a player, half a man.

'I mean,' said he, moving between me and the table, taking hold of the Venus and putting her back in her place on the mantel, 'are *you* weak for the girl?'

'Oh,' I said. 'Oh.'

'Do *you* love her?' he pressed. 'Do you love Mim and wish to marry her?'

I thought I might be sick. I was a mouse being dangled by a foot. I was a frog whose insides were gripped, ready for the yanking.

The strength of my feelings came as news to me too, I suppose. News I'd been doing my best not to listen to. The way I felt about Mim, there was a word for it – a word I've used and always known, but in some far off way, only for others. But the doctor had called it. It was a shot to the chest.

'I don't know what business it is of yours,' I said, blustering, borrowing his lines, but it was too late. You can't keep that sort of thing hidden, can you? You saw it, pig, all along. Even when I hadn't rightly worked it out for myself. You knew and you're nothing but a daft bleeding mudlark who can't count, even for the promise of carrot heads.

'How fascinating!' the doctor crowed. 'What a revelation! And I thought someone like you was only capable of quivering lust.' He leant back on the table and folded his arms. 'The one-arm'd boy,' he announced, '*loves* the girl-exotic!'

The way he spoke of us – as things he had named, things he had decided upon.

'Well, well, well,' he said. His pale face was all brightness now. 'I suppose your answer to my question is immaterial,' he went on, sussing this all out in the talking. 'Because the important thing is, who does Mimosa love?' His look was one of pure victory. 'I wonder who Mimosa wishes to marry?'

Immaterial, eh? I'm supposing that means worthless.

'I believe . . .' said he, 'no! Scratch that! I have proof conclusive of who is at the centre of Mimosa's wishes regarding matrimony. It is all within the pages of her commonplace book, I am sure, for she writes everything there. Shall we read it together?'

I would take no more of his mockery. I would talk to Mim in the morning myself. She had stalled on the stairs when I mentioned the rope and our different future. She was wobbling in the balance. So I shouldered past him, out of the staleness of that airless room, and I tramped back home to you lot.

Home. What a rounded word for not very much at all.

And here I am now with a page of words that I cannot

read. A letter. The bar girl from the Mitre brought it over to our camp after sun-up. I thought she'd come with grave news of Mim, that she had slipped the wind in her sleep, like the landlord said she would. My heart near leapt out my mouth.

'What's happened?' I said, right up in the bar girl's face, making her startled in return. 'Is she dead?'

'Dead?' said she, confused. 'No, not dead, sir. But gone, she is. They wished for me to let your master know.'

'Gone?'

'They are no longer . . .' Her eyes went to the sky in search of the words she'd been given for the delivering. 'They no longer require your master's services.'

'What?' I said.

'They asked me to offer their sincere apologies for taking one of the horses and the carts and . . .' She searched again for her scripted lines. 'And, oh yes, I am to tell you that they are to be married.'

My heart didn't lurch no more, pig. In that moment, it stopped.

'The lady,' the girl went on, a certain sauce to her voice, because here was a scandal she'd entertain her friends with for months. 'The lady, she wanted me to give you this.'

And she put the letter in my hand. A letter. One I cannot read and never will be able to. That's all that's left of her.

So what do I do? Shall I feed the thing to you? Shall I drop it in the fire? I have no need of it. My Mim's feelings are clear – for feelings are shown in the doing, not the talking, not the writing. My answer to that question on love might have been *immaterial* but hers weren't. Mim wishes to marry the doctor and I, the prating fool, pushed him to make it so.

Dear Alex,

I am glad you are not too proud to take this letter to someone who can read it aloud for you.

(& to you, dear 'reader-aloud', whoever you be, do not be too proud yourself. My sentences are as good as my education (or lack of it) allows. Also I have had a knock on the head. But that is a whole other story & not for here. Suffice to say, it took me a good time to get this all down upon paper without crossings-out & with all my spellings accurate, so be accurate in the telling of it. Do not go making your own alterations. I mean it well, even if I cannot write it well)

(Then please forget everything you read here, for all of it is most private).

Alex, I am sorry for us to part on harsh words. I thought about writing to ask your forgiveness for what I said, but when I had a bit of a sit down & another think I came to this conclusion: I meant every word. We _are_ allowed to come to good. All of us. So that is what I am trying to do. Happiness is but a decision, I reckon, as is luck. So I am giving myself big servings of both. I have been made a better offer & I am letting myself have it. When you get your better offer, Alex, make sure you grasp it with both hands (excuse the expression).

George flew away recently, as you know, & this made me very sad. I am disappointed in myself for never bothering to learn his language when he made such an effort to learn mine. But I am being taught by him now, in actions rather than speaking. He left hoping for something better than a cage, a perch & a bell. I want more than slop & old hay & a twice-weekly beating. I know I have had it good these last few weeks but I have the nagging feeling, as it is with anyone who is the apple of Grainger's eye, that my time as top billing will not last forever.

I used to be very scared that Grainger might sell me. Then, as I got to know the doctor, I hoped I would be sold, because though Sebastian is strange in his ways sometimes, he is not so mean & has taught me more in the last few weeks than Hildy managed in years. (& anyway, is it not safer to assume that we are the strange ones, living on the edges of life as we do?)

Last night, Sebastian woke me from my sleep & asked me to be his wife. After the knock on the head I had received, I thought I was having some kind of vision! A highborn gentleman wishing to join hands with the likes of me! Marriage is something I never truly had in my sights. I wished for it certainly & Hildy had trained me to expect it but I always tried to keep my expectations low so I would not be disappointed. When I told you last night that Sebastian loved me it was only my ambition speaking. I was upset & wanted to boast. For it to actually be true – 'tis a miracle!

I asked Sebastian when he made his proposal if he was planning on buying me after all. He thought I was saying this as one of my jokes, but I explained that it weren't. So he in return explained that no payment was necessary because Grainger did not own me. It is not possible for one human being to own another, that is how he put it. Which means, Alex, that you are likewise free. Of course, I do wonder if he speaks in error & that my running away is against the law. But haven't we always lived on the wrong side of right so what difference will this make?

I shall take the risk. George took a risk leaving me, after all. Who will give him seeds & stroke his nose when I am not there? I hope he misses me but I also hope he finds someone new. He has left behind big blue seas before with trees growing out of them, for that is what it looks like where he is from, so he will manage well enough without this girl who is neither one thing nor the other. & so shall you.

I know how awful it can feel to watch others go. Hildy went, then George. Everyone who I thought loved me has left. Perhaps that goes to show I know nothing of what love is.

What does it look like, or sound like, or feel like? Have you fathomed it yet, Alex, with all of your girls?

I am going along with the idea that love is a spark, one that might light a fire if you let it. & that is what I felt when Sebastian did his kissing experiment upon me that very first night. It hurt me some, but that seems to fit the description too, does it not? Of love, I mean.

I wonder if you have some other suggestions. I think I will always wonder. Goodbye.

Your Mim

ACT III

Desperation will drive a man to extraordinary lengths. Often times, blood will be spilled. And sometimes that blood will belong to an unfortunate cow.

An animal is bought. Yet another deduction to be made in the fayre hawker's pocketbook, where the column marked 'incomings' has little to show. Since the doctor ran away with The Electrical Venus, the figures have drooped, drowned, dropped to the bed. They do not have a performance to collect the coppers for. A 'one-arm'd boy', a 'no-legg'd brute' and a 'dwaff' with tricks will not draw the crowds they have grown to expect, a situation that sends the fayre hawker into great monologues of cursing, lambasting the country rabble for having 'sophistications above their standings'. Down into the bottom of his beer tankard he wails, about how the world is not what it used to be, about how modern life moves too fast and will surely come to ill. In this groggified state, the fayre hawker will sometimes sob, until he is asked to leave the tavern because his snivelling is distracting the more focused drinkers.

Without a reason to move on to the next town, the company stay put, saving on energies and the horse feed needed for their remaining two nags. A periwigged parish officer comes to the camp early on to read the Riot Act but finds their numbers – and obstinacy – insufficient to make their eviction a satisfying one.

'Ah, sit down and have a dish of tea, why dontcha,' says the fayre hawker's wife to the officious little man and he obliges, flipping the tail of his coat and taking a tree trunk seat by the fire. He expects to sup a lusty drink made from leaves shipped from China, so baulks when given an insipid soup of whatever leaves happens to have fallen from the nearest tree. Untimely excuses are made. He never returns.

The bread and butter days of electrickery become a distant dream, and once again the company subsists on unpalatable slop, the portions so small it is hard to know whether to be grateful or sorry.

'We just go back to what we does best,' is the solution suggested by the fayre hawker's wife as they guzzle their meagre helpings. 'Menageries and spectacles of human birth. That's what we should stick to.'

'Oh, how can we, you great fussock!' scoffs the fayre hawker, 'when we have sold the hare, the pig, and slaughtered all the geese.'

'Why, we've still got Abel,' says his wife, nudging the fellow in question so his spoon of slop does miss his mouth. 'And Abel's still got his wings, in't ya?'

The man nods, wiping food from his lap, delighted, momentarily, to be considered a thing of significance on this sinking ship, one that will soon be looking for extra weight to throw over its side. But his delight quickly becomes dread. He does not want to be in the middle of an argument between cat and dog. The master's disagreements with his wife so often turn nasty. There could be biting, scratching, the blacking of eyes.

'Oh, well, that's us sorted then, in't it!' says the fayre hawker, mocking his wife. 'That's us singing sweet! We got all we need if we have ourselves a shrimp with wings! Oh, act sensible, woman!'

The small man makes himself smaller yet within the shadows. The boy and his bear boxer companion exchange a look across the fire, one that says prepare to administer forceful restraint or beat a swift exit, whichever seems most wise.

'You will magic them wings back into dancing geese, will you, Jack sprat?' hisses the fayre hawker, closing in on his prey, his question in no way a rhetorical one. The fayre hawker's anger has turned to wild desperation. He wants an answer and is so clearly hopeful of a 'yes'.

But the one-time angel can only shake his head. Yes, he has a pair of beautiful celestial wings, but no he cannot turn water into wine, nor feathers back into geese.

'Fuck it!' bellows the fayre hawker. 'Fuck it to next Tuesday!' And he drops his tin of slop, letting it connect with the toe of his boot and he shoots it directly into the flames of the fire.

When sunrise comes and the booze has worn away, the fayre hawker concedes that his wife had been shoving them gently in the direction of a good idea. They must look to their old act for salvation, to the words upon their former broadsides. They must remember Hildy.

The doctor had told them of other pig-faced ladies he had

seen in fayres up and down the land and how each of them was nothing but an elaborate hoax.

'What a rum sham!' the fayre hawker had exclaimed disparagingly then.

'What resourcefulness!' is what he cries out now. And: 'Isn't it time we played along?'

With the assistance of the boy and a sharp-enough knife, the fayre hawker slaughters the poor purchased cow with a cut across the throat.

'Good Lord above!' squeals the fayre hawker's wife, as the claret gushes from the defeated beast, running rivers through the grass and pooling in the mud. 'I cannot watch!'

Her husband and the boy stand stunned at the disgrace of death, bathed in the red stuff from wrist to neck, from knee to shoe. Their faces are splattered as if they have contracted a peculiar kind of pox. The fayre hawker steps away from the carnage so he might catch his wife who looks set to swoon, but she revives suddenly, sharply, when she sees his bloodied hands reaching to sully her skirts.

'And don't go letting it all run away, you pillocks!' she snaps, back to her old self. 'Think of the decent gravy I could be making with that!'

The animal is clumsily butchered, and for a while a sniff of hope hangs above the camp, along with the stink of congealing blood. It is the type of hope that arrives when your stomach is full, swimming with beef stew, when your teeth are busy with the gnawing of ribs cooked bare upon the fire. Their bellies swell painful from the eating, their organs having shrivelled to nothing by previous rationing, but it is an ache they are able to bear. For here is optimism! And it is promising to stick around as long as there are stores of meat that have not yet turned green.

The head of the cow is carefully set aside and the boy is charged with emptying the neck and the skull of its brains, a task that makes him retch the contents of his loaded guts into the grass to mix with the thickening blood. This is the match in the barrel that forces them, at last, to move camp for the first time in a fortnight, so plagued they are by the flies and the stench.

At their new abode, in woodland further along their route towards the capital, a meeting is held across the fire, accompanied by a soup made of the cow's tail (along with its ears, hooves, nostrils and bum). Each of them wipes clean their dish with the edge of a dirty finger and makes many noises of satisfaction.

''Tis time,' says the fayre hawker, with a certain solemnity when the eating is all done. ''Tis time to try out the head!'

'Yes!' agrees his wife with a gleeful clap. 'Step up, Alex. Let us see how it looks.'

'What?' says the boy, leaping to his feet with an instinct to run, no inkling to oblige. 'I'm not doing it!' he protests. 'I won't be able to stand it! My guts will come up through me teeth!'

'Calm it, would ya!' says the fayre hawker to the boy-hysteric. 'You are strange enough with your missing arm. A cow's head would be a move too far. A moooo-ve . . .' says the fayre hawker, slipping back into his role of entertainer and wit, '. . . too far!'

They laugh along, happy at this reminder of how things used to be. Not good, but better. The boy sits and gives out a sigh.

'I was meaning,' clarifies the fayre hawker, 'that the head should be worn by Lizzy.'

'You what?!' The wife is on her feet now, also not willing, unless the willingness is to stand for a fight. 'How bloody dare you!'

''Tis animal-faced ladies that is the fashion, my dear. Do not take it so personal.'

'I *shall* take it personal!' booms the wife. 'I shall!'

And then comes a sight never seen before – the woman's eyes are wet. The others fall silent at this spectacle, this awful miracle, as if tears were falling from the statue of a particularly sweary virgin.

'I take it very personally indeed, Frank,' she continues, her chin wobbling so much that the skin of her neck joins in. 'I take it as proof, once again, that you do not love me.'

The fayre hawker is silenced. The short man, the bear boxer and the boy look away. Somehow it is easier to tolerate cat-and-dog war than it is to swallow this – tears and talk of love. The bear boxer, when all are not looking, swipes a tear of his own from beneath his eye.

'But what are we to do, woman?' asks the fayre hawker, gentle now. 'I cannot keep you in the manner to which you have become accustomed, a manner that is not the grandest, I admit, but enough. It is enough, am I right?'

The woman shrugs, the tears flow fast.

'I cannot look after you,' croons the fayre hawker, 'if we do not have a headline act.'

All is silence, but for the crackling of the dying fire.

'*I* look after *you*,' says the wife at last, a means to concede to her husband and stand above him all at the same time. "'Tis the other way around.'

Her husband nods, accepting of that truth. The short man, the bear boxer and the boy consider whether to retreat from this exchange, threatening as it is to become a scene more tender.

The fayre hawker's wife sniffs, wipes snot upon her sleeve, and makes her decision. She steps forward and places her hands around the cow's head, its eyes beginning to melt with the maggots. She is the one what keeps this ship afloat, all present know it, and she must save them once again.

'Wait!' cries the boy, just as she is about to lift the terrible thing upon her head. 'This ain't right,' he says, 'for a lady to have to do such a thing.'

There is a certain tilt to the head of the fayre hawker's wife at this word – 'lady' – at the small gift of honour contained within it.

'I can be your headline act,' says the boy, pride rising in him but also, with it, a sadness.

This was to be a secret thing, only for him and the girl, but now he is to give it away. Yet the boy knows, in perfect clarity, that there comes a time when dreams must be acknowledged as exactly that. Practicality must be allowed its reign. She is gone and she does not love him, not even in the troubled messy fashion that his master loves his mistress. So in a final exorcism of his vanished girl the boy confesses his night-time antics and tells his only family, 'I have rope tricks. Let me show you.'

And in this instant, as if marking out a choice well-made or perhaps foretelling something intriguing yet to be seen, a bird alights upon the boy's left shoulder, making him yelp in surprise.

'You're a beauty!' says a voice in his ear, and the boy turns to face the yellow bill of the long-lost disobliging parrot.

MIM

Good afternoon. My name is Miss Mimosa Pudica, but you may call me Mim.

I appreciate you're unlikely to call me anything, and really I shouldn't talk to you at all, but it is too tempting with the room so quiet.

I don't talk to the mice now, do I? – not much, anyway – because that would be unscientific. And it is likewise with you. Besides, you have been sent to me in error and I wouldn't want you to become attached – to the sound of my voice, etcetera, etcetera – before you have to go away again.

Yet you must stay a while, at least until Sebastian returns, until I can confirm you are definitely an inaccuracy. Perhaps you were only labelled wrongly – not a gift for me as it said but intended for a forthcoming experiment.

Oh, don't look so worried! I've become quite experienced at pulling creatures from the air pump at the vital moment then reviving them good as new. What I am less experienced at these days is chatter, for I spend much of my time alone. Sebastian is about the town in daylight, whichever town we are in, making connections, attending to this and that, furthering

163

himself. In the evenings we rarely venture out.

It did not used to be that way.

I was The Electrical Venus, don't you know. I performed and people came from far and wide to see me. They would even pay to kiss my lips. You will no doubt have heard my name upon the breeze – for I was quite the thing. But the act is momentarily rested.

It's not that we did not enjoy the stage life, Sebastian and I – the adulation, the applause, the money – but it was only ever for a while. The show was a means to an end, a way to accumulate a certain reputation. Sebastian has explained it to me in what he calls layman's terms, so let me explain it to you:

We do not do what we do, us natural philosophers, for the adulation, the applause and the money (though it can sometimes very much appear that way). We do it for the betterment of humankind. And your kind too, I suppose. We do it so we might throw out superstition and welcome in greater understanding. We also do it to attract a wealthy sponsor so we can get our own laboratory and buy more minerals and a decent machine to replace our now ailing one. So I suppose the doing it for the money bit still stands, if that ain't a complete contradiction.

Sebastian will return soon and can explain it better, though he's unlikely to be in the market for conversing with a creature. He is still cynical of the theory that you have souls like we do – you and the mice and the geese and the like. He seems somehow willing to allow horses and dogs of a certain pedigree to have a spirit and an essence, which has prompted me to ask, 'Where exactly should we draw the line?' His answer to this he is still preparing.

When he comes through the door, expect him to be in a mood most foul and disinclined to talk to even me. This is how it usually goes:

'What the blazes does a man have to do to get his paper read in this wretched city?!' he'll bellow, threatening to rip said paper in two – a paper he has spent many tallow-lit nights perfecting. 'These old dogs think they know it all, but they know nothing,' he'll fizzle, kicking at chair legs. And sometimes when he is in the rankest humour, he'll spit, 'Who does one have to fuck at the Royal Society to get a look-in!?'

There are no responses that will calm him. You must just step away until he has simmered down and is ready to converse in good humour.

Later he will say sorry for using coarse words – that one beginning with f in particular. He'll repeat the word in the apologising, but gentler, different. He'll look at me in a way that's strange, a look that's alive somehow, pulsing. Then he'll gather himself up again, tight like a knot, and off he'll go to his books, all speaking done.

So, let us converse. It can do little harm, I suppose. I did once know a boy who talked to a pig. What a trifle is this compared to that.

If we are to continue though, I must say something out loud, here and now, so it does not hang over us as a thing unmentioned. In my experience, subjects fester if not spoken of. Fester and turn stale, then descend into an almighty bleeding argument.

So here it is: you are supposed to be a parrot.

165

I mean it as no insult. You are a fine example of your species, I'm sure, but there is an order to things in which we all have our place. It's exactly like a ladder. And on that ladder, you are not a parrot. You are not prized as a bird-exotic, and there isn't a thing you can do about it. Your circumstances are fixed, not like us humans who are able to climb, so feel no shame.

I know for sure that you were supposed to be a parrot because on a rare day out together in Oxford this week, Sebastian and I passed a cagemaker's – a place with many brightly coloured birds for sale. I was cock-a-hoop at the sight of them, all sitting there in the window, cleaning their feathers and watching us walking by. Never had I seen a shop like it! I begged my Sebastian that we go inside.

You see, I once owned a bird like that – or rather it owned me. The price of those creatures on closer inspection – well, it was quite blindsiding. A year's fortune! It seems I was the one thrown in with the deal when Grainger bought the parrot, not the other which way around.

(But that is a whole other story, and best saved for another time.)

Before our visit to the cagemaker's, I had held hope in my heart that I may, one day, replace my darling George, my lovely green Amazon what flew away. I had no idea how. George was from an island thousands of miles from here; you will not bump into his sort often. And, anyway, 'replace' ain't quite the word I'm after. George could never be replaced. I had a yearning for an understudy – that's a more accurate means of putting it.

As I whirled about that tiny shop in my excited state, I confessed all this to Sebastian, saying how much I missed the bird.

'Really?' said he, watching me with his face contorted, as I rubbed my face against a large blue-feathered fellow perched regal on a wooden stand. 'I think I have had quite my fill of his verses about dildoes,' he said under his breath.

I laughed at this remembrance, for I'd quite forgotten about George's ability to recite the poem by the Earl, and as I moved on to stroke the neck of a grand white bird with a lovely yellow crown, I said to my Sebastian, 'What is a dildo anyway? I have been meaning to ask you, for I have always felt certain you would know.'

I did not bother myself with soft tones as he had and, on hearing our conversation, the shopkeeper roared with laughter. I turned, quite surprised. My Sebastian, meanwhile, jaw gritted, pierced me with that stare of his, the one that says, *you have let me down.*

'Please excuse my wife,' he said, almost bowing to the traderman. 'She has quite the unique sense of humour.'

Wife, he called me – wife! A sound I had not heard from his mouth yet in relation to me! It almost allowed me to forget his fury.

'No apology needed,' the traderman replied and he gave me a wink which, though friendly enough, set me ill at ease.

Sebastian was then somehow more eager for our talk to return to the parrots so I explained further my longing for a new feathered friend, how I missed the texture of George's cheek upon mine, the feeling of him lifting a seed from my fingers most gently with the hook of his beak, the way he could mimic Lizzy's laugh, and Grainger's hawking, and Alex's swearing.

I know it was him – Alex – what taught George to say 'numbskull' and 'nob' and I know exactly who he was speaking of. But I have chosen to forgive. For what is the point of carrying that grudge around upon my shoulders?

(Again, this is another story you need to hear, but not for now.)

My Sebastian did make all the correct noises to the shopkeeper in response to my pleading.

'Whatever the little lady doth wish for . . .' etcetera etcetera, making his language just that little bit fancier than usual, to cover up for the moment with the dildo I presumed – a moment which, even now, makes not an ounce of sense.

I was utterly convinced that he had taken my request to heart and I would be in for a surprise gift in the close future. So when the covered cage did arrive this morning, my name upon it, the embers still hot from our ferocious argument last night, I thought – aha! – here is that 'sorry' I deserve, all wrapped up in feathers.

But, no. It was you.

Still, while you are here, let us make the most. Let me search for you in Sebastian's library and record the peculiarities of your behaviour in the pages of my commonplace book.

I have become adept at looking things up. When we first met, Sebastian took delight in doing research on my behalf or explaining things to me from the vast amounts of knowledge already up there in his head. But as I said, he is not around so much these days. And my questions, when he is present to hear them, have come, I fear, to frustrate him.

The other day, I discovered something quite by accident and

was fit to erupt with the find by the time Sebastian arrived home. I had spent the afternoon testing the reactions of different metals, exposing them to degrees of heat, seeing what happened when I dipped them in various substances, that kind of lark. Running short of hands, I had absentmindedly placed a stick of copper in my mouth and then, while reaching for my quill to make a note, did the same with a stick of zinc. And –

ZING!

Through my tongue shot the most tremendous fizz. I spat out both sticks immediately, of course, onto the pages of my commonplace book, smudging all my latest words. Then I picked those sticks straight back up again, and tentatively placed them either side of my tongue once more.

ZING! ZING! ZING!

There it was. Every time. For sure.

'Why does that happen?' I gasped at my Sebastian when he returned, grappling to help him remove his jacket so he might join me at the table straight away. 'Why does it make my tongue tingle like so?'

He was calm, not excited at all. 'Because of the effluvia,' he intoned, beating my hand from his neck where I was endeavouring to speed up the removal of his cravat.

'The gross particles, yes,' I said. 'Like when we use the machine or the jars, but why?'

'Why what?' said he, arranging his clothes upon the hook, irritation rising.

'Why is effluvia present when no rubbing's been done to create it? Why is it there? And why does it do what it does?'

Mysterious things, I have been taught, must be put down

to the ways of the Lord, but Sebastian says believing God is behind everything is equal to closing your eyes to nature.

'Why does the effluvia create that sensation?' I implored.

But he could not be drawn in. 'It just does,' he snapped, taking himself off to his cot to read, like always. End of conversation. Which to me was no better than Lizzy barking, 'Cos God said so!' and bidding me gone with a flick of her spoon.

I left it be – with him, I mean. I am not done with the copper and the zinc. I have been thinking about the electric kiss I used to perform, about the sensation that created, and how, though more powerful than this, it was very similar. Was it truly just effluvia passing through me all those evenings on the stage? Or is the effluvia already there, within me, and the Venus act was what brought it alive? I have decided that this will be the foundation of my experiments to come – and for that I do not need Sebastian's assistance. I can look things up for myself.

Here are some examples, if you are in doubt:

I searched for a reference to 'dildo' in Sebastian's books as he will not provide me with an explanation. A very thorough investigation I conducted, which led me only to definitions for 'dilatory' (given to causing delays), 'diligence' (the application of persistent effort) and 'dilemma' (a difficult choice between two alternatives). If I was feeling superstitious, I might think Sebastian's books were making some kind of wry commentary on my life as-is.

The pages were, meanwhile, more free-flowing and direct on another search – the true meaning of my name. The Pudica part of Mimosa Pudica, did you know, means modest. Pudica means pure. It means chaste.

Well, all those things, I still am. For though Sebastian called me 'wife' in that cagemaker's shop, we are not yet married. This was why last night we quarrelled.

Each time we move to new lodgings and he gives our names as, 'Mr Fox and his student Miss Pudica' with the coda 'I am her guardian. We shall be requiring two separate rooms' I challenge him as soon as we get to the top of the stairs.

'Let us marry, for goodness' sakes,' I'll gripe, 'if only to save us the double cost of lodgings!'

For a time he presented our lack of nuptials as a problem wholly caused by circumstance, a problem completely beyond his fix.

'We must announce the banns three weeks in a row at the same church,' said he, 'but we cannot stay in one place that long, my work will not allow it.'

Then it became an administrative issue, one that I must take the blame for.

'What is your place of settlement?' he asked me, only to prove the point. 'In which parish were you born? Where were you baptised?'

All of a sudden my God-shunning man is most interested in my christening. Of course, I had no answers for any of those questions.

'Well, this will make our union troublesome,' he told me. 'Let us begin the search for a minister who will adjudicate my marriage to such an unregistered citizen.'

I did believe for a short while that he meant it – that this search was being undertaken. Now I am certain it never commenced in the first place.

Last night his argument shifted once more. By not marrying me, he says, he is improving my mind.

'You will have to stop with your studies once we exchange vows,' said he.

'How so?' I replied. 'You told me that the wives of learned men did support them in all they do.'

'By taking caring of the home, yes,' he countered, 'by managing the servants.'

'But we have no home, no servants, and anyways, that is not how you set it out to me.'

'I set nothing out to you at all. I don't know what you are speaking of.' He raised his voice, thinking it would quell mine. 'What I am saying, Mimosa, is that you must leave behind the bigger subjects. Once married you will be compelled to find a pursuit more ladylike.'

'Compelled by who?' said I, a question he ignored, infuriating me further, pushing on with his crooked line of reasoning.

'You will have to remain with the delicate arts,' he went on, 'like botany, perhaps, if needlework is not sufficient.'

'No, it ain't bleeding sufficient!' I yelled, only realising my feelings on the subject after I had shouted them aloud.

Ain't it funny how it would have been quite sufficient for me but a few months ago? A few months ago it would have been an overflowing of riches to be wedded to a highborn gentleman, occupied only by the darning of the holes in his breeches. But now . . . Sebastian has introduced me to certain feelings and a certain knowledge, or rather the promise of knowledge, and I feel I must cling to it very tightly. I have read articles in Sebastian's periodicals saying how education in a woman is a damaging thing. And here I am as the proof, I suppose.

And here you are – there is a picture of your likeness in this book, all brown and plump. *Passer domesticus*, that's your given name. You are indigenous to this country – which is a word that means you were born here and you belong, in case you were wondering. You are a sociable sort who likes to wash with friends, then preen and sing. You are thought of as a blessing to the farmer for your insect-eating but also as a pest when you go at the grain. The Romans did, long ago, keep you as pets. So not that far removed from the parrot after all.

But you are not a parrot, I'm afraid – my mistaken gift, my small chirruping friend – I cannot grant you that. No. What you are, and what you will always be, is a sparrow.

This is to give Notice to Gentlemen, Ladies and Others

that in this very Place before sunset there shall be the Opportunity to see the most
EXTRA-ORDINARY *and* SURPRISING *Feats of Activity by*

THE GRAND TURK
ALEXI

This Boy who does hail from the sultry Shores of the East is able to do much impressive ROPE DANCING never exhibited before, as follows :

A startling Piece of Performance where he does walk with ease across the swaying Rope, stand upon one Foot and then upon his Head and then balance upon one Hand upside-down.

To which he will introduce a PIPE and play a Ditty of the Audience's choosing while continuing his Rope Walking.

To which he will introduce BALLS and do juggling while continuing LOFTY TUMBLING.

After which he will balance a CHAIR upon his NOSE and then balance himself upon the Chair making it stand on just the one Foot resting upon the Rope.

And all of this will be done with most impressive Balance as the amazing Alexi does have only the one Arm after losing his other to the Teeth of a Tiger.

SECOND, you shall see

A MAGICKAL ANGEL

A celestial Dwaff who has flown down from the Heavens on giant Wings to impress us with Sleight of Hand (and Wing!) with Cup & Ball and Deck of Cards. There will be the Opportunity for serious Play if any Man believes he may beat the Angel at his own divine Game.

LONG LIVE THE KING!

ALEX

This, George, is what the good life looks like.

An animal wagon freshened up and all mine, Hildy's mirror propped and candle-lit for my using, and a small glass of something waiting for me at the end of a show. I even have water warmed special by Lizzy so I might wipe my ugly mug clean of all this clay.

'You're a beauty!'

Very kind of ya. But who can say for sure, since there are no girls here to tell me so?

All that's forbidden now. If I did let them in once the applause was done, they would rumble the humbug. What a lie they'd see we've got going on! From a far view it looks exactly like I've had a faceful of foreign sun, but up front no one is fooled. Besides, the clay stops at my collar and cuff. When my shirt and breeches come off, the rest of me is as pale as moonshine. One kiss and this sham of a moustache would be stuck to their lip, n'all. I worry every time I go upside down on the rope that it's likely to fall southward. Though I might perhaps be grateful if it does. The thing smells to heaven – a mixture of cow skin and my own souring sweat.

If Lizzy ever catches me complaining she says: 'Well, grow your own moustache then,' and that sets her to sniggering, cos she knows full well I've tried and bleeding can't. My master and her have some right belly laughs about that one.

'Enough of your lip!' he'll go.

And she'll say: 'I just saw a hairy caterpillar, kid, shall I fetch it to live on your face?'

A right comedy act.

I ain't complaining. It is good to see Lizzy happy. As happy as she'll ever be. Her face at rest is one of a cat just poisoned, I swear it, but for the time being there is no pressing danger that she will murder my master, or he in return will murder her.

So, this is it, George. This is how it is when your name's writ biggest on the handbill! My name, that is, with a little jiggling. An extra letter at the end makes me sound more exotic, my master says. Makes me sound more expensive is the important thing. He charges an extra duce per person for the entry on the basis that I'm from overseas and you don't bump into the likes of me every day.

Yet, I regret telling them where the idea for the rope tricks came from. If I'd known we'd be mimicking the whole affair, going the full Turk, I might have kept my lips buttoned. Cos it means I can do no talking; can't announce me own tricks, can't ask the crowd to suggest the tune I play upon my pipe, guiding them subtle-like towards something that works well when you've only got the one set of fingers for playing. I ain't got the kind of voice that hails from the desert, or the mountains, or whatever it is they have over there.

At least it gives Joe a job though, helps him keep his place. If he did not do my announcing in that big boom of his –

'Ladies, gentlemen and others!'

Admirable, George, but you're nothing compared to Joe's thunder. If he did not do that, what worth would he have in our company? Displays of his heavy lugging just ain't exciting enough in the presence of a tumbling Turk or an angel who stings you for your wages with his loaded dice. I think I might have managed to earn a crust if I had been dropped from the cart, but Joe . . .

I'm beginning to understand how it works, George. For one man to do well, another has to lose. When Hildy was queen, the rest of us ate like poor kedgers. Then when Joe and me did our fighting, our bellies were the fullest while the others went hungry. Then when that nob, that doctor showed up, I went without so he might be rewarded.

I have long peered in on those fancy folk who ride in sedan chairs and felt yellow in my envy. If ever I got the chance to be in their position, I told myself, I would grab it. Never did I spare a glance at the poor fellas who carry those chairs. Is it right for them to break their backs so others might not get shit upon their shoes? Should I be getting bigger servings while Joe gets only small?

It's my duty to help Joe make himself useful, now I'm not available to box. He would do the same for me if our roles got switched.

I bet you could do it though, George, the Turkish accent.

Off you could fly, hang out with them fellas for a spell, then come back speaking fluent gibberish.

'Je m'apelle George. Enchanté.'

Bonny-soir to you n'all.

'Avez-vous un animal de compagnie?'

Yeah, stop it now, ya show off.

Ain't it funny, though, how I am altogether the wrong fella for the gig. The more I do it, the more I reckon the rope dancing is truly minor to everything else. The audience wants a Turk, that's what brings them flocking, and you, George, are far more skilled than me in the tongue department. Mim, meanwhile, she would have had the perfect shade of skin, no clay-smearing needed. How they would have loved her up there on that rope, hair wild, chin high, bellowing out a verse of *Rule Brittannia* . . .

Oh, look it, bird. Look what I've done. I have made mention of her, and now will come the blues.

'Stupid you!'

Come on, distract me. That's your skill, isn't it, your headline act – butting in with them rude little ditties you've picked up along the way? Distract me now. Tell me where you've been, for you have never rightly said. I have a hunch, of course, from the new voices you have brought back with you. All your new laughs are of the female variety.

'Oh, you are most awful!'

You've been keeping company with ladies what keep company, in't ya? Go on, spill it, bird, what have you seen?

'That is extra, sir.'

Oh, George, you dirty bird! Whatever brought you back here, when you could have stayed there? Were they feeding you the wrong kind of seeds? Or are we the devil you know best? You must be like one of them pigeons I've heard mention of. Tie a message to its leg and off it'll fly to deliver, coming all the way home on instinct.

Though I have to say, I thought your home would be her, not us.

Perhaps that is what I should do – tie a message to that little pink claw of yours and send you Mim-wards. Oh, don't look worried, you lazy git, you ain't going nowhere at this time of night. Besides, another skill I lack, along with speaking Turk and having the right shade of face, is putting the King's English down on the page. And even if I could, what would I say?

I have a letter from her, though, did you know that? I was all fit to feed it to the pig or stick it in the fire, much good it was to me but, I dunno, I kept it anyway. I like to read it sometimes and by that I mean, just look at the shape of the words and know that she chose them so they're probably ones of some distinction.

She'll be married now. They'll be Jack and Jill, bedding

down in London in a place of reputation. On the dresser will be a wig two foot taller than her last one, now that they keep all the money they earn. His share of the notes he'll have flashed on rats in bottles and rude statues that he'll swear are educational. She will have quite the collection n'all, I imagine. That robin will be stuffed, mounted and sketched. Perhaps she will do a drawing of me from memory – the strange one-arm'd boy she used to know.

'He is a kind of beautiful.'

Don't be cruel, bird. Not her voice. Not that.

'He is a kind of beautiful.'

I'm sure he bleeding is but that don't mean nothing in Grainger's lot. The gold's more plentiful in this kind of life if you're strange-seeming. Beauty only holds its value if it's in the smooth line of a tumble or the steadiness of a balance. You'll find no importance here given to a chiselled chin or fancy shoes. That Mim has given merit to those things, that she probably always did, adds a fair bit of salt to my sadness.

'He is a kind of beautiful.'

No, he is not! He is a nob and a numbskull!

'Ah, fuck off!'

No, you fuck off, George. You fuck off!

No, don't.

If I truly had no one to talk to, no creature at all, I'm not sure where I would be. Throwing myself from the next church steeple, perhaps. You, and the pig what came before, you keep me from going touched in the head. After every show I must scuttle back here to the animal wagon and hide, must not let the sham be discovered. I cannot be who I am no more, for that is not who they want. It used to rankle that people only valued my act because of my missing arm, but wasn't it better than this? At least it was honest. At least I weren't lonely.

In the wagon by myself I have nothing to do but pick fresh lice eggs from the seams of my breeches. Can't even bury my pain between the legs of a girl like I have before. And despite all of that, I do imagine them happy – Mim and her doctor – not to torture myself but because she wished for me to come to good, so I must wish the same for her in return. I know they must be happy. Being top billing is just the half of it. Having a someone to share it with is what makes it complete.

The other night, out of the crowd flew a cabbage, right at me head, knocking me clean off the rope. Did you see? There were laughs enough and plenty applause, especially when I got straight back up and did the trick with the chair. But my pride took a dent, I must confess. How could it not? That cabbage was bleeding heavy.

I would have liked to have commiserated on it with someone after the show, but no one was there.

'Mercy!'

Then another night, some smart fella tried knocking me off with a potato. He hurled it in the general direction of my gob, but his aim was fair disastrous. So I flung one hand in the air and I caught it – just like that! – not even a wobble. The crowd went wild at the trick of it. If I had seen it done myself, understanding what I do of this business, I would have reckoned it a con, a sleight, all arranged from the start and practised over and over. But, of course, it weren't.

And who was there then? Who was there afterwards to be as thrilled as me about what happened, to clap me on the back and call me a hero?

The others are too busy post-show, working the crowd while they're still giddy and more likely to part with their coppers for a game of cup and balls.

So I come back here, to a glass of gin left by Lizzy and

'Je m'apelle George. Enchanté.'

Yeah, and you, George.

If I could write Mim a letter, if I possessed that skill, I would likely recount the story of the flying potato. I am sure it would make her laugh and I miss that sound. Can't you do it, George? You can mimic Lizzy's cackle something wonderful, ain't Mim's particular kind of chuckling on your tongue too?

I would tell Mim about the potato and I would describe how nice I've got things now, mention the way Lizzy brings me warm water and booze, and then she would see that I have come to good. I want her to imagine me happy. I cannot bear any sort of pity.

And it wouldn't be a lie now, would it?

Look about you, George. If you do decide to head off and look for Mim, make sure you tell her what you see:

An animal wagon freshened up and all mine.

A small glass of something waiting for me at the end of a show.

The good life, George. Tell her, this is what a good life looks like.

MIM

Remember that order of things, bird? That ladder I told you of?
Consider the happenings of the last few weeks a demonstration,
if you will. Theory in action. Right exhausted am I from all
the upping and the downing, for though it might be a subject
scientific, that don't make it one without feeling. Sebastian
will not have it so. To him, a study of the arts leaves no room
for emotions, no room for error.

I, bird, think differently.

I am willing to be moved by what I discover, but more than
that – I am desirous of it! For ain't that part of the thrill? I am
also willing to confess my mistakes so will start by admitting
one to you. You are not stuck as a common creature, like I once
said. You may never be a thing-exotic, certainly, but observe
how recently you were upgraded.

'The bird is for you,' said Sebastian when I went to him
with news of your arrival.

''Tis a sparrow,' I said.

'Yes,' he replied, nodding slowly as if to a child.

'But I wanted a parrot.'

'You also wanted, my Mimosa,' he returned, 'a wedding

ring upon your left hand, yet none of the consequences that come with wearing it.'

My jaw fell open. That he would labour his argument in this way, in so cruel a fashion. 'Then why buy me anything at all?'

'Because a sparrow suits a girl like you,' said he. On his face was the most superior grin. How pleased he was with his silly joke. He wished for me to bite, I am sure of it, but I would not give him any kind of satisfaction. 'A learned girl,' he concluded, 'has no need for a band of gold. A live specimen is of much the greater use.'

So you see, bird, you are no longer a mere 'inaccuracy', you have been promoted to the rank of 'deposit' – a thing put in place until I behave in the right way to deserve the real prize. Or perhaps, in truth, this is not an upgrade but the opposite. You have fallen. No longer are you a 'mistake' but an 'insult'.

Regardless, I have decided to appreciate you, if only to spite my Sebastian. And as time goes, I have grown most fond, charmed by your quick movements, the small black jewel of your eye and the sharp preciseness of your beak. I have fed and watered you well, have I not? Sebastian's books have been my guide, telling me exactly what you need: seeds and little insects to eat, water for bathing, or dust, if I can find it. And in lodgings such as these it has been a substance most plentiful.

For this is where the true shift comes. You may have been downgraded but 'tis nothing compared to the great shove southwards that I have undergone.

You've experienced our routine as it is now. We ride from town to town unpacking long enough for Sebastian to go wherever he goes all day, then we pack again and move on. At the last place, we did all this in the dead of night.

'Are we tipping them the double?' I said as we headed off at fair gallop, the stars doing our guiding.

'We shall not be tipping at all!' he said, quite furious. 'That residence was atrocious.'

This was the truth, for it wasn't just the one rat I spied in my bedroom, but as a place of lodgings it was no better than the place before, nor the place before that. And anyway he had not understood me. I was asking if we were doing a runner, a moonlight flit. I didn't bother to illuminate him. He is the one who explains things to me, bird. He will not stand for it the other which way around.

I let it go. Hadn't I sought adventure by leaving Grainger's company, and wasn't this that – us playing thieves in the dark?

After our bolting though, life became pure humdrum. I have been most grateful to have you to care for. My experiments with copper and zinc keep me occupied certainly, but it used to be that I could leave our lodgings a while during the daytime, take the air while Sebastian was away, observe the shapes of the buildings, the stylings of the people, the bending of the river along the edge of each particular town. Now I have strict instructions not to leave our rooms at all. I must watch the books, the jars, the models and the machine, whenever he is out. Which is always.

The standings of our lodgings have slipped, you see, and his precious cabinet of curiosities cannot be left unguarded. Who knows what class of people are allowed up the stairs in these abodes. Sebastian believes they're the sort who might want to make off with his human skulls and pickled frogs. He does not know people. He does not know them whatsoever.

He thought I had not noticed this falling by degrees of our accommodation. Because, it being by degrees, I was tricked into staying silent. The awful stale smell in one place went unspoken of, then did the extra grubbiness of the walls in the next. All of a sudden, an excess of bugs in the bed seemed too trifling a thing to mention when I had endured all that had gone before. Perhaps he thought that, being of unfortunate upbringings, I simply did not care. Or that I did not deserve any better.

I let the disappearing wigs and dresses go unmentioned too. The first dress, I assumed, was left behind in my error so did not want to bring it up and have him chide me. Then when a wig vanished, I suspected a serving girl, so kept my lips buttoned so she did not lose her position. Then when another dress and wig were seemingly filched, my doubts began to rise. Would I walk outside the four walls of these lodgings and find them in the window of the local pop shop? Is this, I wondered, how we funded ourselves now?

For not a single farthing have we collected since it's been just Sebastian and I – no performances, no new broadsides printed. The idea of Grainger wasting the last blast of summer, a time when people leave their hearths with the goodest of grace – 'tis unimaginable!

Yet I let my suspicions fall away. Why should we be bothering with the gathering of money, I told myself, when Sebastian is a gentleman born to pots of the stuff? The hard bargain he pushed with Grainger and our quest for a wealthy benefactor I disregarded. In experiments, I once noted in my commonplace book, we often alight upon the answer we go searching for, rather than the one that's true.

Then at the last town the dull life of guarding got the better of me. I felt fit to suffocate. I wonder, bird, if I do not know now how it feels to live within the confines of a cage like you. So I shut the door of the rooms behind me, did a quick prayer for the keeping back of housebreakers and headed down the stairs.

I did not expect to wander far – I had seen on our arrival how surrounded we were by fields and sheep, no buildings of great interest to stare up at – and this was to be just a token act of disobedience. I would at least meet some faces in the bar below, I thought, other human beings who might share a 'good afternoon' and a 'nice weather' to break my infernal boredom. Yet, when I descended, not a soul was present, besides the cross-eyed landlord. All was washed wood and motes on the air.

Still, feeling defiant, I ordered a small-beer and sat beside the window, half shuttered, taking cautious sips. I was just beginning to convince myself that this was entirely usual, to be a woman alone, taking weak ale in a strange bar in the afternoon, when a girl came and sat opposite me, her own mug of something on the go. I hadn't heard her come in from the outdoors so she did right surprise me, especially as every other seat in the place was there for the taking.

'Don't I know you?' was her greeting.

I shook my head. How could she, when I didn't know her?

'Yeah, I do,' she went on. 'How would I forget your face!'

Her own face was pale with dark rings of no-sleep beneath her eyes. Her hair was the colour of wet straw, stabbed through with fabric flowers, wilting and dirty. She was my age, I reckoned, if I knew what mine was exactly.

'What about my face?' I asked.

'Well, it's the kind people remember, innit.' She grinned at me, not friendly, nor unfriendly either. A look of business, perhaps. And then it landed – she had seen our show! Sebastian and me! Somehow and whereabouts. Or she had seen an etching of me on a poetical broadside. Perhaps she could not put her finger on who I was exactly, for I do look right different when I'm powdered-up and in my wig.

I smiled and leant towards her so I might say this hushed and not seem too proud. 'I'm The Electrical Venus,' I announced.

Her blue eyes went wide at that and I leant back, arms crossed, nodding my confirmation. I might have even winked.

'Oh yeah,' she goes, grinning, 'and what does The Electrical Venus do?'

So she did not know me after all. Or she was being playful, wanting me to put into my own words how it feels to be celestial royalty. I decided it was the latter.

'I wear a glowing crown of sparks,' I said.

'Right . . .' she replied, not impressed at all. Confused, maybe. Her manner was that of someone sozzled though she spoke cleanly enough and did not smell strongly of the liquor.

'I pull the stars from the sky,' I said, trying to win her back.

Her face was still askew. 'And what in gawd's name,' asked she, 'does that do for the fella?'

'The fella?' My turn to look askew. 'Well, it gives them a nasty shock, dunnit, when they kiss me.'

'Oh,' she said, a smile threatening.

'Because that,' I added, 'is what true love feels like.'

Her laughter came in a great big shout, filling the space. I joined her with a quiet chuckle so as not to seem odd but I understood what her laughter meant – she thought me ridiculous. And wasn't this what my experiments with copper and zinc were leading me towards too? A conclusion thus: metals and machines may be the source of electricity, a conduit perhaps, but they cannot make us fall in love. Us living creatures are the only source of that.

Still, I had started upon a certain conceit with the girl and you know I can be stubborn, bird. Proud, too. I would not let myself go back.

'We are taking it to London,' I boasted. 'We were in Buckingham and have come by Oxford and now we're here on our way to the capital.'

This drew more barking laughing from my drinking companion.

'Right, you are!' she squealed.

'No,' I said, 'we are.'

'Going the long way, is ya?' she asked, sniggering into her mug.

'And what would the likes of you know about it?' I said, drawing myself up. Some time ago, me and that girl might have been of the same rank, the same rung on the ladder, but I believed I'd climbed a step or two. Only, she didn't see it that way. Slamming down her mug, she yanked me by the arm and insisted I follow her to the end of bar where a fading map of the countryside was framed behind glass on the wall.

'I stare at this all day when business is slow,' said she,

sticking one finger on our capital city and announcing its name – 'London!' Then with another finger she traced a line from Buckingham to Oxford, then upwards – UPWARDS! – and most definitely away from the capital, across this vale of bleeding sheep.

'That nob!' I spat. 'That numb-bleeding-skull!'

And I was away, stomping back up the stairs, to get ready for my attack. The girl yelled for me to wait, don't go, to talk a while. She must have known I was ready for violence, for she called after me with godly allusions.

'You can't do anything round here,' she warned, 'without the agreement of the Abbess.'

But holy consent or no, I was bent on fighting – doing something physical and real. Sebastian was leading me on a merry dance and I did not like the tune – making me believe he was raising me up, when in truth he was keeping me small, keeping me in the dark. Perhaps I should have been scared, bird, that I had been dragged across the country on a false excuse, perhaps I should have feared a sly motive and my own untimely end, but it turned out I was far too angry for that.

When my very own dastardly libertine returned, I was waiting, sitting at the table in his quarters in the dimmest candlelight so he might not see me and be prepared. He closed the door behind himself, and I struck, moving with slashing force. I took up the glazed model of the Venus and I threw it as close to his head as I could manage without taking out his eye –

CRASH!

It shattered its headless self against the wood of the frame.

191

'Good Lord, woman!' he bellowed cowering amongst the shards. 'What is with you?'

'With me?' I parroted. 'What's with me? Nothing! And ain't that the bleeding problem. You are never here and when you are you are full of nothing but flam!'

'"Flam?"' he enquired, still shrinking.

'Flim-bleeding-flam! We're supposed to be going to London but we've gone 200 miles in the wrong bleeding direction. You call yourself a man of means, don't think I ain't noticed how the rats get fatter and the bugs get more numerable at every consecutive lodging house. And as for the whereabouts of my wigs and frocks – you must think I came down with the last shower!'

I put a hand to his precious pickled rat and shoved it from the table to shatter upon the ground. The poor dead thing swam, sort of, across the floorboards towards the wall, towards dozens of its relatives living there behind.

'Will you stop!' he cried. 'These things are of great value.'

'And what of me, Sebastian? Do I have any value at all?'

'Yes!' he cried, though I thought he only said it to make me stop. Then, 'Yes,' he said again, quieter, and with more meaning. 'Greater value than I had ever anticipated.'

He looked to his shoes, decorated as they were with flakes of the Venus and I felt a small stab of guilt for the things broken that could not be put back together.

He took a great breath. 'The pursuance of a career in the philosophical arts is not limited to the independently wealthy,' he began, as if explaining one of his lectures to me in layman's terms, though the subject of this one was more heavy than any that had gone before. More personal. 'It is a vocation that values rational and inquisitive thought above all else, the willingness to experiment, to attempt trial and error. You may think it entirely democratic and open to all, but it cannot be ignored that those who have the liberty of time, who are able to fund a laboratory, purchase equipment, use their influence to gain access to societies for advancement, they will see their ambitions prosper with alacrity. While their fellow man . . .' He was shamed by the telling of it. He shook his head, looked me in the eye. 'I am of the middling sort, Mim,' he said. 'I never claimed to be anything more.'

'The middling sort?' I asked.

He nodded.

'What's that then?'

'Why, the people who exist between the highborn and the . . .'

'. . . likes of me,' I finished.

He nodded again.

The idea that there were people living grander than my Sebastian was at the same time a revelation and downright bleeding obvious. For when had I ever seen him yell 'chair!' in the street so we might not smut our shoes? When did he ever curl his hair the right way or talk short to a liveried lackey trailing in his wake? I had been mesmerised by more than the man's electricity. He was a convincing mimic with his lovely vowels and his excellent shoes, but more than that. The smoothness of his skin, the cut of his jaw, that dark brow – they were all a distraction, a sideshow, one that sent sensations through me like metals on the tongue.

'But if you are climbing as I am,' I ventured, shivering a little as the juice from the rat jar seeped into my stockinged feet and climbed the wool, 'what do you want with the likes of me?'

He considered again the broken Venus on the floor, and as he did, I watched him weigh up the two alternatives. A dilemma. To tell the truth or to soothe me with a lie. He decided upon the former.

'You are my greatest experiment yet,' he croaked.

'Experiment?' My voice was a husk but I would not cry. In that moment at least, I swore to remain coldly scientific.

'I thought I might write a paper on you,' said he, his head hanging as it should. 'I have been telling all the learned gentlemen with whom I have corresponded when I ask for their audience and their patronage and sometimes . . .' He cleared his throat. '. . . the hands of their daughters in marriage.'

I bit hard on my tongue and tasted metal of a different kind – the bitterness of blood.

'I have boasted to them about how I have managed to transform a poor illegitimate vagabond girl into a . . .'

I think he wished for me to finish his sentence, define how I saw myself now, but I could not speak, could not open my mouth, for if I did I think I would only have wailed. Not love then. What I felt was not his love. I had slid from the ladder entirely, bird. I lay at its feet as prone as a mouse in the air pump, no air to breath.

'. . . into a lady with a great mind,' he finished, no flourish, only disgrace.

Downstairs the bar had begun to fill – we could make out certain bellowed words, hoots of laughter.

'But . . .' Sebastian moved towards me, crunching the pieces of the Venus beneath the soles of his shoes. 'But I did not imagine such success.'

Now I would strike back I thought, tell him of my hurt, but he bid me stop, by clasping my face in his hands. My breath came in great hitches at his touch, tears spilling heavy down my cheeks.

'You have charmed me, Lady Mimosa . . .'

'Mim,' I managed, 'my name is Mim.'

'You have stirred within me a feeling that I have found hard to resist. I feel compelled at every glance, compelled to . . .'

And then he kissed me, very hard. No snap of electricity, no fizzing of the tongue, but something. A surging of something. I seized his face too, returned the kiss with all forcefulness, let his tongue stray into my mouth, pushed mine deliciously into his. I let him tear at the laces of my stays, as I ripped at the buttons of his shirt, seeking desperately the warmth of his chest. And when we were both fully naked, he stepped away, so he might take in the whole sight of me, observe me as he never had before, tell me how beautiful I was, that part of his body standing tall as he did, ready for what was to come next. He guided me towards his cot and I fell with eagerness, with an urgency, no thought allowed. Quite unscientific.

There was pain – Hildy had told me to expect it – but beyond that, there was pleasure, or at least the promise of it to come. I felt that spreading of warmth I had achieved for myself alone, but with an intensity I had never before experienced. When two people come together like that there is a strange magic.

We lay there afterwards quite silent, staring at the sagging ceiling, embarrassed, perhaps, that we could be that way, so base and animal, then have to return to our civil selves, once the spell has lifted. We delayed our getting dressed again, for that would mean having to go about the rest of our day as if nothing had happened. And in that silence, I thought of the copper and the zinc creating a charge, of the force I believe must live within all of us, ready to be moved. And also I thought of Alex, his voice in my head, those words we exchanged at the tavern in Buckingham, telling me that I am but a sideshow of a sideshow.

'It's done to you,' he'd said to me. 'That's not you. It's done to you.'

So where am I now, bird, in the order of things? For certain I shall never be a lady, great mind or no. A skill for knowledge is worth nought; I have handed over my greatest asset, my chastity. In the days what followed I saw my Sebastian watch me with yet fresher eyes, the way he edged around me, avoided my gaze. I was goods soiled, an experiment gone awry. We rarely engaged in any kind of conversation.

Still, lowly as I was, I understood that I now held a tremendous power over him. A new force, one just discovered and in need of investigation. I am able to strip him of reason and restraint. He may have stopped me from becoming a lady proper, but I am able to take away his gentlemanly values in return, with a touch, with my body. I went back to guarding his possessions if only to have the time to think on it.

Then circumstances came crashing through the silence that we had created for ourselves.

All can be utterly transformed in an instant by the smallest of things – a drop of a certain liquid, the tiniest spark. And in this situation – a piece of paper. An invitation – to speak, to show, to demonstrate. At last, an invitation!

Sebastian came home last night clutching it like a beacon. He wished to embrace me with the joy of it, I'm sure, yet did not dare in case we should fall back upon his cot again. And there is no time for that. No time to even think or sulk upon it. We must give ourselves entirely to preparation. He runs to the nearest town right now to sell some of his curiosities so he might buy a suit befitting the summons.

And there it is, bird, theory in action. Some of us start humble and choose to climb. Then comes the fall, a momentary loss of balance, but we get up, we brush ourselves down, we bathe in dust and we ready our feathers. For soon, I believe, we will sing, bird. In ways quite fantastic, we shall sing.

To discover the entrance you must first negotiate the twists and sweeping cambers of a winding maze of trees. At the last bend, the soft ground will become elegant cobbles – and there it is. A pale stone house of enormous proportions rising up suddenly from the landscape, as if it wishes its visitors to gasp.

The girl-student dressed as a girl-exotic obliges.

'Gosh, Sebastian! Bleeding hell!' says she, a lady's way of speaking quite forgotten in her awe. 'I ain't never been anywhere so fancy as this!'

''Tis a lie, though a trifling one. The girl has enquired at the kitchen doors of places of exactly this type in her past at the behest of the fayre hawker's wife, seeking out a commercially minded cook who might sell on leftover dripping and discarded candle stubs for a reasonable price. She has never, it is more accurate to say, advanced upon such a place in this style – that is, via the front entrance, their route in the covered cart punctuated by hedges shaved to resemble all the shapes geometric.

Holding steady the sparrow in its cage upon her lap, the girl pushes from her mind the shattering of the Venus, both literal and metaphorical. As the mansion – this castle! – grows larger before them it stands as proof, in bricks and mortar, that her man is not one entirely made of flim, or indeed flam. Of the middling sort he may be, but he has the means to persuade nobility, if not to be it himself.

'The fellow is a lord,' narrates the doctor as they continue their approach, expressing it as something quite workaday, which only excites his companion more. 'He often dines with the king.'

'By George!' the girl exclaims.

'Indeed,' returns the doctor, and overflowing with anticipation, they share a nervous laugh.

At the mouth of the house, the doctor bids the horse stop and, to impress the waiting man-servants, he puts on his formality, as if it were a dress jacket.

'Mr Sebastian Theodore Fox,' he announces, vowels en pointe (he will not be known as 'doctor' here. This crowd will not be gulled that way), and he hands a waiting lackey his beautifully printed calling card.

Then, beneath the bug-eyed gaze of gaping gargoyles, the setting sun spilling orange across the scene, the equipment is prepared. The sparrow is set upon a back shelf and the machine brought forward. The philosopher cranks the handle, swallowing his curses each time it sticks, the contraption quite tired from all its travel. Slowly, each of the lead-lined storage jars is charged.

They were told to expect a small salon space in which to conduct their learned demonstration, no room for large contrivances, and this they took as a blessing. The jars will hold power plenty and will be more reliable in the moment than the machine and its belligerent actions. It must stay in the cart, like a disagreeable child.

In their rehearsals at the lodgings the machine had proved itself exasperating, faltering when it should fire, discharging when it should be spent. Yet still the girl had found a certain joy in the repetitions of their practice, in its necessary inventiveness. Up on her resin block, she recalled the promise of adulation and applause. Though they were performing dry runs for an audience of boxed mice above the fireplace, she still experienced an overwhelming sensation, one she recorded in all eagerness within the pages of her commonplace book – the feeling of being 'at home'.

A small salon space seems improbable now as they stand before this fortress, loading the blue-cuffed arms of servants with the necessities of their show. How can anything, they fathom, within these four walls be of piddling-size?

The large resin block goes first, cradled by a fellow of dumplin height who sways with the carrying of it. Then a glass tube, just in case they should require it, is placed in the white-gloved hands of dumplin's elderly colleague. The storage jars go next, in the grasp of a tall, spoony attendant. They are secured in a wooden box, to keep the charge intact, with fierce instructions from the philosopher as to which parts must absolutely not be touched.

'Or else – boom!' says the girl, leaning in towards this gangly servant, making him jump. She giggles to see his wig shift uneven, obstructing one eye, and expects the other gathered servants to join her in her mirth. But it is only the philosopher who laughs, and in a shouty fashion, huge and false, to throw a damp blanket over what she has started.

'Forgive my cook!' says he to these underlings, giving the girl a glance that says she has let him down. 'She can sometimes be too playful!'

As the lackeys trail inside, the girl looks about the driveway, searching for this 'cook' mentioned by her teacher, her almost-fiancé, by this man so in control of everything except his own hot passions, which she consumes voraciously whenever they burst free.

'Cook?' she enquires and the philosopher's face runs pink.

'I may have called you that within my letters to the lord,' he says quietly, ensuring the footman who waits at a distance may not hear.

'Not student?' she asks.

He shakes his head.

'Not experiment? Not girl-exotic?'

'Experiment perhaps,' he concedes, 'but cook also. I did not want the lord offended by your presence.'

And before she can respond, object, the philosopher is striding towards the footman, calling him 'Dear fellow!' as if he had been heir to a lordship himself.

In the opulent lobby, with its candlesticks and ticking of clocks, another liveried slavey arrives, seemingly from an endless provision, to take away the philosopher's coat – and the cape belonging to the most glamorous of cooks. The girl steadies her towering wig and ensures the black spots upon her white powdered face are sufficiently affixed, as they are led along a broad hallway, the eyes of the house ghosts following them from portraits on all sides. Down a stone staircase they descend, towards the guts of the building, where the corridors become narrower, the girl's hairpiece collecting any missed cobwebs from the ceiling. Then they are brought to a halt by a recess displaying an urn and a collection of ancient cornices, so the footman can throw open a door and announce their arrival.

The philosopher turns at this moment to issue the girl with some hushed, eleventh hour advice.

'We do what we do and our future is safe,' says he, his tone gentle, a roundabout apology for downgrading her to cook. She smiles tentatively, and searches his face for reassurance more, perhaps for love.

'And remember,' he adds.

She nods expectantly.

''Tis distracting when a woman opens her mouth.'

And in they go, on the heels of the footman's announcement – 'Mr Sebastian Theodore Fox!' – into a room that is small, dark, red, full of men and their laughter. Smoke curls from the hot tips of ornate pipes, heady with vanilla, slinking through the candlelight and swirling in one great fug against the low, decorated ceiling.

'Sebastian!' bellows a man, stout of chest and gills, and he pulls himself through the horde – a horde that can only be a dozen-strong yet feels double in a room so tight. Why they are confining themselves, these men of corporation, in one small corner of such a vast palace isn't clear. All there present have relieved themselves of their frock coats and wigs. Their stocks, jabots and solitaires hang from the backs of chairs instead of around their necks. The overall effect, particularly upon the girl who cowers behind the philosopher as best she can in a wig so tall, is the feeling that they have stumbled into a male bathhouse as the collected are midway through the act of disrobing. She swallows hard. The man is upon them now, their lord and saviour.

'Wonderful of you to join our little club!' he roars, kissing the philosopher sweatily upon both cheeks, sloshing a honey-coloured liquor against the brocade waistcoat of a nearby fellow as he does. A fellow who notices but shows no care.

'We are looking forward to some enlightenment – are we not, brothers?' says the lord, a wave of ayes and yeas rolling back towards him. More liquor is poured. More liquor is sloshed.

'And what do we have here!' he bellows, using a fat paw to push the philosopher aside. 'Let the hound see the hare!'

The girl, as she has been instructed, does not speak, only kindly smiles – in the way of a cook to begin with then, remembering how she is adorned, she smiles in the manner she imagines befitting of a girl-exotic.

'Wherever did you find her!' exclaims the lord, as if she is a pretty shell collected from a beach or perhaps a stray dog that is remarkably mild of temper. The heads of the men about them turn. Lips are licked. 'Such an exquisite blackamoor!'

The girl looks to the philosopher for a polite introduction, a small serving of respect to elevate her from the lord's dubious summation, from the drooling of his cohorts, but she sees only reddened cheeks, the philosopher's gaze upon the buckles of his shoes. So she breaks with instruction and introduces herself.

'I am The Electrical Venus,' says she, a name she hopes

will wield some authority, but the lord laughs heartily at her pronouncement, his friends joining in, as if she is a child convinced that one day she will be king.

'*Fais ce que tu voudras*, my good man!' says the lord, clapping the philosopher upon the back in some kind of congratulation. '*Fais ce que tu voudras!*'

Mystification fills the eyes of the philosopher and the girl sees it. Knows it. The philosopher does not understand the motto. He can no more speak French that she can speak parrot. She would like to pull him to her, hold him close, whisper in his ear that they are more on a level now than ever. She would also like to slap him, hard, right across his cowardly mug.

But there is a show to do.

The resin block is set. The dial on the first jar is turned to its lowest notch, the glass tube set upon a dresser amid bottles of liquor. The girl steps up and arranges the plaits of her wig so that they sit neatly on the small shelf of her bosom. It is an action, in her naivety, she believes translates as modesty.

The philosopher begins.

'You are about to witness, gentlemen, the flow of a force, an electrical fluid that is not yet understood by all. But it is a force that I believe, with shrewd patronage, could be investigated and developed for the future advancement of men – an advancement that will be intellectual, yes, but also spiritual and economic.'

The last word is given most gravity, and as they have practised, at its utterance, the girl snatches hold of the metal appendage rising from the top of one of the lead-lined jars with a flourish. This does not lend drama to the moment as they had hoped, only whoops and titters at the sight of her hand, tense, upon that stiff pole.

'Now who,' calls the philosopher, rising above the chatter, 'would like to experience this flow of force at close quarters? A kiss upon the lips of The Electrical Venus, I can assure you, will be most illuminating.'

All are willing – and they take their jolly turns at her mouth, flying backwards at the sensation, laughing heartily, then returning for another try. But it is not enough. The jars are swapped and the charge increased so the men might try two kisses in quick succession with more sensational results, then two kissers at once. They are delighted. They are in ecstasy! But the girl is not.

''Tis too strong,' she hisses to the philosopher.

'How can it be?' says he. 'I'm using the lowest setting,' he lies, 'barely sufficient to burn wire.'

The next kisser descends, his breath made of ash and suck, and the girl's complaint is lost to his jellied lips as the jar is turned to a yet higher setting. Back for second servings, he goes, this corpulent man with the popping eyes of a frog, and he has a plan in mind – he will withstand the charge, stay connected to the girl, push his tongue between her teeth, feel the charge sizzle between them in an elongated way, as bacon does in the pan.

The crowd cheers his efforts.

It is unbearable. She pushes him away, quite dazed, and lifts the back of her hand to her nose to feel the blood dripping there.

''Twas too strong,' she says, too loud, 'I told you so.'

The philosopher is aghast, at the red spilling down her dress, soiling the scene, but also at the girl's admonishment, that she has dared shame him in public. Already he had ranked himself as the least important man in the room; he cannot stand to be reduced any further. He whips a handkerchief from his pocket and thrusts it to her face, instructing her with a stern nod to hold it there.

'Ah, I see that the capacity for love in this room is too vigorous!' quips the philosopher, and the laugh he was seeking comes big and belly-led.

'Have we broken her, dear boy?' calls the lord. 'I thought girls of her breed were savages by nature and made of stronger stuff.'

The girl looks fiercely to the philosopher to defend her, to tell them the show is all done.

'Her father was of Africa, via the South Americas,' begins the philosopher, attempting a tone anthropological, 'but her mother was of our kind. Of your kind. Blue-blooded. She –'

'For I do feel,' says the lord, not interested in this lecture, 'that we should see which other parts of her body give out the thrill.'

The girl's eyes widen as mutters of grave agreement fill the room. She lets the handkerchief drop, not caring that her face is all smeared with blood.

'But . . .' says the philosopher, 'but I came here to –'

The lord bids him stop with the palm of his hand. 'My patronage is yours, of course, whatever you require.'

The philosopher's eyes widen now – in astonished delight.

'But,' adds the lord as his caveat, 'we must be free in our investigations, must we not?'

The girl stands stunned, dripping blood upon the carpets. The philosopher cannot speak. Here is everything he has always wanted – but with a human price. What flashes before him in this moment is the image he holds of himself working from his very own laboratory, dashing from jar to flame, scratching down vital words for his first great printed work, dining in the evenings with other learned fellows from the society. And a mirror image flashes across the girl's mind too. For her ambitions have become the same as his – except her evenings would not be filled with the opinions of men. She would rather hear the cheers and the gasps and the applause of a crowd, one she has shaped to her will.

The philosopher turns and, quite outrageously, as if they were alone, places his forehead against the girl's brow, leans into her in surrender, closing his eyes. He twists his face, as he has before, so he might rub his cheek against her skin, send hot breath upon her.

'Sebastian?' says she, ignoring the jeers of the men witnessing this bizarre gesture. 'Sebastian?' She takes hold of his shoulders and shakes at their limpness. He swoons, she thinks, but then no, his hands are moving. They are there at the laces beneath her dress, beginning their work.

'What are you doing?' she pulls away from him, tries to, but he is heavy and he is persistent.

'Take off your dress,' he murmurs.

'No,' says she. 'This is not what we came for. Remember what we have worked for.'

'It is all for the taking,' he says. 'It's all there, if only you will . . .'

And here is where their dreams must finally come apart.

The girl knows that success upon the stage, scientific or

207

dramatic, means nothing to her without others there to share the joy. Your true worth is not measured by papers published or applause at the end of a performance, but by the love you let yourself receive, the trueness of the love you give. The philosopher holds no such knowledge. Within his fervid visions of a life lived with success, was there never the clear imaginings of a wife. There were no imaginings of anyone else at all.

'Stop,' says the girl. She pushes his hands away but they return, like the nose of a dog that has got scent of the meat.

'Please,' he begs, quietly, in sorry desperation. 'Do it for me.'

'No!' Her voice rises so they all might hear.

'If you loved me well . . .' he dares to say. 'Don't you love me well?'

But she is considering another question, one she has asked herself and others so often without resolution: what am I worth? And this time comes an answer from within, one that she knows is the truth with absolute clarity: she is worth more than this.

She is worth far more than this.

She frees herself from the philosopher's weight with an almighty shove and stands back, on the furthest edge of the resin block. She swipes the ridiculous wig from her head and wipes blood, snot and tears from her face with the back of her hand. She observes before her the man she had once wished to marry and she makes her decision. Years of performance have taught her that you must sometimes give the audience the unexpected and sometimes exactly what they have always desired – and right now she is in the market for some savagery. She takes her dirtied hand, makes it into a fist and she drives it into the slender line of the philosopher's nose. There is blood, shooting like sparks. The men howl, excited.

'If you loved me well?!' she yells, appalled. 'If *you* loved *me*!'

The philosopher trembles, astonished, over the bloody bucket of his hands, stuttering: 'You . . . you . . . hit me!'

The girl leaps from the block, seizing the glass tube, making casualties of nearby vases. 'Ain't that the truth!' she cries, swinging her crude glass sword to clear a path through the smoky throng. 'And how does it feel, Sebastian?' she calls back over her shoulder as she navigates the dark, narrow corridors to the wild outside air, to the covered cart which she will claim as her own.

Her words will bounce from the cobbles of the carriageway as she disappears into the night.

'How does it feel, eh?' she will hoot. 'How does it feel?'

ACT IV

A hum vibrates across the marketplace. This is the sound of expectation.

From one pillar of the corn market to the fixings of a nearby building, a thick, woven rope has been hung, and tourists gather to view it. Some offer opinions on the strength of the attachment. Others, feeling bold, step forward to give the rope an exploratory nudge. All believe they are the authority on why it has been suspended there in the first place. But trust them not.

These are the same folk, the same tourists, who travelled here specifically to view the castle, the resting place of that Henry with the wives. Then later, when wandering the market town, they pronounced that there was nothing more to see.

''Tis no wonder,' they tutted to their companions, 'that His Majesty did not take a seat at Windsor.' The place is so devoid of shops and other means to spend one's money, they declare that a fellow at leisure here, so bereft of entertainment, may simply die.

But they are mistaken.

There is much more to see – this evening, at the very least.

213

And the existence of the rope suggests it will be every bit as thrilling as a hanging.

As the sun lowers on this September day, the summer having stretched itself languorously into autumn, the street hawkers get word of the cable hanging upon the high street and of the gathering of people about it. They bring their wares to the ginnels of the Guildhall, and up goes the call for peascods and pyes, for oranges and gingerbread, and to get 'em quick, while they're fresh. The wealthy and the middling sort hand over coins, while the poor salivate enviously and the cut-purses make use of these foodie distractions to slide their hands into pockets unseen.

Then, once the lamps are lit, a voice breaks the hubbub to announce: 'Gentleman, ladies – and others!'

'Tis the fayre hawker in fine lung.

'He is here!' he roars, bringing about a momentary hush. 'Lift loud your applause for the Grand Turk Alexi!'

They do, cheering with the utmost enthusiasm, then cooing in unison as the celebrated man skips across the marketplace in breeches of the most unusual design, billowing in the breeze. He strikes a pose by the rope, one hand poised in the air as if plucking an imaginary bloom. The other hand might have rested upon the hip of his leg thrust forward, but there is no other hand, no other arm. Word of this absence ripples backwards through the crowd in all varieties of astonishment as the Turk jiggles the extraordinary moustache that sits upon his strangely bronzed face.

Next comes the pipe, the sound of it curling upwards, in a key that suggests the beginning of things (and that those things-beginning will be entirely foreign). The Turk takes this as his cue and moves behind the rope. A twitch, a breath and he launches himself into a run, making his stomach a flat plane to land upon the cord, his feet lifted. The crowd adds *oos* and *ahhs* to match the motion of his swings. Some audience members back away, concerned that they may get struck, while others shoulder forward for a better view.

This is what the girl does, with elbows pointed – the girl dressed in the filthy skirts, a man's jacket upon her shoulders. Forward she pushes, treading down upon the heels of those in front with the hard toe of her boots, ones that once belonged to a farmhand and are muddied all the way up to her stockings. The sore-footed ones turn to admonish the man that has harmed them, not expecting to find a lady – of sorts – her hair decorated in a cursory fashion with feathers tucked into its wild knots and tumbles. They swallow their insults. The girl gains ground.

Upon the rope the Grand Turk Alexi pulls himself to standing, feigning imbalance so what will follow may seem all the more remarkable.

The girl is now but three rows back. She looks up at this spectacle as a holy sister might gaze upon a visitation. Her face is all dirt and exhaustion, but her dark eyes are bright – never brighter – and for the first time in many weeks a smile threatens to break across her lips.

She had given up hope.

Never would she find them – this is what the girl had told herself. Her home was gone. The sun-soaked fields of harvest were to be considered home now. She must believe that she belonged out there, tying the barley, bagging the turnips, keeping her tale short to those who asked for it when they paused in the shade to brush husks from their skin and to sup from the river. Then the harvest ended, and she had to move on, to another possible home – to a town of blanket weavers where she earned enough for crusts by working in a factory, broom in hand. As she swept about the feet of the men and women at their benches, she watched them perform their particular tasks with a lightness of fingers and an endurance for repetition, all part of one process. This must be her new ambition, she presumed, to be promoted from broom to scissors, from scissors to the operating of a machine, one that produced something more useful than sparks.

But it was in that town of blankets where the girl saw the scrap of broadside pinned upon the weighing house, turning brown in the air. The mention of a Grand Turk capable of 'rope'-something (the tear in the paper robbing her of the exact information) and 'lofty'-something-else did not excite her at first, but 'a magickal angel', 'a celestial dwaff'. . . She snatched the fragment from its nail and to the amusement of passersby, brought it to her lips for an elaborate kiss, witnesses pulling their children protectively from her path.

In every tavern, in every shop, she asked. Who had seen the show? Who had talked to the fayre hawker? To his wife? Perhaps even to the Grand Turk himself?

'Did they say where they might be heading next?' she demanded.

And then she enquired, 'This Grand Turk you saw, did he have only the one arm?'

Rumour and hearsay she pieced together and so began a

paper trail along the southern drift of the Thames. Her former family had continued their journey London-bound, it seemed, though she had not. Or at least they were circling it, keeping the capital in their sights, ready to pounce, with what appeared to be a brand new act.

Days of begging followed, of a little stealing and much sleeping by the roadside. There was nothing left in her covered cart that she wished to sell. She had pawned the birdcage, setting free the sparrow soon after her own escape. Seeing a quarrel of *Passer domesticus* upon a rooftop and remembering the line in the philosopher's book about how her friend preferred to sing and preen with its fellows, she had stopped the cart and let the bird take flight. Off it had fluttered without a moment's hesitation. She had disposed of her elaborate clothing in exchange for skirts more simple, and later bought a moth-chewed outfit reminiscent of the philosopher's garb that she wore with her hair secured beneath a continental hat acquired by sleight of hand. How disappointed she had felt when the boy had told her, all those months ago – months that felt like years – that she must learn to love breeches. How reluctant she had been to dress as a man. Now she was most grateful for her masculine get-up for it allowed her to make her way through the countryside with barely any harassment at all. In the fields and in the blanket factories, she had always had access to a sturdy instrument of some kind to fight away the advances that besiege a girl who was once described as 'exotic'. Her glass tube sword had long since shattered. The only other items that remained within the cart from that daytrip to a lord's castle were the girl's commonplace book, which never left her possession, and a truly untrustworthy machine. The book she believed held no value to anyone but her and, with its many blank pages still to fill, it remained a companion to her mind, allowing her to record the discoveries of her travels. But the machine . . . She might have eaten well from the quids of its sale, yet she could not allow herself to let it go.

In a town of brewers and iron she came across another scrap of broadside and in the cluster of villages to its east, more. Then was Windsor, where she swapped breeches for her linen dress, wishing to once again resemble a lady. Whether she could still lay claim to that title, she was beginning not to care.

And as she stands in the crowd now, she gives no notice to those around her, how they view her. Every piece of her attention is on the boy with the one arm and the strangely brown face.

He hangs from the underside of the rope, our Grand Turk, by two feet, one hand and, less apparently, by the strength of the muscles within his stomach and chest. Then, with small movements in his grip, he squirrels his way quickly from one end of the rope to the other, bringing laughter to the square. Then he is up again, upon the rope, walking forwards and backwards with an ease that elicits gasps. Wooden balls are launched at him for juggling, which he does one-handed while standing upon one foot. A lady in the front row is persuaded to relinquish her fan for the purposes of balancing upon his chin.

'What tune should the Grand Alexi play upon his pipe?' demands a gruff, bearlike voice, and though she cannot see this announcer from her vantage point, the girl recognises him by sound.

'*Rule Britannia!*' she bellows. 'Have him play *Rule Britannia*, Joe!'

But it is decided that the call for an obscure yet simple ballad, playable with just the one hand, is the louder and the Turk obliges, dancing upon the rope as he plays. With his final note, he turns forward to face the crowd, and plays a self-fanfare. The girl puts two fingers in her mouth and whistles this move, perhaps the only person present to understand how very difficult it is. The applause goes up, the girl whooping as she claps, joyful tears spilling down her face and displacing the dust.

He is found! And, oh, how marvellous he is!

The Grand Turk holds his position to drink up the crowd's admiration, thirstily, as if it is water on the tongue after a long, dry day in the corn. Then he tumbles, suddenly, but quite deliberately, from the rope to the ground. And he is gone. From her view, at least. Gone.

She pushes frantically in the direction of the corn exchange, forward and left, where she believes he may have exited. She had spied the animal wagon parked beyond there before the crowd became strong and thick.

'Watch yourself!' people bark as she tramples toes in her urgency to reach him.

'How rude!' come the spits.

'Alex!' she hollers as she swims against the unyielding sea. 'Alex! It's me!'

She can see the top of his head – his hair grown long – and she uses this as her guide to pull herself through the bodies, emerging at last at the crowd's fringes. He is unbuttoning his ornate shirt, damp with sweat, making for the steps of the animal wagon. A snatch of the flesh of his chest is exposed, so much paler than his hand and face, and she breaks into a run, a desperate pelt, through the arches of the corn market, past the stone pillars. Oh, how she will seize a hold of him! Pull him towards her, smut her clothes with the stuff he has plastered upon his skin. And once she is there, breathing hard but safe within his grasp, she will impart with urgency the greatest thing she has learnt.

'I know it now, Alex!' she will tell him. 'I know what true love feels like!'

But she stops. Dead. As if her muddied ankles were still locked in the mire.

A girl emerges from the animal wagon. Not a 'girl-exotic', but certainly a pretty one, with hair the colour of a shiny pan. The Grand Turk picks up his pace on sight of her and, meeting on the wagon steps, he places one, able arm around the waist of his coppery love and pulls her close for a long kiss. They go inside.

The girl stands rigid in the shadows of the corn market. For days she has been propelled forward, ever forward, and now comes a halt. A nothing. All compulsion gone. She lacks even the desire to walk away. That is until she hears the husky grate of the fayre hawker's wife, a voice coming ripe in her ear.

'Well, clonk me sideways with a dew-beater!' says the woman. 'Look what the bleeding cat dragged in!'

ALEX

She is back, bird, but she has changed.

Hoggish, she is, and I ain't even talking about her appearance – though she made quite the eyeful when she came upon us that night in Windsor. I'm certain even you would not have recognised her. I ain't rightly over the shock of it myself.

Annie and me were here in the animal wagon when we heard Lizzy squawking, desperate for the master to see. Joe and Abel got vocal too, full of *well-I-never*s and *bleeding-hells*. The last thing I expected to see when we stuck our heads outside, the very last thing, was her.

Her.

A long, warm summer and it hadn't made her rich. She was fair staggering on Lizzy's arm, my mistress in no mood for holding her up. We ain't the most finicky of people, I know this, but Lord above, George, she was filthy. There was a man's jacket on her back full of holes, her dress was the colour my face is when I'm dancing on the rope, and her hair was nothing but a bird's nest. Those boots, n'all. I've seen fancier things hanging off the toes of beggars.

We were all soft to her, of course. It would have been a

meanness not to, finding her like that, tears streaming down her face from some ordeal, the details of which we hoped to prise out of her once she got herself calm. Everyone was doing her running, hither and thither from the fireside, fetching water and food, hot rag and clothing. She was still the celestial queen, all right – even my Annie was at it, and she has no clue of that girl's electrical fame.

We have not talked of Mim, you see, except in the most fleeting fashion. It never seemed right, to make one girl yellow by talking of another.

When I got myself alone with Mim a moment, that first night by the fire, the others all off in search of some bit of comfort she might need, I reckoned I ought to ask the important question. I felt sick to do it, but with the others avoiding it, more fussed with her health, it was down to me. So I said: 'Did you get yourself married then, like you wanted?'

And do you know what she said, bird?

'Ah, fuck off.'

Close. She looked up from her huddle of worsted and she says to me: 'What the bleeding hell do you care!'

It stung me, George, like a wasp might, because I'd asked it gentle. With her face all mussed and streaked with the crying, she looked like a tormented animal, one that might attack if I came any nearer. And that weren't fair. It wasn't me who upped and went, stealing the master's horse and cart in the process of it. If I were she, and I'd limped back into camp after leaving the lot of us in the lurch, I would have been full of

222

sorries and good stories. But there's none of that. She seems to have some counsel with Lizzy on the matter of where she's been and what she's seen, but it ain't being shared wider. Whatever's happened, it's touched her mind, made her hard. She is hulver-headed now and I like her not.

Once cleaned-up, at least, she became less terrifying. We all headed west from Windsor, from the castle surrounds, purposely to find ourselves a place for bathing. A perfect spot we landed on – a stream not too fast in flow and up to our middles. It must have reminded you of your sunny home, bird, with that light upon our backs.

The ladies went first, and when they did, I thought of asking Annie to look for marks upon Mim's body, bruises and the like, things that might tell us of what had been done to her. But that would have meant giving Annie more of the story of Mim, of that numbskull Fox. Maybe Mim would've been more willing to say to Annie what'd gone on – girl-to-girl, woman-to-woman, someone who didn't know her as she was, only as she is now. But I couldn't ask it. Annie and me are to be married, if you don't count the tying of hands Lizzy did while drunk with the idea of it (and also actually drunk) that night in Maidenhead.

I owe my sanity to that girl of mine. I'd do well to not forget it.

'Ah, fuck off.'

I know I thought her pushy at first, her following me to the wagon that night after the show, not taking my 'no' as an answer – given as a silent Alexi shake of the head. But her need to escape, George, her desperation to get away – it swung me. You must understand that feeling having done your own flit, for certainly I had sympathy. Often I have craved to go. It's just I ain't never actually done it. How Annie knew for sure that I was the right man to do the escaping with, I can't explain. I was only someone she had seen from a distance, balancing upon a rope. Perhaps I should have thought her mad and cast her out, but I had a kind of admiration for her certainty. For the way she did not wait. She grabbed the thing she wanted and she made it hers.

It helps, of course, that she is smock-faced with that great mop of sunshine hair. I never thought my tastes would go in that direction, a girl so pale you can see the blueness of her veins, no richness there, no dark shades licking at her limbs, soaking up the light. She is small-shaped too, not tall, her gaze as pale as her skin, but I like her well. She is more than willing for a bit of dancing under the blankets too and that does not go against her.

'A lady should be chaste!'

That's as maybe but before Annie, George, you saw me. I was so bleeding lonely.

'We need to do it proper,' she says – Annie – meaning getting wed. If anything should happen to me when I am upon the rope, if I should die for example, Annie says without a ring on her finger she won't be looked after.

'But Lizzy tied our hands,' I told her. 'What more do you want?'

224

''Tis not binding,' says she, 'because you have only the one.'

It was the first and the only time she has mentioned it out loud – what's missing – and right embarrassed she was too. I don't know how we had allowed it to become a thing that can't be said. *Oh, you ain't got no arm!* It's as easy as that. No injury done. In my experience, when a thing goes unmentioned it grows large and difficult, impossible to master.

Maybe it was easier with Mim because she knew me when we were small. She'd ask me almost every day: 'Where's your other arm gone?' I would tell her the whole story of the horse and the cart and the post, me trapped against it, the sight-bending dose of laudanum and the dirty beard of the barber what did the slicing off. She liked to hear it, especially the bloody parts. Some days I would change it, just to play with her, tell her a great dragon had swooped down in the street and bitten me proper.

'And it was so tasty, my hand,' I'd tell her, 'that he came back for the rest of my arm!'

It would make her laugh or it'd get her cross.

'That's not how it happened!' she'd fizz. 'You're a great fat liar!'

I don't know what good it would do the likes of me and Annie to get proper wed anyway. She has no dowry coming, hotfooting it from her parents like she did. And I have no roof above my head to offer in return, alive or dead, cos I don't reckon the animal wagon really counts. Getting married makes two become one, but isn't there some kind of comfort in numbers?

'Love is all what matters,' she says, and I reckon she's right.

Anyway, that day beside the stream, I decided to spy upon Mim myself. I climbed a tree saying I was after a better view of the road ahead, only I spent most of my time up there looking in the opposite direction, back over my shoulder at the water. I reckon Abel did clock it, but he didn't blow the gab. If he'd had the length of limbs to be climbing too he'd have been right up there with me.

Now, I have seen my Annie in the naked way, of course, and over the years I have caught unwanted glimpses of our Lizzy in her birthday suit, but Mim – I've only ever seen that outline of her in her nightgown. Hildy always made her play the lady. But there she was, in the broad sunlight, in all her colours, the full shape of her, so different from the other two. The water sat like diamonds against the skin of Mim's arms, the soft brownness of her belly.

Oh, don't cock your head at me, bird. Don't make out like I was doing something wrong. I was looking at her for her own benefit, to know if that numbskull Fox had hurt her in a way that showed.

What I would have done with that kind of information, I did not rightly know. Would we have gone in chase of him and had our revenge? I couldn't see my master agreeing to that.

'Seen anything juicy on the horizon, green lad?' Abel called up, and I told him no, nothing at all, just leave me be.

Maybe I was looking because I wanted to find something. Was that it, George? Did I want there to be cuts and bruises upon her? Did I want to be proved right? Be able to say for sure that Fox had been a sad dog all along? Did she deserve to be bodily hurt in return for the pain she'd caused? If that's so, then I am a sad dog n'all. For what kind of fella wishes ill on a girl that way?

That is not how it is.

I have loved Mim so hard I have thought it might destroy me. And I love her still. You know it, bird. I love her still. I wanted to somersault down from that tree right there and then, wade into the waters and grab a hold of her, push myself against her, push myself inside of her. Not to cause her damage, no, but because I want us to be one. With Mim there is no comfort in numbers at all.

But she has changed, George. Her time away has made her treat me with a fierceness I do not know or deserve. If I had made to embrace her she would have pushed me away or crushed my bones, I am sure of it.

Or if I am not sure, I am scared. The way her eyes shine when she looks upon me – she is all at once filled with a fever, but yet so distant, so disappointed. I could let myself believe I am the cause but it is a path I've followed and fallen down upon before. Besides, I have agreed to love another, a promise I shall keep. For what else is there for me to do? If I am not to be a sad dog? If I am to be a good man? If I am not to be lonely again?

I must tell myself, remind myself, often and loudly: Mim is hulver-headed and I like her not.

227

MIM

Say it again, George. Say it all you wish.

I know very well the voice you are mimicking but I do not care. You cannot make me weep.

'She is hulver-headed.'

That so?

'I like her not.'

It was plain to see from the moment I returned. I need no duplication from you.

'Ohhh, Alexi! Uh, uh, uh, Alexi!'

Nor duplication of that either!

If you wish to make me weep, that is the phrase to do it – tears of disgust. Or you could come rub your cheek against mine instead, and make me shed tears of joy.

Oh, to be with you once more, my feathered boy! Did you

return because you knew I would too? Did you know I would be so very sorry? Sorry that I did not keep my ear to you but instead listened to the great quacking of a weak man. He said you were not wise but I am beyond certain now that you are. To have found your way back to Grainger's camp, no scraps of handbill to do your guiding – how very clever! Or are you just as stupid as me? We had our freedoms, George, and we messed them up. Back we slide to the place we started. Back to this sorry bunch, with its one more sorry addition.

'Ohhh, Alexi! Uh, uh, uh, Alexi!'

Yes, her.

Perhaps you might go squawk some of your intelligence into the ear of that Grand Turk, for he has been gulled. The girl is a fayre-follower, a flossy, someone more smitten with the great gleam of fame than the ordinary man beneath it. You may think me harsh, envious perhaps – not so. I understand her ways, is all. I was her but weeks ago, wooed by a fancy pair of breeches, and the use of what was within them.

'A lady should be chaste!'

Sorry, George, that ship has sailed.

I'm no honest virgin but still I have some truths to give. I doubt Alex would welcome my counsel though. So I'll keep quiet. 'Tis his choice, his bed to lie upon. And she lies upon it with him with much gusto from what I have heard, even without your faithful repetition. The animal wagon does shake with it. Lizzy thought I should bunk up in there too when we were first redividing beds. But, zooks, could you imagine! There is plenty room certainly, but I am not so tolerant as you, George, of the ceaseless grunting.

I like my tent, gifted to me by Joe and Abel after returning to them their covered cart. It is of good and sturdy shape, well-oiled against the rain. It housed a gentle giant and a mighty dwarf, so it will be plenty enough for me. I am happy to lie alone. All this time I have survived by depending upon my own wits. Why should anyone wish to care for me when I am most capable of the task myself?

Indeed this very week I have, with my fine-tuned skills of persuasion, secured my immediate future. I have convinced Lizzy, and she, in turn, has swayed my master. The Grand Turk must quit his sulk and take the decision upon the chin, as he has so many punches in his previous line of business. There is no matter to quarrel over. 'Tis a decision that is purely economic.

'How much money did you make of an evening when Mr Fox and I did top the bill?' I asked Lizzy as we bathed that day by the river. It was not an idle question – a scheme was already brewing within me.

'Mind your own buttons,' was her reply, and weren't that to be expected. She still has her fury for me, bottled like jam, made tarter by my taking off with the horse, the cart and their significant income. If she could, she would bend me over and whip my backside for what I've done, just like she used to, but she cannot. All of a sudden, here I am, grown up. She would not dare. If she were to strike me now, I have the guts and the permission to strike her right back.

Yet still she did not send me away when I staggered upon her that night in Windsor. In a blink she could convince my master that there is neither money nor room for the likes of me. But she sees that I have value. 'Tis not that I'm a fellow woman; if she requires friendship of the female variety, she has Annie now. The two are of similar minds, they cackle the same way at the same things. But this fresh girl, this fayre-follower, she lacks an important quality that I possess.

'Took what he needed, did he?' That's what Lizzy said to me, proud as a peacock, as we swam out that day.

Annie, the flame, was splashing and frolicking for our spy in the tree who we were supposed not to have clocked. But I saw him. I knew his game. Hildy's voice was all haughty in my ear – *a lady should be chaste –*

'A lady should be chaste!'

But what weight does that hold now? And besides, I have recent learnt, George, through harsh experience, that to throw off a challenger you sometimes need only give 'em what they demand. When you do, they will likely realise they never wanted it in the first place. So I undressed with no apology, kept my neck long, my chin high and I let him see what he came for.

Let him see what he does not have.

The exact same cards I dealt to Lizzy, giving her the answer she'd be poking for, took ownership of it so she could not use it against me.

'Did our Mr Fox run away with my womanly goods? Is that what you're after asking?' I said. 'For if it is, the answer's,

231

yes. They're gone. Scrammed. I'm about as pure as you, Lizzy dear.' Then I gave a nod to our frolicker, throwing water upon herself in the shallows in no fashion that would make her clean. 'About as pure as she is.'

'Oh,' said Lizzy, 'I see.' We swam a little further from the reed bed that grabbed at our ankles. 'Well, it comes to us all,' said she, spouting water. 'One minute you're the girl, the next you're the hag.'

I let her own that in return. Hag may not be a position anywhere near the top of the ladder, but it is rungs above a jilted one like me, someone who clearly ain't, as Lizzy had always said, the marrying sort. So this is my value. Lizzy is my bad weather friend. She needs me here so there is someone to feel superior to. This I am prepared to shoulder.

'She is hulver-headed.'

Yes I am. I will accept the limitations of Lizzy's love just as I will take the spiteful words of a Grand Turk and all of it I throw aside.

'How much does he bring you in?' was my next question for Lizzy, jerking my neck towards our peeping Tom. 'How does a tumbling Turk compare to an Electrical Venus when the sums are done?'

We stopped to tread water.

'Which horse exactly are we saddling here?' asked she.

And that's when I told her I still had the machine.

We broke the news to him by the fire at night and off he went,

232

as I expected, perhaps even as I had hoped, spitting and fizzing, into the dark, that moony girl of his calling after him, always with his rope name not his real one.

'Alexi! Alexi!'

'Ohhh, Alexi! Uh, uh, uh, Alexi!'

One more time, George, and I swear I shall reconsider the cage!

She could not find him though. He had gone deep into the woods or deep into the town. Deep into a jar of something I guessed, for he has a taste for the gin now. Only small glasses but enough to be on the path to becoming his master. Annie had to be convinced to go to bed alone, steered like a wayward, honking goose into the animal wagon by Lizzy. Her noisy tears were as much for herself as they were for him. She cannot be the wife of a celebrity, can she, if she has no celebrity to leach onto?

Her Alexi surfaced eventually, beyond midnight, bursting into my tent with no word of warning.

'It's late,' I croaked, soaked in sleep. 'What the bleeding hell do you want? And go careful with that candle, or this whole tent'll go up!'

'Is this your idea of revenge?' he snarled, kneeling over me, close enough to bite the very nose off my face. Hadn't I thought, not that long ago, that we might go back to our days of fighting upon the ground, Alex and I. Well, there we were, except there was no laughter with it. The boy was straight rage.

I pushed myself to my elbows, thrust my face into his, made him back up.

233

'Revenge for what?' said I.

His mouth bobbed open, no answer inside.

''Tis an idea for making more money,' I clarified, 'nothing more.'

'And for making mincemeat of me!'

His freckles are still there, aren't they, George, when the clay comes off. I could see them with his face so near to mine. I could also smell the booze upon his breath.

'Doing a good job of that yourself, in't yer,' I said, with a sniff. 'Quite a spree you've been on by the looks of ya.'

'You drive me to it!' he slurred, and wasn't that a familiar phrase, one that flies from the gob of our master almost every evening, spittle landing on the face of Lizzy.

He gulped as he said it. I shook my head.

'No, don't you go making me out to be like him,' he said, fighting back. 'That ain't fair. You are the bad apple, Mim! You are the one what brings rot to the camp.'

I smacked my hands against his shoulders, shoved him away. 'Tastes sour, does it?'

His face twisted in response, his gaze travelled down me, making new judgements.

'Not enough for the both of us, was there?'

'You what?' said I, pulling close the ties of my shift that had loosened at the front. I thought he spoke of my body, that he knew I had given myself to Sebastian, that he was suggesting I should have given him a taste too. But I had him wrong.

'On the bill,' said he. 'Why did you not suggest we make a double-header? Twice the price.'

'Oh,' I said. My turn to work a silent jaw, no phrase landing that seemed to do the job.

'You could have fought for me too, Mim, made us both come to good, but you didn't, did you? Someone must win and someone must lose, eh?'

'No. It don't work like that,' said I. 'We can all climb high, but your fate ain't my business. Your mistakes are your own.'

'Mistakes!'

He lunged forward in the dark, his hand catching hold of my leg beneath the blanket. I could feel the warmth of him, the memory of it, a fresh wave of anger washing over me, that he should come upon me like this, sozzled and mean. That he should touch me and remind me of a path not taken.

'It would not have worked,' I said, fierce, 'the both of us on the bill.'

'Why not?'

Because you are to marry another, I could have said. Because if it isn't the two of us upon that rope then I can't bear any rope at all. But instead I said: 'Because I am to talk of learned things, to demonstrate great wonders and 'tis distracting when a one-arm'd boy starts tumbling.'

I am an excellent mimic, George, just like you. An excellent student. I sought to knock him out with my bile, send him running for his flossy, but his grip only tightened upon my leg, his fingers digging into flesh. I reckon the contact of his hand upon me had reminded him too, of what we were before, and he also wished to forget it, to replace it with a feeling more memorable. Pain.

'Why did you come back?' he spat, his body trembling,

the vibrations going through me. 'Why did you have to come back?'

And he began to cry in great glubs, as a child does. I have never seen Alex that way before. Not never. I always thought that losing an arm so young meant he had faced the worst, got it all out of the way, that nothing more could ever hurt him. But that wasn't the true measure of him at all. I gripped hold of him right back, my fingernails driving into the firmness of his arm, as if he were to fall any moment from a cliff edge and I was the one to prevent it. Or perhaps the one to lift him up and throw him over.

'You could go,' I said, sobbing now too. 'With Annie. Take your act on the road alone. Make your own money.'

'Leave?' he said, his bitter breath hot against my mouth. 'Just leave you?'

I thought that he would kiss me and that there might be a spark. Then arrived a more terrifying thought – that he would kiss me and there would be no spark at all. For he came at me like those who push and shove, who pay their penny and care only for the thrill. Or would it be like it was with Fox, him coming to me in surrender, like I was a strange force upon him, one that he did not rightly believe in. Stray hairs may cling to a yellow stone and feathers will fly to the hand, but those things can be made to move in the opposite direction too. They can be repelled.

So I turned my face from his, abruptly, pointedly, as if the presence of him appalled me. I would not let him reject me first.

'I hate you,' he said through his tears, confirming all. 'I hate you for what you've done to me.'

And we let one another go, feeling the imprints in our skin disappear.

And then he did too.

Disappear.

'I love her still.'

What, George? What did you just say?

'I love her still. I love her still.'

This is to give Notice to Gentlemen, Ladies and Others

that in this very Place at Sunset the proprietor

Mr FP Grainger and his MOST MUSICKAL WIFE

are honoured to present

THE ELECTRICAL VENUS

MISS MIM, a lady of some Distinction and Heritage, from Birmingham, a Student of Natural Philosophy and an Expert on the Language of Birds, desires to share with all Members of the ordinary Publick (who are willing to pay Tuppence for the Enlightenment) her Knowledge of the æthers electrical. She will take to the Stage with the Assistance of an extraordinary Parrot who is named for the King and does speak the English Tongue most tolerably and also:-

A PHYSICKAL ANGEL

Miss Mim will make small Objects float with the Angel of their own Accord, cause great Sparks to fly from her own Scalp and, on the payment of ONE PENNY, Gentleman will be permitted to kiss the Hand of this most distinguished Scholar and experience the shocking Sensation of Electrickery for their own Selves (a Sensation some have compared with the Shock of true Love but, as Miss Mim will explain to all gathered, this also has a most rational Explanation of the scientific Variety).

All followed by bare-Knuckle Fighting
for your Entertainment and serious Play!!!

BETWEEN:

THE ONE-ARM'D BOY and
THE NO-LEGG'D BRUTE

LONG LIVE THE KING!

'Tis the night for electrickery to rule again!

And all hell is loose.

It begins with the fayre hawker's wife attempting the accidental murder of the lot of them with a slop more toxic than any of her previous achievements. The redhead flossy and the physickal angel fall the foulest, casting up their guts at every opportunity, while the others nurse stomachs that growl like wounded pups.

To pour misery upon misery, the rains come down – in great, biblical ladlefuls – as if September has remembered, all at once and too late, that summer is not its business and it must make up for lost time. The ground around the camp swells with puddles, and as the men attempt to erect the performance tent, adjusted to the new philosopher's specifications, no pole will stick proper in the soupy mud. The bear boxer throws additional logs about the place to create a dam, but still the tent sways, more queasy than the poisoned performers beneath it.

It is the boy who says it first, though the thought has pestered every one of them – ''Tis all bad omens and we should abandon it.'

'No!' The new philosopher steps forward in her strange arrangement of lady's frock and gentleman's jacket. 'The handbills are out and we have promised a show.'

The boy squares up. 'But the machine can't be trusted, especially in weather like this. We've seen it before when that nob did do it. The wet gets in.'

'"The wet gets in"?!' The new philosopher parrots the boy and laughs loud in the doing so. '"The wet gets in"?!'

She looks to the others to side with her, against this cod's head of a boy, this noodle, this chub, but they are too busy wafting away the smell of the latest venomous fart to issue from the fayre hawker's arse.

'The wet gets in!' says the parrot himself, incidentally, as if in agreement, but with whom it is not clear.

'You know nothing about it,' says the new philosopher to the boy. ''Tis not how it works at all.'

'Then how does it work, oh doctor? Why don't you educate us little folk.'

She shakes her head. 'Don't you go making them turn against me. I am saying *you* know nothing, not them.'

And away they soar, arguing again.

Which is a shame after a day passed so pleasantly.

That morning and afternoon there had been a relaxing of the war. The new philosopher had behaved more kindly, more curious, around the boy, since the parrot's late-night admission. The boy, seeing this shift, had been mellower in return.

Could he really have uttered those words? wondered the new philosopher as she watched the boy go about his tasks.

And if he did, could she allow herself to absolutely believe that he spoke of her?

For though this new philosopher seems superior and strong, she holds within her a secret belief – that really she is a monster. The boy, with his particular shrewdness, she suspects, has found her out. How could she not be some kind of changeling? All that has happened to her – from the moment her real mother placed her as a squalling baby in the arms of a vulturous fayre hawker, right through to her recent rejection by a dubious doctor – all this has created the creature she is now. And how does the new philosopher see this present-day shape of herself? As a beautiful, exotic, learned ogre.

Nothing within the boy's actions that day had confirmed the parrot's words of love nor her dark beliefs of otherness. But nothing had contradicted them either.

As he speaks to her now though, in the shelter of the tent, in blocks and insults, her mind becomes fixed. Her affections for the boy she throws upon the coals in a desultory fashion. This is her grand opening night, her name writ largest upon the hill, and here is the boy wishing only to scupper it. The conclusion she arrives at is that he cannot love her in any way.

'I know enough,' says the boy in his defence.

'Stupid you!' says the disobliging parrot from its perch upon the new philosopher's shoulder.

Then in unison the boy and bird do cry, 'Ah, fuck off!'

So the girl turns to the fayre hawker and asks in all reasonableness, 'Can we afford not to perform?' The cheap state of their dinner and the punishment of their stomachs is evidence enough. 'I say,' she continues, not waiting for the hawker's nod, 'that we cannot.'

The quarrelling does not cease though, for there is the matter of a missing angel. A system is suggested by the fayre hawker's wife, keen to make amends for her deadly cooking, whereby they suspend the ailing man from a rafter still, but place, quite tactically, a bucket beneath him to catch the sick. All do groan at the mere imagining of it and agree it will not suffice. An understudy must be found.

'The next lightest is what you're after,' says the bear boxer, who knows a thing or several about lifting heavy objects.

'Annie,' says the fayre hawker, working down the company in size.

'But she has it coming through her teeth worse than Abel,' remarks the wife. 'It's Lady Bountiful here who's next, but if she's doing the talking then . . .'

Every eye lands upon the boy.

'No,' says he. 'I ain't doing it.'

The new philosopher fixes her stare upon him, this stubborn goat, this obstacle to her success.

The boy fixes his stare upon her in return, this cocky hen, this hulver-headed bitch.

Her instinct is to attack him, to call the boy upon his sullenness at being usurped, to question the substantiality of his balls for not taking his act and his flossy on the road by himself. She could tease him for his vanity, for not wanting to look ridiculous in the strap-on wings of a goose-feathered angel. Or she could, being the excellent mimic that she is, bribe his affections.

'*If you did love us all,*' she might say, '*without hesitation, you would do it.*'

But a fight is not what she wants. She wants to perform. She wants to stand before a crowd and speak to them, in that way of hers, tell them all she has learnt – including the reason why a rainy day may indeed make the sparks less impressive than usual. She wants to feel the audience hang upon her words and action, hear them gasp when she impresses them, laugh when she tells a joke. She will hold them softly and move them at her command. Tears could fall from their eyes or hoorahs launch from their lips but only if she guides them there. Because this is her skill, ogre or no. On stage, she will find a way to be proud of herself.

So instead she says: 'You, Alex, are the one amongst us who is most capable with heights. It will be nothing to you to swing from those silken threads. We could haul you higher than we ever could Abel, and make a great dropping entrance of ya, because you have a head for it. You have proved yourself on that rope. My goodness how you have.'

The rain's rattle upon the tarpaulin roof, once loud, grows dull. The evening's birds – sparrows perhaps – sing a song of its decline. There is the burble of people, not deterred by the drizzle, gathering on the grass outside in readiment.

The boy shrugs, tempered by the way the girl has talked (in that way of hers). She has seen him for what he is perhaps, seen his worth and he repays her observations with his assent.

'I will do it.'

The others give weary cheers of relief so do not hear the coda to his acceptance.

'For you,' is what he adds. 'I will do it for you.'

They scatter to take their posts. The fayre hawker's wife

claims charge of the erratic machine. The bear boxer gathers cup and balls – and hopes his fingers nimble enough to match his small, trickster friend – and he wheels himself outside to the waiting crowd to rid them of their pennies. The fayre hawker joins him, making a plan to collect money of his own.

'Come,' says the new philosopher and she takes the boy by the hand and leads him to where the threads are ready to be wound about his body. He looks down at her hand as they walk, grasping his, then to her face, seeing that she has made this contact unthinkingly, simply. It is the easiest thing in the world. He could confess all to her now if she asked, he would do anything, but he knows that when he does, when he finds the courage to speak honestly of his heart, he must have her listen. Right now her mind is upon the show.

So he stands before her, and she takes up the ball of filament and begins to bind his torso, passing the ball behind him with one arm then, in a momentary embrace, her breath quick upon his neck, collecting the threads with the other.

'How high might you go for me?' she asks.

'As high as it takes, Mim,' says he.

The tent fills and the tallows are lit. The sight of the striking new philosopher, her peculiar costume belonging to neither man nor woman, quietens the people. She moves before them with a flick of her jacket tails, a flourish of her hands. Already she can feel it – their attention, their love.

'Gentlemen and ladies!' she cries.

'And others!' adds the parrot, from his nearby perch, as rehearsed.

'We gather you here tonight under the folds of this unremarkable tent to show you something we know to be, on the contrary, most remarkable!'

She takes her pause. She makes them wait. She exchanges a nod with the fayre hawker's wife standing to attention by the wooden machine, then another with the fayre hawker at the opening of the tent tipping coins into his inside pockets, and finally she acknowledges the bear boxer who is ready, hands on the pulley, to haul the angel skyward.

The angel himself watches her in a serious way that cannot be read. Does he love her? she asks herself once again. Has he forgiven her? If he was to open his mouth and declare that his hatred remains, that he still wishes her not returned, it would come as no surprise.

She turns back to her audience.

'I am The Electrical Venus,' she intones, 'and I will confound your eyes with the most extraordinary electrickery!'

She points a finger close to the metal rod of the machine and –

ZAP!

– the residual power there jumps to her finger, sending a flash through the air.

There is a gasp from the audience and a smile upon the mouth of the new philosopher, then a grumble of thunder as the rains begin again, the girl seemingly the conductor of every natural element this evening. The eyes of her onlookers skitter from the echo of the flash to the tarpaulin above them that is being played like a drum by the downpour. The girl makes use of their distraction to signal that the bear boxer should now begin the angel's ascent. The boy in the goose-feather wings is lifted from the ground and he rises, pauses, rises, pauses, with the rhythm of the boxer's heft. Also to this rhythm sways the tent, the pole from which the boy is suspended. Imperceptible is the movement at first then, as the boy gains great height and the momentum of a pendulum, it sways distinctly. It is enough to draw the attention of the audience, have them *oo*-ing and *ah*-ing the motion, as they had the Grand Alexi in that Windsor square when he had swung belly-down upon a rope.

'Mim!' hisses the angel from his vantage point, high, high above them.

'Shush!' she hisses back and returns to her patter. 'Behold this angel that comes floating towards our earth!'

The new philosopher nods to the bear boxer, signalling that he can now let the boy descend but her assistant is not waiting for the prompt. He is watching the angel rocking with the most sickening motion. The wooden post that holds him begins to bend and complain.

'Alex?' cries the boxer, upwards, as the boy spins upon his threads, grasps for something to hold him steady but clutches only at mist. 'Alex? Should I let you down?'

'Yes!' snaps the new philosopher.

'No!' cries the boy, the angel, growing frantic, not knowing what is best. If he is moved downwards, then the bracket won't stand it. But the only other way free is to release himself from the threads, and if he does that he will certainly . . .'Tis his greatest fear. And at such a height, more would be broken than a singular wrist.

The new philosopher repeats her line to the audience as cover. 'Behold this angel floating towards our earth!'

But the angel only wails. 'The pole,' he cries, 'it will not hold!'

'He is a kind of beautiful! He is a kind of beautiful!' chants the disobliging parrot, sensing danger, needing to voice it, but not having the words. The new philosopher, her focus only upon her own demise, her show so carefully crafted now descending into chaos, does not see the situation – hear it, feel it, know it – for what it truly is.

'Crank the machine more!' she instructs the fayre hawker's wife, believing she is able, with the power of her language and drama, to make everything come to good. But the wife stands frozen, eyes skyward, swallowing air at the impending horror.

'Lizzy!' The new philosopher snaps. 'Lizzy! Are you listening?!'

She is not.

But the next sound they all hear.

CRACK!

The pole gives way. Then comes the terrible scream of an angel descending as he was told to, but too fast, too fast.

'He is a kind of beautiful! He is a kind of beautiful!' gabbles the parrot as the boy tumbles through the air in the seemingly stretched-out motion of a dream.

The new philosopher turns, likewise trancelike, to see that the bird's words are correct. There is a beauty – a certain majesty – to the revolutions the boy makes as he slips through the air, a delicacy to the dance of the silken threads as they tangle his wings, arm and legs, preventing him from making any effort to break his fall.

The green parrot takes flight to join the boy, to coach him perhaps, on the magic of flying.

The audience's faces are upturned, a sea of expectant Os.
Then there is another deafening –
CRACK!
– as a body hits the floor.
Time returns to its usual terrifying pace with a wild cry of despair. The dream ends.
An angel lies broken, head bleeding, upon the ground.

MIM

Alex, you sod! You blighter! You useless tumbling Turk. Zooks, I am so furious I could pluck you feather by feather.

If you still had those useless wings.

If only you'd had wings.

You are dead and all is lost, that is what Annie says, and I am imagining – because it is soothing to me somehow – that you have done all of this to spite me. If that was your intention then, bravo, well done. 'Tis the performance of a lifetime! A tumble like that with George dancing in your wake, the passions of the crowd entirely at your mercy – it is exactly as you say. Someone wins – you – and someone loses – me. The One-Arm'd Boy shall be the headline act forever more. Perhaps in the next life, all bets get paid.

But you are breathing, and you mutter. Sometimes in this endless sleep of yours you move about in a fitful way. So I keep my hope alive that you will wake – and not fall right back into a mutinous stupor at the immediate sight of me.

The physician said we should have sent for a priest not him, that there was nothing to be done. Your soul, said he, not your body should be the focus of our efforts. 'Tis a worthy motto certainly, for a healthy being, but I do not stand by it where you are concerned. Instead, I return to the many words that I read within Sebastian's library. He was a nob, yes, a numbskull too, but one with an impressive collection of journals. One article said that talking to someone who is unconscious might lift them upwards.

If we have not had our fill of upwards-lifting for the time being!

All this I said to Joe and Abel, the joke included, but they did not laugh. Both sob without any embarrassment when we talk of you, even hard-hearted Abel. He feels as responsible for your downfall by his ducking out of the show as Joe does for being the one with his hands upon the pulley.

''Tis easier to laugh than cry,' I told them, a little shame-faced. And then I said, ''Tis my fault not yours. I take the blame completely.'

I therefore must claim all responsibility too for hauling you from your deepest sleep, by continuing this chatter, and by bringing warm bricks for the bed. I will also say a little prayer, though I am beginning to doubt the existence of a God that would bring this upon you. I had strengthened my faith some by studying the sciences, even though Sebastian felt it should steer me towards the opposite. All the wonders the Lord has placed upon this earth for us to discover – a spark of light, a fizz upon the tongue, the particular behaviour of one bird when compared to another. Some treasures he leaves in plain sight, others are hidden to make the finding of them all the more thrilling. But if he is a fair god then I should be lying in that bed, not you. Pride goeth before destruction and a haughty spirit before a fall, so the accident was rightly mine. Or do I receive the greatest punishment having to watch you fade away?

You shall not go.

The next step – and I remember this most distinctly because it is a thing quite startling – is that you should have a naked body beside you in the bed. Do not crow nor scoff! 'Tis proven as a thing scientific upon the continent that a natural warmth of this kind can revive a person who has almost drowned in a canal. Annie is the acceptable candidate, of course, for you know her body well, but she is spooked by your trance. She will not venture any closer to you than the door jamb before running to hide inside the animal wagon.

She may yet be convinced.

In the meantime let me pour liquor between your lips to revive you. A glass of gin, said Lizzy, was what you enjoyed after each show. No more than a glass though. We have little need for another brandy face round here. The master keeps up the task. He pushes us to move on, to perform once more. Cash runs low.

I did protest on your behalf by the fire last night. 'And leave Alex in the lodgings?' I said. 'Is that what you're suggesting?'

'Be sensible, girl!' he sniped, using the voice he usually reserves for Lizzy. 'We cannot afford his rent no more.'

'So we leave him to die, is that it?'

'He will do it anyway,' breathed our master, 'with or without us.'

I looked to Lizzy, to Annie, but they would not give me their eye. They go with Grainger to the tavern to drink to their sorrows. This is an expense they make a priority. Sometimes they come back singing and I suppose it must be like my efforts at laughter – so much easier than crying.

Their hopes might fade, but we stay strong – Joe, Abel and I.

I use my words and my reason in your defence, and they demonstrate their allegiance with their very selves. They go into the town and look for work. I told them of the sorts of places where I had swept the floors this summer – how these factories of fresh brick were a feature almost everywhere I travelled. One man pulls a lever upon a line of production, I explained, then the next performs a small task while seated at a counter, before passing to his fellow to act out another particular skill. Abel has always been light of fingers, Joe strong of heft. They begin new positions next week and have pledged a part of their wages to keeping you warm.

You live the good life, you see. Open your bleeding eyes and take a look about you, save me the breath of elucidation. Your sleeping quarters are the finest you've ever seen, all you could wish for. 'Tis a crime that you see fit to snooze your way through it. Above your head is an actual ceiling, beneath your bum a mattress and a real bed. Atop your chest a decent-enough blanket for the price we're paying. Play your aces right and we might spare some pennies for a tavern supper so you can swerve the slop. But that is wholly dependent on your coming-to, you understand.

Do we have a deal?

Grab it quick, Alex, do not wait.

Or must I try a different tack?

I know how little you appreciate my talk of the things I have observed, collected and organised, but I warn you, that is what I will speak of, if only to have you leap from this bed to escape my monologue.

Flowers and birds, animals and minerals – so many new varieties have I recorded within my book. Such is the detail I could share with you. But perhaps I should talk of the subject that intrigues most, that eludes me still.

Love.

I wish to catch it like you can a butterfly, Alex, pin it down, sketch all the intricate workings of its wings, but it does not wish to be caught, nor examined, nor told where it sits in the order of things. Where we sit in relation to it. But still I try.

I imagine the love my parents might have had for one another to have deceived their mutual master so. Perhaps they only felt the stirring-up that comes when your body is close to another whom you find somehow fascinating. 'Tis a powerful sensation, a something I have experienced – judge me for that all you wish – but 'tis not love. Not the entirety of it at least.

I look to my master and mistress to see the love they share beyond the booze and the bickering and the money in the tin. Why do they stick together? I ask myself. Why do they go a-bed at night in hatred of one another, then rise the next day to try out love all over again. It is like the feathers that fly up, they are compelled to be with one another. Maybe Lizzy should be convinced to resist such a force, to find a someone who does not rub up against her and create those particular sparks. Certainly I should have resisted the pull of the doctor.

But how do you know, Alex? How do you know until you are right there within the grips of it? And then when you are there, gripped and spellbound, you are entirely the wrong person to be taking the rational view.

So I look to you and Annie next, and I see that she is vigorous and pretty, and that the stirrings do flow between you, yet still I do not know why you chose her. I watched you very closely before your fall, the way you moved about one another. I was seeking some kind of understanding. In my proudest moments, I decided you picked a girl that looked the least like me, in skin and hair and build, so as not to be reminded of how astounding I am. In my lowest moments, I thought the same, that you could not bear to be reminded, because I was the monster you would rather forget.

Annie has gone.

I suppose I wished to break this to you gently. Today I was to talk of her reluctance to be in the room. In a few days, I would say she had gone into town like the men to find work. Then a week or so more, I would talk of a suitor who has asked for her hand and justify her decision. But I have no stamina for the lie.

She wept at what happened, do not think her heartless, but you were her means of escaping a family who had trapped her like a slave. To be your nursemaid forever was a fate she could not accept. A band of musicians came travelling through some time past, collecting coins at the tavern for the audience they drew with their rowdy ballads and dances. Their company was joyous and the fiddler among them had a certain charm, I suppose, a welcoming smile.

I believe she loved you – not the man that lies here, but the man that dances and tumbles upon a rope. Because, oh, what an easy man he is to love! Up there you are something wonderful, Alex. I only wish you did it with your own face, your own name, that you spoke in that way of yours.

Because I believe you are something wonderful upon the ground too. I think you are a kind of beautiful.

The bird has told you this many times but it is as if you will not hear it, that you do not believe it can be meant for you.

George has words for me as well, ones I am unsure whether to own. He tells me that I am hulver-headed and that he likes me not. He also tells me, in your voice, that he loves me still.

A repulsion. An attraction.

I know of an æther, an effluvia, that makes those things happen. An electricity, if you will. I also know that love can make them possible too.

No longer have I the stamina for this lie, nor the energy to run away from something that I know could be most remarkable, most magnificent, most wonderful, if only I let myself be pulled towards it.

I am taking off my clothes now, Alex, so I might lie beside you. Only for the reviving nature of my warmth, just for that. But once I am beside you, I will kiss you. No simple kiss, no everyday show of affection, for another quality that grows within me despite my studies, along with my faith, is a desire for magic. I will kiss you and you will wake exactly like that princess in the folk tale when the prince came upon her. Then, once revived, the prince and his princess will go back to the rope. Every night. Dedicate themselves to it. To the success of each other. Imagine it, Alex, behind the closed doors of your eyelids.

I'm climbing into bed with you now, for it is cold without my frock and warmth is what I am supposed to be bringing, not a chill.

We don't take it to Grainger, this is what I'm thinking. Once we're perfect, it's a ticket to London. To Paris. To Venice.

We name ourselves. We give half to no one.

This is my deal.

And this is my kiss, a spark of life, a fizzing upon the tongue, a sensation that you will know instantly because it feels exactly like . . .

ALEX

. . . Love.

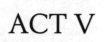

ACT V

Music plays – a waltz with a tune both grand and merry. It is only the chords sounding beneath that suggest there may be danger ahead, that the evening's entertainment will not be entirely of the waggish variety.

To this chiming accompaniment, she climbs, slowly, deliberately, rung by rung. And once she has achieved the height she desires, she steps out, chin aloft, walking upon the rope.

The people down below have received no notice of the show's commencement, no hawker has made cry. It is her responsibility to pull them from their gossip.

'Ladies, gentlemen and others!' she calls. 'Look up! Look up! Let your sights be high!'

They all do, and the flummery they'd been exchanging, chatter about fans and frocks and infidelity, is replaced by cries of astonishment to see her there, so far above the ground.

She feigns imbalance, just for a moment, just for them, so that what follows may seem all the more impressive. A few steps further and she holds her position in that dip in the rope, and executes a perfect spin upon one set of her toes, landing it unbelievably, impossibly two-footed, to face the mighty crowd. The round of applause she receives is not as great as the achievement, but only because she has made it seem like nothing. No matter – she needs them quiet. It is time for her to address them, in that way of hers.

'Ladies and Gentlemen, we gather you here today under the folds of this remarkable tent, to show you something we know to be more remarkable still. Most magnificent! Most wonderful.'

She turns to the side and slides herself, effortlessly – or so it appears – into split legs. The rope sways but she holds her position, arms correcting the balance. The applause comes louder now, accompanied by cries of bravo. She turns her neck, gives them her face.

'But do not expect us to confound your eyes. Oh no, ladies and gentlemen! We gather you here today not only to make you see, but to make you feel.'

She gives up the splits, swings and is up again, walking once more. Her goal: the platform and the throne there residing. To reach it she has to work in opposition to the upward line of the slack rope. 'Tis not easy. She must push against it, absorb the kickbacks, right her poise. The audience senses the difficulty and holds its breaths until she arrives, exhaling as one, in time with the three-count of the music, as if it were rehearsed.

'I have made it,' she announces as she sits upon the throne, arranging her skirts, slit through to allow for movement. She places an elaborate crown upon her head and grasps hold of a sceptre. Then a green parrot swoops down to make a perch of her shoulder and finish this regal scene.

'Look at me!' she boasts.

'Look at me!' says the parrot, using her voice.

'I am a queen upon my gilded throne, a crown upon my head, high above everyone.'

'Ruuuule Britannia!' coos the parrot and his mistress joins him in brief and joyous song, 'Britaaaannia ruules the waaaves!'

There is a ripple of gentle applause which she breaks with more narration.

'What an ideal place this is to observe you all.' Her head snaps to the right, to the side. 'And,' says she, 'to observe him. My love.'

A sea of heads turn, a great wave of wigs and powdered faces.

'He is a kind of beautiful,' announces the parrot and she nods her agreement.

Together they watch as he steadies his feet at the other end of the unforgiving line. He takes the downward slope, rides the sway that threatens to shake him free, and he walks, one precarious footstep after the other. To steady himself he extends his one arm, and it is enough. It has always been enough. His gaze is not on the remorseless rope beneath him but on her – his love. She is his destination and she is becoming closer, closer . . .

'What will it feel like?' announces our seeming-queen to her audience, 'when he reaches me, my one-arm'd love?' She offers them her palms and shrugs. She expects answers but receives exactly none. 'Will it feel as sure as a punch to the jaw? Like the sting of alcohol upon a wound? Will it be as certain as the teeth of a goose? Or as sound as a beating with a wooden spoon?' They laugh, her listeners, if only for a moment. 'As dull as an ankle twisting beneath your weight? As hot as skin pinched in desperate violence?' The tent falls a-hush.

'If that is the case, then how peculiar, that we should be in such longing for it. The pain. Would it not be better if it felt exactly . . . like . . . this . . .'

The parrot clatters into flight and the crowd cries out at once. She is alight! The crown upon her head glows blue, spitting sparks like a firework. The sceptre in her hand ignites at its tip into a fiery heart. The light fizzes and it throbs and the people below her croon astounded, a little afraid. She tosses back her head, delirious with the sensation, the golden rain pouring down upon her.

At the centre of the rope, the lover stops to admire this spectacle too, his hand placed upon his own heart, which throbs invisibly beneath the skin, in the average way. And as the flickering glow fades, he steals the attention of the crowd by turning himself upside down, firstly into a balance upon the head, then into a cartwheel. An explosion of cheers greets him as he restores himself, unbelievably, impossibly, two-footed upon the line and continues his perilous journey towards the throne.

'And you people will ask,' she intones, grasping the focus once more, 'because you always do – have I ever fallen? This you will dare to ask of me – a lady by all appearances, a sovereign, radiant and invincible, a–'

'So?' he calls as he walks, loud and brash, interrupting her flow. 'Have you? Have you ever fallen? A girl as exotic as you.'

'A lady should be chaste!' adds the parrot from the leftfield, eliciting titters from the crowd.

The question holds, as does he, in a solid stance at the upward slant of the rope, hand upon his hip. Her gaze holds also – her eyes narrow, her nose resolutely skywards.

He is the one on uneven ground, she is the one who sits safe, so she scoffs, 'How could I possibly? Someone like me! A goddess! A deity! A celestial being!'

He refuses to be impressed and her face droops. What good is it to ascend to the status of heavenly creature if he will not worship? If he will not be on her side. The audience watches this exchange enthralled.

'How could you possibly,' he repeats, parroting her, his voice and balance flat and steady.

'How could you possibly,' says the parrot himself, mockingly, from his perch up high and far away.

Defeated, her shoulders wilt, her neck too. She bends at the waist as if all muscle and marrow have leached from her being and she tips forward, forward, until . . .

She falls! She tumbles through the air, she whirls. The parrot lifts off immediately to join her in the dance. The sceptre with its now ashen heart falls with her and the crowd has no choice but to gasp in anguish. Her body hits the ground with a sickening –

THUD!

The waltz trails off in a way that insists no man, woman or other must clap. The room is full of gentle wails.

He keeps his balance, our lover, his composure upon the rope, as he looks down at the broken shape of her. His gaze is cold, considered, triumphant even, as if this is what she has always deserved. The crowd grows restless and distressed, that she should lie there unattended. Someone must do something! But before panic can take its grip entirely, he bids them fiercely to be quiet.

'Yes,' he says, 'you are right. Something should be done, for she has fallen, the goddess has fallen.' He takes his pause and contemplates once more the pile of skirts upon the floor, shrouding his sometime queen. 'So I will,' says he. 'I will do something. I will not wait any longer . . .'

He closes his eyes, he arches his back, and he tips his face, his heart, to the heavens beyond the tented ceiling. That arc of movement continues until his legs can no longer sustain him. That arc is the lover's undoing. Removed of all equilibrium, he falls, just as she did, body limp, entirely at the mercy of the yielding air. The parrot squawks in his own language as the boy lands –

THUD!

– beside the girl, heavy upon the floor.

The crowd who had momentarily calmed descends into agony. Two lovers destroyed! Such heartbreak! The women fan their heaving chests. The men tremble at the seeming consequences, at their own culpability for letting this disaster unfold.

Then, against all odds, the girl lifts her head.

'So how did that feel?' she asks, so matter of fact, to the crumpled body beside her.

Confusion passes through the audience as a buzz.

The boy lifts his head too. 'Bleeding painful,' says he.

The pair leaps to their feet in unison, with a bounce and a flourish, as if no harm had ever come close. The parrot flies about their heads in huge, green, celebratory circles and the waltz strikes up once more, its chords now as merry as its melody.

266

It takes a moment – the time needed, say, for a minute hand to slot, click, into position at the top of the hour – before realisation hits. They have been fooled! The crowd erupts into cheers and clapping. There is whistling done with the use of fingers and teeth. Oh, how they thought they had faced tragedy this evening! And, oh, how pleased they are to be wrong! 'Tis comedy! they say to one another in that looping language of theirs. 'Tis a happy ending!

The two performers smile at this glorious reception, though they would disagree that anything that went before should be considered a trick, or a piece of wit. The crowd was not fooled in any way. All did occur. What the audience felt when they were right there in the grips of it was real, no matter the outcome. How easy it is now to take the rational view.

'Painful, yes,' the lover tells his audience at the settling of their applause, 'so let us experience something new, something . . .'

'Remarkable?' offers his companion, removing her hand from his. 'Magnificent?' she tries. Then, 'Wonderful?'

Wonderful receives his nod and he turns and he kisses her SNAP!

A tremendous spark lights up the stage, blinding the audience momentarily, delighting them yet more.

'Ladies and gentleman, I am The Lady Electric!' says she, before translating swiftly, '*La Signora Elettrica!*'

They step forward together to take their bow, hand in hand, the bird upon her shoulder.

'And I am the Amazing Tumbling Man,' says he. '*L'incredibile uomo acrobatico!*'

'And though you may have understood very little of our words . . .'

'*Signore e signori* . . .'

'Take with you the feeling . . .'

'*La sensazione* . . .'

'Of a spark . . .'

'Of falling . . .'

'Of love.'

'*Grazie, Venezia!*'

'Thank you, Venice,' says the parrot. 'Goodnight.'

This is to give Notice to Ladies, Gentlemen and (especially) Others *that in this very Place, on the payment of Fourpence, you will be able to experience the most wonderful Magick of true Love, in the illuminating Presence of:*

THE LADY ELECTRIC *& The*

AMAZING TUMBLING MAN

MISS MIM, a Student of Natural Philosophy, Human Nature and Magical Electrickery, and her Partner, MASTER ALEX, a lofty Tumbler, Rope Dancer and Acrobat of some Distinction will demonstrate the accurate Disposition of the Heart via the most extraordinary Means. Celebrated at the grand Fayres of Paris and Venice, English Audiences will be permitted to experience their remarkable Act for THREE NIGHTS ONLY before they depart to impress the Audiences of the Americas with their considerable Skills.

The Show will also feature:
AN EXTRAORDINARY PARROT

who is named for the King and does speak the English Tongue as well as His Majesty's Subjects and can be petted and talked to at the end of the Performance.

Any Person who is desirous to know more about the Magick of Electrickery and how these exceptional Forces may be used for the Betterment of the general Publick can purchase a Book written by Miss Mim on this Subject on their Exit from the Hall.

LONG LIVE THE KING!

Letter extract: Erasmus Darwin (1731–1802), physician and leading thinker of the Enlightenment to Matthew Boulton (1728–1809), manufacturer and fellow thinker.

December 1799

. . . *word abounds that Volta's pile of copper & zinc is no new proposition & the particular current this combination enables was first proposed some time ago by a circus player – & a woman to boot! You may laugh (as I did) but this claim comes not from a single source. There is repetition. To extract truth from rumour I sent word to this much-adveris'd entertainer known as the Girl* [sic] *Electrick offering my audience and my ear. Her reply came promptly via Sadler's Wells thus: 'How kind an offer, sir, but I have a surfeit of audience members, and twice the supply of ears (if you do make the calculation). You would be most welcome to buy a ticket and join said audience, of course. You are sure to be enlightened.' Now, dear friend, you may let forth your laughter! I think we may assume these rumours are nothing but puffery . . .*

Origins and Acknowledgements

The first spark (ha!) for this story came while stuck in a traffic jam on the M25 listening to Melvyn Bragg's *In Our Time* on Radio 4.

The programme's scholarly chat usually bamboozles me, but that morning I found myself not only understanding everything, but entranced by it, as the contributors explained early electrical discoveries and the inventive ways natural philosophers demonstrated them to royalty, benefactors and the general public.

Immediately I was transported back to my secondary school science lab, that physical memory of my hand on the shiny dome of the Van de Graaff generator, the peculiar sensation of my hair flying skywards, the painful delight of zapping a friend with the poke of a finger.

My favourite childhood books, returned to over and over, were never fiction but ones that explained how things worked. Why do clouds form? Where does lightning come from? What makes a light bulb glow?

No wonder I was enthralled by Bragg's enlightened guests. The programme described in detail Nollet's hanging boy experiment with its silken threads and floating feathers. Then came an explanation of a salon trick where a woman was placed upon an insulated block, charged with static electricity, before kissing the men in the room so they might feel the thrill.

I was stunned. Was this obscure moment in history the reason we describe love the way we do today – as a spark, a charge, as a current of electricity flowing between two people? I had to find out who this woman was upon the block and know her opinions on love. Had they been shaped by her visceral experiences – did she think of love as nothing but static, or as powerful as an electric shock?

I first developed Mim's story for BBC Radio Drama and am very grateful to my producer Emma Harding for helping me shape all this science into a compelling historical romance, and also for casting, where possible, actors whose physicalities matched those of the characters. As Miranda Sawyer summed up perfectly in her review of the drama in the *Observer*, 'I like the idea of all that effort, that authenticity, for something we don't see. We sense it instead.'

Being in the studio with Hannah John-Kamen (Mim), Arthur Hughes (Alex), Mark Edel-Hunt (Fox), Michael Bertenshaw (Grainger), Jane Slavin (Lizzie), Peter Burroughs (Abel) and David Cann (Joe) made me yearn to spend more time with Grainger's lot and develop their lives on the page.

I'm very grateful that my agent Louise Lamont, and the Hot Key team, in particular Jane Harris, Tilda Johnson and Jenny Jacoby, were as excited about the prospect as me.

I am no historian or scientist, and I do not possess the same physical characteristics as my characters, so in writing this book

I am indebted to those who shared their personal perspectives and expertise as I wrote.

Dr Patricia Fara (who I heard speak on *In Our Time* all those years ago) invited me to Clare College to expand upon her knowledge of, and enthusiasm for, the natural philosophers of that era.

Mary Whitehouse, Honorary Fellow of the University of York Science Education Group, was my physics teacher, diligently checking my manuscript to make sure Fox and Mim's experiments were, in all senses of the word, earthed. Any errors that remain are mine.

Fellow Hot Key author Lydia Syson, a published expert on electrical sex in the 18th century (seriously – seek out *Doctor of Love: James Graham and His Celestial Bed*), guided me towards the most illuminating reading matter, and my former mentor, author Maria McCann, an authority on the Georgian era, helped me banish any glaring anachronisms when shaping the language Mim and Alex use when talking in that way of theirs. Thank you also to my friend Nicola Everritt who, in her capacity as a science teacher, helped me get my head around the uses of a Leyden jar.

I am lucky to have met Kate Marsh while working in my hometown, Peterborough. Kate is a dancer with a disability and her upfront views on defining yourself as different were a true guiding voice in telling this story. Kate's Change Maker blogs at www.MetalCulture.com on this topic are worth seeking out.

Deborah Bent at the Limbless Association created a reading group for an early draft of the novel. Thank you Adam Lala, John Harrison, Christine Ross and Roy Haycock for taking the time to read, to tell me your experiences and to challenge my views of amputees.

Actress Miranda Heath read an early draft too and was generous in talking about how the acting world perceives her as a mixed-race woman.

Of all my beta-readers, it was Fleur Sinclair who gave me the fiercest notes and questioned me most furiously on my portrayal of Mim. The book is so much more adventurous because of her. If she wasn't busy running the amazing Sevenoaks Bookshop (go, buy books) she'd make a formidable editor.

If you want to experience something of Mim's world, you could do as I did and live it vicariously through London's museum exhibits.

The perfectly preserved Sir John Soane's Museum in Lincoln's Inn Fields, helped me imagine a decadent basement den at the lord's house, while Fox's lodgings I supposed might compare with the interiors at the utterly magical Dennis Severs' House in Folgate Street.

For scientific exploration, past, present and future, the Wellcome Collection on Euston Road is endlessly vibrant, always accessible and sometimes seemingly psychic. Their temporary exhibitions as I wrote *The Electrical Venus* coincided precisely with my points of interest. *Bedlam* provided me with valuable social context, particular of the lower classes and women who did not conform, *Electricity: Spark of Life* displayed static-generating amber and early Leyden jars, while *Making Nature* plotted our longstanding human desire to organise the natural world so we might understand it. Early versions of Carl Linnaeus's taxonomy (the 'ladder' system that Fox uses to categorise plants and animals, a system still in use today) were on display in *Making Nature*, alongside a poignant art instillation about parrots that utterly transformed my perception of, arguably, the most important character in the book, George. *The Great Silence* by Allora and Calzadilla with text by Ted Chiang, paired film footage of a Puerto Rican parrot sanctuary with footage from the Arecibo Observatory as it pings out a signal to potential life on other planets, showing us the wisdom of nature here on earth and our human foolishness in ignoring it.

To view specimens in jars, like the ones in Fox's collection (if you have the stomach for it) head to the Hunterian Museum, also in Lincoln's Inn Fields, which additionally houses that large and beautiful book containing a naked Adam and Eve that (almost) shocked Mim. The Natural History Museum in South Kensington, meanwhile, has digitised the pages of the commonplace books of the early philosophers, male and female, for you to virtually leaf through in their Darwin Centre. The book that Mim reads describing her 'homeland' is quoted verbatim from *A Natural History of Nevis* by Reverend William Smith (1745), on display at the NHM.

The British Library's *There Will be Fun* exhibition was a great resource on fairground and circus life and helped me understand the desires and disappointments of Grainger's troupe, while the Museum of London at London Wall offers an 18th century pleasure garden to stroll through, and an authentic, wooden-walled gaol, lifted from the basement of a nearby pub, where you can read the hauntingly poetic graffiti of its inmates.

Much of Fox's early boasting in the book is based on the attitudes of Hans Sloane and his peers, which you will find quoted on the labels in the 18th century rooms of the British Museum. Fox's cabinet of curiosities, his shell collections and box of cures resemble the artefacts (or 'arte-farts' as Grainger would have it) displayed in that room.

If an adventure in London isn't possible, then you can submerge yourself further in Mim's world on the page.

As my epigraph suggests, I am grateful to Peter Adamczyk and Paul Francis Law's *Usborne Understanding Science: Electricity and Magnetism* (Usborne, 1993) for bringing me back up to date with all the science I had once learnt as a child and since forgotten, along with David Bodanis's *Electric Universe* (Abacus, 2005). Dr Patricia Fara's *An Entertainment For Angels* (Icon Books, 2003) is your first stop to learn more about electrical experimentation during the age of enlightenment, while Jenny Uglow's *The Lunar Men* (Faber and Faber, 2002) is an impressively thorough journey through the lives of the most prolific natural philosophers.

For a better understanding of life as a person of colour in 18th century Britain, I turned to Kathleen Chater's *Untold Histories* (Manchester University Press, 2009), David Olusoga's *Black and British* (Pan Macmillan, 2016) and James Delbourgo's essay *Slavery in the Cabinet of Curiosities: Hans Sloane's Atlantic World* (downloadable from http://www.britishmuseum.org). For more insight into the position of women in society, Bridget Hill's *Eighteenth Century Women: An Anthology* (George Allen & Unwin, 1984) is a book of bite-size joy (and woe, as you would expect) while Colin Barnes' *Disabled People in Britain and Discrimination* (C Hurst & Co, 1992) paints a history of inclusion and exclusion.

Ricky Jay's brilliantly entertaining *Learned Pigs and Fireproof Women* (Hale, 1987) provided me with endless insight into the lives and acts of early performers, as did Ian Kelly's delicious romp *Mr Foote's Other Leg* (Picador, 2012). Eighteenth-century sexual mores are laid bare in Julie Peakman's *Lascivious Bodies* (Atlantic, 2004) and for the slang words to describe all those bodily parts, Louise Allen's *Regency Slang Revealed* (Amazon, 2016) is an accessible treasure trove. Emily Cockayne's *Hubbub: Filth, Noise and Stench in England* (Yale, 2007) is excellent on the day-to-day foulness encountered by the average Georgian, while Paul Carter's *Parrot* (Reaktion Books, 2006) will lead you to a borderline religious affinity with our feathered friends.

The Electrical Venus is a book about science and love, yes, but also about our human inclination to mimic what we see and hear, good and bad, and repeat what has gone before. As such, my characters frequently parrot the words of real-life people. As well as speaking like Hans Sloane and co, Fox's patter at the lord's house borrows from the handbill for Anna Eva Fay, a spiritualist performer of the late 1800s. Author and abolitionist Thomas Day also conducted an experiment to improve a girl of low social standing, two in fact, and his accounts of this helped me better understand Fox's motivations. You will be pleased to hear that Day's subjects did not bend entirely to his will either, much to his frustration.

Hildy's phrase 'A lady should be chaste' is inspired by actress Peg Plunkett's writing of the 1790s in which she acknowledged that chastity is certainly a female virtue. 'But may I be allowed to ask,' she went on, 'is it the only one?'

The line George recites from the 'poem by the earl' is taken from the ditty *On Cary Frazier* written by John Wilmot, 2nd Earl of Rochester, around 1677. The poem gets even ruder beyond that line so, with the ghost of Hildy at my shoulder, I won't repeat it here. His pornographic verse is available in various collections and online. Have a google.

The advertising broadsides closely copy contemporaneous examples, which can be found in The British Museum's online collection and at the author Mike Rendell's excellent blog of 18th century ephemera (http://mikerendell.com/blog/).

I could go on.

These references I list to honour my sources and to guide readers hungry for more, but I suppose I hope to speak more directly to any girls or young women who have read this far. If you are, like I was, fascinated by how clouds form and where lightning comes from, or what silent women from the past would have said if they'd been given more of a platform to speak, I hope you might think about pushing forward with your interest in history or science.

We have come a long way since the days when girls like Mim were kept in their so-called place but we've also come no distance at all. In writing this book I had to ask myself, in all seriousness – why hadn't I pursued my love of science and history early on? I think the unpleasant answer is that I believed, back then, that they weren't suitable subjects for girls. Or at least, they were only for the posh girls. This is, of course, bunkum. I am no historian or scientist. But you could be.

Julie Mayhew

Julie Mayhew is the author of *Red Ink* (shortlisted for the 2014 Branford Boase Award), *The Big Lie* (winner of the 2016 Sidewise Award for Alternate History) and the critically acclaimed *Mother Tongue*. She also writes for the stage and for film, and has been twice nominated for Best Original Drama at the BBC Audio Drama Awards for her radio plays – including a 2016 recognition for the *The Electrical Venus*, the drama on which this book is based. Julie grew up in Peterborough and originally trained as a journalist, then as an actress, before turning to writing because she couldn't find enough brilliant roles for girls.

www.juliemayhew.co.uk
Twitter: @juliemayhew
Instagram: JulieMayhew

HOT KEY BOOKS

Thank you for choosing a Hot Key book.

If you want to know more about our authors and what we publish, you can find us online.

You can start at our website

www.hotkeybooks.com

And you can also find us on:

We hope to see you soon!